For now Seoc could appreciate the pink tone to Barabal's round cheeks, the dark framing of her eyelashes to her dark eyes.

And bless the sunlight, for she'd warmed enough to not wear that monstrous cape that hid the bounty of her curves. Oh, her dress was mud splattered and leaves seemed crushed along the hem, but she was here before him, and he wasn't wrong.

She was like the last ember in the darkest of fires.

"What do you want?" She frowned.

You, he almost blurted. Swallowed hard on that word. Had he lost all control of himself? But then, being near her, he wanted to lose that control. To talk to her about anything. What was it about her?

She put her hands on her hips. "Are you here to run me off?"

Her tone was acerbic, but there was that delicate flash in her eyes. That little light of vulnerability she covered up so skillfully, he couldn't believe it to be true.

Author Note

If you read Hamilton's or Camron's stories, you'd think I'd have Seoc hunched over a giant cauldron mixing herbs and honey like he's in some laboratory. So for him to have any love story, some woman would have to be trapped in a mead-infused barrel for him to notice her.

That absolutely does not happen here.

What does happen? Barabal, who arrives on Beltane night full of hope and contrariness. Seoc notices her immediately, doesn't let go and holds on to her for dear life.

Eventually, she notices him, too. How could she not, when he's absolutely gorgeous, and asking for a kiss the moment she marches up to him?

THE HIGHLANDER'S MYSTERIOUS MAIDEN

NICOLE LOCKE

HISTORICAL

If you purchased this book without a cover you should be aware that this book is stolen property. It was reported as "unsold and destroyed" to the publisher, and neither the author nor the publisher has received any payment for this "stripped book."

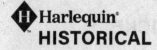
HISTORICAL

ISBN-13: 978-1-335-83147-7

The Highlander's Mysterious Maiden

Copyright © 2025 by Nicole Locke

Recycling programs for this product may not exist in your area.

All rights reserved. No part of this book may be used or reproduced in any manner whatsoever without written permission.

Without limiting the author's and publisher's exclusive rights, any unauthorized use of this publication to train generative artificial intelligence (AI) technologies is expressly prohibited.

This is a work of fiction. Names, characters, places and incidents are either the product of the author's imagination or are used fictitiously. Any resemblance to actual persons, living or dead, businesses, companies, events or locales is entirely coincidental.

For questions and comments about the quality of this book, please contact us at CustomerService@Harlequin.com.

TM and ® are trademarks of Harlequin Enterprises ULC.

 Harlequin Enterprises ULC
22 Adelaide St. West, 41st Floor
Toronto, Ontario M5H 4E3, Canada
www.Harlequin.com

Printed in U.S.A.

Nicole Locke discovered her first romance novels in her grandmother's closet, where they were secretly hidden. Convinced that books that were hidden must be better than those that weren't, Nicole greedily read them. It was only natural for her to start writing them—but now not so secretly.

Books by Nicole Locke

Harlequin Historical

Lovers and Highlanders

The Highlander's Bridal Bid
The Highlander's Unexpected Bride

Lovers and Legends

The Knight's Broken Promise
Her Enemy Highlander
The Highland Laird's Bride
In Debt to the Enemy Lord
The Knight's Scarred Maiden
Her Christmas Knight
Reclaimed by the Knight
Her Dark Knight's Redemption
Captured by Her Enemy Knight
The Maiden and the Mercenary
The Knight's Runaway Maiden
Her Honorable Mercenary
Her Legendary Highlander

The Lochmore Legacy

Secrets of a Highland Warrior

Visit the Author Profile page
at Harlequin.com for more titles.

Annabelle Anders and Deb Marlowe,
I absolutely cherish our friendship and
can't wait to share in a lifetime of adventures.

Chapter One

April 1297

'Anyone feeling we should let the fire die?'

Seoc of the Clan Graham threw on another log, squatted next to his bench and poked the fire with a thick branch. The fire sparked to life, unlike the dead empty space inside his chest where his heart used to be.

'Feels good.' Hamilton sat on the dense log while his twin brother, Camron, shifted on the other makeshift bench.

Since their return to Graham land a little over a fortnight ago, the three of them often sat here in the empty fields at night. They were near their childhood homes, but far enough away not to be disturbed. Their inability to fall asleep with the rest of their clan went far beyond their years of scouting and keeping night watches together.

For Camron, now he'd returned to Graham land, he was again tortured by Anna, the woman he'd loved for most of his life. Always methodical and stalwart in everything he did, Camron's one weakness was their childhood friend. Everyone knew of his longing, but Anna seemed incapable of returning that love. In recent weeks, they'd spent some time together, even journeyed to another clan, but given Camron's grim expression, Seoc didn't believe his friend fared well with her.

8 *The Highlander's Mysterious Maiden*

As for what kept Hamilton, Camron's twin brother, awake, that was a bit of mystery and a welcomed distraction. But Seoc surmised Hamilton's restlessness must have something to do with Camron and the unerring sense something was wrong and must be righted.

Hamilton was constantly meddling. If he wasn't pulling pranks, he was trying to repair the consequences. If he was up to another scheme, one that especially dealt with his brother, Hamilton was likely to make matters worse before it could be righted.

But then there was also the fact that for the last few weeks, Hamilton had been spending time with their friend Beileag. Seoc wondered, not for the first time, what was happening between them.

As for himself, well, he'd rather not reflect on what kept him awake at night. He'd rather seek distractions, not obsess over those times he, too, wanted a wife and children. This past year, he hadn't been without comfort, a few women, a few hours here and there, but he could never be as fortunate as his friends to find someone to spend the rest of his life with. What woman would stay at his side long enough to ease the terrors plaguing his dreams?

Seoc swung his gaze to his friends. They'd been talking while his thoughts wandered. 'What was that again?'

He caught Hamilton's eyes sliding to his brother's before his friend answered, 'Last I said was that the fire felt good.'

Did it? Seoc stared at the fire and grunted. He didn't think anything would warm him again. At least the night was crisp, clear, and the sky was lit by uncountable stars. It wasn't raining and he had some distraction because his friends were near.

'What feels good is not drinking your mead.' Camron stretched his feet.

'Nothing's wrong with my mead,' Seoc argued out of habit. He'd been working with different herbs and spices for his metheglins, or spiced meads, most of his life. In his opinion, he'd perfected metheglins in all their many forms. As long as no one interrupted his methods or stole any of the herbs he needed. Or worse, pulled a bung and ruined the months-long process of a good fermentation, then all was good.

What his friends forgot, though, or maybe flirted with, was the indisputable fact he brewed his mead strong. Though it irked him he couldn't get it stronger. If he had time, or the strength of interest like he used to, he knew he could make it better. There was something he was missing. But then, for over a year, he'd been missing much.

'Nothing wrong with Seoc's mead, as long as you don't drink that much,' Hamilton said. 'And let's not forget drinking such quantities was your choice, dear Brother.'

Camron groaned, Hamilton snorted and Seoc forced a chuckle.

Which pulled at his ragged scar on his chest. Would the ache, the reminder, never end? It was bad enough he'd been carved clear across his body at the Battle of Dunbar a year ago. He'd fallen before he could save Sir Patrick of Clan Graham. Their Laird was the only Scotsman to die that bitter day and it had been Seoc's duty to watch his back.

And he'd failed. He deserved to be carved in two. He deserved to have died at his Laird's feet. What he hadn't deserved was for these two brothers to have rolled him on to some sort of stretcher and drag him the miles to Ettrick Forest.

Each bump and rock across those cursed fields had felt like knives drawing him closer to death and he'd welcomed every one of them. He had wanted to die, but Hamilton and Camron had brought him to safety and denied him an hon-

The Highlander's Mysterious Maiden

ourable death, or at least one he deserved. For the rest, his brutish body, built like a mountain and just as strong, pulled through the rest. His scar, though visible from any distance, was healed.

What he was left with, however, was an empty husk inside. It seemed as though his friends knew it, for they constantly watched him. As if they feared he'd be split open again.

Couldn't they tell there was nothing left inside him to worry on? He eyed the twins. Both of them had gone quietly sober. Were they lost in their darker thoughts like him? Maybe it was his turn to be a distraction.

'So, Camron, when will you tell us what happened on your travels to the Clan Colquhoun with Anna?' Seoc sat back on his own makeshift bench.

'Not much to tell.'

Hamilton stretched his hands to the fire and clapped them. 'I've been trying for days to get him to confess.'

'And he's stayed silent?' Seoc said.

Hamilton nodded. 'A certainty something happened between them.'

'Ah, maybe he had to fight for her hand while she was with those Colquhouns,' Seoc tried to tease. 'You know how they are.'

'Persuasive red-haired devils.' Hamilton turned. 'So was that it? Did a Colquhoun notice Anna's beauty, Brother?'

Camron scowled and Seoc felt immediate remorse. Anna was a lass worth fighting for, but Camron was younger than her and a few years ago she'd gone and fallen for a scoundrel. Now, she didn't seem to have any trust for another man.

That was his fault. Alan of Clan Maclean was a man he had vouched for. Until Dunbar, him introducing Alan to their clan had been his biggest regret. Not that anyone blamed him, but he'd blamed himself well enough.

Laughing, Hamilton pointed his thumb. 'See, this is how my brother's been. Especially as Anna's been avoiding him since they returned.'

'You going to ask me whether she's worth it?' Camron retorted. 'Aren't you going to say I told you so? It's not as though I wasted years thinking of only her. There were other matters keeping us occupied.'

'Dunbar, Seoc,' Hamilton said, then rattled off more words that Seoc couldn't hear from the sudden roaring through his ears. But he did see the look Hamilton shared with his brother again.

Seoc knew what this was about, but there was nothing to be done for it. Hamilton had blurted the truth out, that's all. He might have returned to Graham land after April a year ago, but for months he was plagued with fever and constantly on the cusp of death. It'd taken a year for him to be as well as he was. Through it all, the twins had stayed at his side and, when he could scout again, they'd watched him all the more closely. Probably because of his nightmares. Fortunately, they didn't talk of it; he didn't think he could even if they asked.

As Hamilton kept conversing with his brother, Seoc tried to keep his expression neutral, knew he failed, so he turned his gaze to the open fields. It was the darkest part of night and their fire ruined any chance for him to see the more subtle shadows in the fields.

He liked staring off into the various shades of grey and black. It helped him not to think of the disfigurement across his chest or the deadness inside him.

He knew he wasn't the only one plagued with dark thoughts. All Scotsmen had had to flee the English that day at Castle Dunbar. The battle was hard enough when they had to flee and losing their Laird, Sir Patrick, was a harsh reminder that, though their hearts were strong, they were still

12   *The Highlander's Mysterious Maiden*

only men. He knew Hamilton and Camron were also plagued with last April and with the decree they were to ride to Stirling in September to face another battle.

Between then and now was Beltane: a night of celebrating spring and abundance.

He'd missed it last year because of fevers, maybe he'd skip it again this year. How could he celebrate when all he thought about was battle, death, pain, loss? Yanking himself from those thoughts, he turned again to his friends. Camron's expression was full of loathing and Hamilton's with worry.

'I stopped questioning your feelings for her years ago,' Hamilton said. 'Certainly I teased you about it when you were so obsessed with Anna before our balls had even dropped.'

'Careful,' Camron growled.

Hamilton rolled his shoulders. 'How could I doubt how you felt about her when you saw her happy with Maclean and you stepped back?'

'When we *thought* she was happy,' Camron growled.

'Face the truth, Brother, that man did make her happy,' Hamilton said.

Ah. They talked of Anna still. Anna, a few years older than them all, had fallen in love and had seemed happy with Alan Maclean. Though he'd felt terrible for Camron, Seoc thought them a good match. Then it was discovered that Alan played with other women's hearts and bodies. They'd run Alan away, but Camron still struggled to gain her attention. He deserved happiness and so did she.

'I have been occupied teaching her brother to swim.' Camron pulled his feet in.

'Thinking to gain her heart by befriending her brother?' Hamilton said. 'That's clever.'

Clever, but no doubt the truth. 'We know you love the boy as much as you love his sister,' Seoc said. 'If you could see your expression, as we do, my friend, you would know we don't need the details to wish you congratulations.'

Camron's expression eased and Seoc felt something like warmth. Something that made him want to pay attention to his friends. They were there for him—maybe he could try to be there for them and not lose his thoughts to grey shadows and darkness.

'I wager he hasn't kissed her yet,' Hamilton remarked. 'There's too much tension in him.'

He could do with more laughter. 'Agreed.'

Camron rubbed his face. 'Don't you have any of that mead?'

Seoc raised a brow. 'Haven't learnt your lesson? Maybe you should try my new spiced ale. I've done—'

'You poisoned us with the last ale you spiced,' Hamilton interrupted.

'I've perfected my recipe,' Seoc insisted.

'The way you perfected that grass water concoction?' Hamilton quipped.

He'd been a child then and his mother had been alive. His mother, knowing her son had already outgrown their little home, had often taken him to the alehouse where she and the other women brewed. He'd learnt much with her, but that didn't mean he didn't also experiment.

'You didn't have to drink that, just as you didn't have to drink my mead,' Seoc said.

Hamilton groaned. 'It's been less than a fortnight since we returned here and celebrated and my head still hurts. Why didn't anyone stop us?'

'I couldn't get you to stop drinking the grass water either,' Seoc pointed out.

'That's because there was a wager made,' Camron said.

14   *The Highlander's Mysterious Maiden*

Hamilton rubbed his stomach in memory. 'Only made us stronger.'

'You two should stop making wagers.' Seoc stood, stomped out his large feet and sat again. It helped with the tingles in his legs, but didn't help with the deadness weighing down his limbs. Would any part of him feel alive again?

'Then where would you get your amusement at our expense?' Hamilton said.

'True!' Seoc laughed, felt the pinch in his chest and clenched his teeth against the pain.

Camron slid his eyes away from him to his brother. 'How's Murdag, Hamilton?'

Hamilton looked away. 'Better than ever.'

Since they were little, there was always the six of them. He, Camron and Hamilton, Murdag, Anna's sister, and Beileag, their friend. When Anna wasn't doing more adult matters, she joined them.

It wasn't unusual for Camron to ask about Murdag, but it was unusual for him to ask Hamilton about her. Maybe here was a distraction worthy of attention. 'Murdag? Don't you mean Beileag?'

'Last I knew my brother liked a certain woman with a thin chemise who stood on a boulder the night we first returned,' Camron said.

'How did I miss Murdag wearing a thin chemise?' Seoc said, but realised that was missing the point because all he'd seen was Beileag and Hamilton sneaking off to the forest... alone. 'You have a strange way of wooing Murdag, Hamilton, by hanging around her friend Beileag,'

Camron's expression grew perplexed. 'I agree with Seoc. If you like Murdag, I'd stop hanging around her friend.'

Hamilton looked flummoxed, as though he hadn't realised

Nicole Locke 15

what he had done. Nudging Camron with his shoulder, he answered, 'Doesn't matter. I'll win.'

'Win what?' Schemes and meddling? Hamilton *was* up to something, which couldn't be good, especially with Camron's darkening expression.

'Brother,' Camron warned.

Hamilton tilted his head to Seoc. 'Ach, come on, he's got to know some time. He'll find out when it comes to the happy moment anyway.'

'What did you do now, Hamilton?' Seoc yawned. Now things were interesting, he was tired? Curse his body.

'It wasn't me,' Hamilton said. 'Odd, I know, but this was, and has always been, Camron's idea.'

'Now you have to tell me,' Seoc insisted. 'Is this another challenge or a jest on someone, and why would your twin, Lord of the Calm and Reasonable Manor, suggest something that has you filling with mirth?'

The twins shared another glance. Did they know they did that often? Side by side on the opposite log, they looked alike until their personalities gave them away. But the one thing they shared was Hamilton getting them into trouble and Camron getting them out. However, there was something else besides a typical joke playing on here. Camron was looking stony and Hamilton somehow pleased, but also wary.

'Not a chance we're telling you,' Camron said.

'Not a chance for what?' Seoc said. 'Equal frowns on your faces and it's as though I've been hit on the head. I'm seeing double and seeing double of you doesn't do it for me.'

'Seeing double of Una's treasures likely would,' Hamilton said, referring to a particularly voluptuous widow in the clan.

'Another truth from you, my friend.' Seoc forced another laugh, but this one hurt more than most. Una was a fine woman and, though she had no expectations of him, of any

16   *The Highlander's Mysterious Maiden*

of the men she invited to her bed, he knew he wasn't being as honest with her as he should. Though they'd had relations for years, he feared now he only lay with her for distraction. She didn't deserve that.

A year since the battle and this was the kind of man he'd become. Maybe he was more tired than he thought. Stretching his arms over his head, Seoc asked, 'I'm getting weary. Will you two tell me what's going on?'

'We made a wager to marry before we leave again in September for Stirling,' Hamilton said.

Seoc was glad he was sitting down. The twins made wager all the time and the six of them often participated in them. But marriage was not a game.

'The less bright one with sentences is attempting to marry Murdag and I'm to try to marry Anna.'

Camron was always trying to wed Anna. Why would he need a wager? And if Hamilton was serious regarding Murdag, why would he spend hours with Beileag? And why, why, why would they make wager when it came to women's hearts and souls? When had they turned cruel?

Something of his expression must have registered for Hamilton raised his hands apologetically. 'It was Camron's wager. Thus I'll win this one.'

'When have you ever won a wager from me?' Camron said.

Hamilton scoffed. 'We'd be here all day if I regaled all my winnings, Brother.'

'Are you sure this is not a jest?' Seoc said, pointing at each of them. 'Because I've had to bear enough of both your jests and your wager all my life.'

Camron raised a brow. 'Bear the brunt of our jests?'

'I must have been hit on my head.' In what world would reasonable Camron escort Anna to Colquhoun land because of a wager? Could it be true they did something so dishonourable and laughed about it? That they both wagered with Murdag and Anna, whom they'd known all their lives, as if they were playthings?

He'd take any risk for love, to scale any peril to have lasting happiness with someone. If such a woman for him existed, he'd follow her to the ends of the earth. Hell, he'd follow her around if she'd just make him *feel* anything at all. And these men thought souls and hearts so worthless they could make a game about them.

'Your head's fine, our friend.' Hamilton chuckled. 'This may be the most awe-inspiring wager yet.'

Seoc felt something then. Rage. Standing to his full height, he glared at Camron. 'This is true? You offered to travel with Anna, to be alone with her, so you could try to win a *wager*?'

Camron nodded.

Seoc looked at both of them. They'd planned games when his Laird Patrick fell, when the blade that should have felled him failed. When he'd returned all but dead to the world, and wished, begged, prayed he'd feel anything except for nothing during the lonely days and terrors at night. These two played games as if a life filled with love wasn't precious and easily lost.

'You fools!' Seoc stormed off.

Chapter Two

Barabal of Clan Colquhoun couldn't see a cursed thing. Walking at night over Graham land had to be one of her worst decisions. But she was still late and there was nothing to be done about it. Hitching her satchel containing all her possessions over her shoulder, she trudged over uneven terrain around vast and well-ordered homes and buildings.

Beyond those structures, huge bonfires, their funnels of smoke billowing, lit the night sky announcing Beltane celebration. A time to welcome summer's growth, abundance and new beginnings with utter revelry.

Even after all her planning for her journey and arrival here, Barabal was late to help with any of the preparations. How many more belittling words did she need to hear, how many more punishments did she have to take before she learnt to be better? Hurrying her steps, the slight weight of her bag hardly any hindrance, she held back pitying tears.

No, never again. Certainly she'd had some mishaps in the past, but she always persevered. Always. The alternative wasn't thinkable. How many times had she worked harder and spent longer hours to get the task, whatever task she took on, completed? Too many to count. She always got back up, improved her skills, and kept moving. *Moved* on.

Not that anyone in any of the clans she'd lived with appreciated her hard work and attention to detail. Which might be part of her difficulties. It was certainly the reason she had arrived late to Graham land actually on the eve of Beltane instead of a day or two before like she'd meticulously planned.

Not that anyone on Graham Clan would know she intended to be here earlier. It was that Beltane was a perfect opportunity to introduce herself and her work capabilities, to truly show how useful she could be.

The celebrations required vast preparations for meals, drink and games. Livestock was rounded up and immense, carefully constructed bonfires were lit and spaced wide apart enough to run the cattle through it.

It was a night when everyone in every clan in Scotland was needed so that the celebrations could be as outlandish and free as possible. To welcome summer's abundance from spring's blossom the revelry must be immense. It was a perfect time to arrive, to have her own new beginning. Everyone would be so busy preparing they'd accept when another set of hands suddenly arrived. She'd be absolutely indispensable, barely sleeping or eating. She'd prepare some of her favourite dishes, or bake the most bread, or weave the prettiest flower garland and the Grahams would beg her to stay.

She'd finally belong.

Being late wasn't her fault obviously, it was that the clan she had stayed with over the last year, Clan Buchanan, hadn't taken any of her suggestions in their preparations for Beltane and she couldn't leave them to stumble their way to celebrations.

In fairness, the whole Buchanan Clan was in upheaval with the Laird changing from one brother to another and unplanned council meetings and whispers of secrets. She didn't have time for gossip, or caring that there was a new laird.

So maybe their disorganisation wasn't truly because their

20   *The Highlander's Mysterious Maiden*

head baker refused to agree with her on the correct way to make burnt bannock for Beltane. But some of it was. As was their insistence on the timing of the flower garlands, and the preparation of the lamb. She'd travelled to more clans in Scotland than any of them, so she picked some tips along the way. Couldn't they have listened to at least one of her suggestions?

They wouldn't listen and she couldn't be useful. She knew months ago it was time to leave Clan Buchanan, but she kept hoping matters would change. Hope, which she'd admit as a fault of hers, was a folly she couldn't shut off inside her. Her heart, her soul, her will to continue was both motivated and devastated by hope.

But if she didn't have hope, then what? Was she simply to sit somewhere between clan borders in places where no clansman lived and stop?

She needed to stop. More and more, that despondency she'd carried since childhood grew heavier. It was a weight, a sadness she couldn't ever put down from one clan to one rejection after another. It was a burden she'd gladly let go and something that she wished she'd never had to pick up. When she was five her parents died and her two older brothers were taken in by the Colquhoun tanners. She, however, was carried off from Colquhoun land to MacFarlane and placed in the hands of her dead mother's cousin, Ciorstaidh. Why she was given away, she didn't know. She'd received no answers and could only conclude that a five-year-old girl was not useful to tanners or to two brothers.

On MacFarlane land she knew some bits of contentedness, but not much. Ciorstaidh and her husband, Gillespie, already had six children, and though she wasn't a burden when she was small, she grew bigger, ate more, needed new clothing. She grew emotionally, too. Enough to understand they weren't cruel, but weren't affectionate either. That the emotion flittering across their features was reluctance when they placed a bowl of soup in front of her. By the time she was nine, the entire family was rationing. Maybe the entire clan was, she didn't know. She did remember them talking of terrible rains, but it didn't mean much to her then. What mattered was the look Ciorstaidh gave to her husband. A look of understanding, of worry and sometimes of fear.

So when she was nine, she was not surprised they talked of one of their cousins in the north who was willing to take her. She didn't protest, didn't know if she had the right to. Thus, with her few pieces of clothing, Gillespie took her away to the Clan Macnaghten.

By then she'd learnt her lesson. She'd been useless for Colquhouns and for the MacFarlanes, but she was determined to be useful for the Macnaghten Clan. She wanted a home, a family, friends, so she'd learn every trade, helped at every turn. And even as she did so she'd show them how much she could do. She'd be helpful and she'd make them notice. She wouldn't be put aside ever again.

Except the Macnaghtens weren't pleased with anything she did. She was always wrong, always needing punishments, always passed from one family's table to another until...until she'd had her first bleed at thirteen and one family wanted her a little too much.

Barabal shuddered. She refused to think of those years again. She'd taken her freedom from them, hadn't she? She'd pulled through all on her own and left in the middle of the night. Who cared if her earlier hopeful eagerness was battered until she was abrupt and too direct for most people? Her heart was in the right place. She'd been weak before and tossed around. Now she was strong, shouldn't she therefore truly voice her helpfulness, her skills? Her ability to do things better? It shouldn't matter if the MacDougalls or the Campbells hadn't exactly warmed to her no matter how long she stayed because the Buchanans had seemed friendly enough in the beginning. Which was the reason she insisted on helping them since she'd arrived late last year.

At first, they'd seemed enthusiastic upon her arrival, but soon, like at all the other clans she'd tried to help, they became less amenable to her direction for changes. So as Beltane approached, she'd found the state of procedures completely chaotic.

It never occurred to her to return to the Colquhoun Clan or to find her brothers. That clan's tanner family had made it clear she wasn't wanted. And her older brothers—if they'd wanted her, they would have fought for her, or when they got older could have retrieved her from the MacFarlanes or anywhere else.

It didn't stop her faulty hope they'd want her back, which was why the last year on Buchanan land, which was adjacent to Colquhouns', was agony. But they never came and she'd been too ashamed to even ask about them.

When she knew it wouldn't work at Clan Buchanan, she'd had nowhere else to travel except east to the Graham Clan. And here she was with loads of skills and prepared to be useful. She knew how to bake, cook, sow her own seeds she had in her purse. She would be ready for anything.

But she wasn't ready to arrive late and not make a good impression. She'd done her utter best at the last four clans and those didn't work out at all. Maybe staying with the Graham Clan would be her shortest—

'Move!'

Barabal jumped to the left before she even knew what she was about. A male rider yanked his reins the other way. They barely avoided each other.

As she righted herself, she saw it wasn't a lone male rider

since a woman rode on his lap. She had one of the large bread sacks over her head and most of her body. Barabal couldn't hear what the woman was screaming, but she was pounding her fists against the rider.

Beltane was known for its bawdy jests, but the horseman didn't look mischievous. Instead, he looked lit by some fevered determination. This couldn't be right.

Barabal scanned the dispersing crowd. Four of them stood eying each other and nodding as if this screaming woman with a sack over her was expected or warranted. Two people looked joyous. No one appeared alarmed. Did they not care how one clansman treated another? Wasn't it clear that the woman did not want a sack over her head as though she was a bag of turnips?

But maybe they didn't. Maybe this was what the Graham Clan did. Perhaps their men trapped women in sacks and carted them off against their will. Suddenly the raucous crowd looked sinister. Maybe those bonfires weren't there to light the night sky so people could enjoy dancing and the swirls of flower garlands swaying in the slight breeze.

Maybe they were there to trap people in the centre. Maybe there was a perimeter of Graham men waiting along the tree line to encourage any stragglers back to the centre for darker, lesser-practised rituals.

Barabal tightened the satchel over her shoulder. Maybe she should leave.

And go where? What other clan would accept her? She'd been to most of them in the north, and just came from the west. All she could go was east, and even so, she'd have to journey through the Graham Clan. It was terrain she'd never traversed before, let alone at night.

This day she'd already travelled far on to unfamiliar territory. And the fire's smoke and giant trees obscured the exact

24   *The Highlander's Mysterious Maiden*

position of the moon. She could go in some vague direction, never knowing if she travelled in circles.

She had nowhere to go. She'd have to stay here for the night, with a clan that might have ill intentions. A loud cheer swung her attention to another crowd of people. What were they doing there?

She took a step, felt the panic inside her and stopped. On her way here, she'd still held hope she'd arrive in time to be helpful. With no obvious task to introduce herself, what was she to do?

She'd already passed most of the homes and buildings. Other than some mothers holding infants to their chests, there were no people carrying trays of food, or small jugs of ale.

This clan appeared efficient. Another wave of worry sped through her. Surely there was something else she could do here that would be helpful? She hadn't survived this long, learnt so much, that she couldn't impart some considerate direction.

She needed to find something to do or someone in need and offer help. It wasn't much, it was the least she could absolutely do. And she'd start tonight. She had a few healing remedies—maybe someone had already imbibed too much.

She scanned the crowd again. People eating, drinking, dancing. No one else appeared to be trapping other women in overly large bread sacks. Perhaps it was only that man and woman. It still unsettled her that no one came to her defence.

Maybe they didn't think to? She gave herself a nod. Maybe some well-pointed words to the people surrounding them at the time, those ones who'd looked to each other and nodded as if in some agreement. Where were they now? It was night, but the fires were bright. Surely she could recognise some of them. Actually, there had been one man, one very notice-able man—*there*.

It was laughably easy to find him. Partly because he was the largest man she'd ever seen and that was saying something when there were giants among them.

Partly, also, because he stood alone. He wasn't dancing, drinking, or jesting with friends. The crowd had dispersed, the others who she thought were his friends were gone.

But there was something else arresting about him. Maybe it was the careless way he held his arm to his chest, as though he'd lifted it, splayed the fingers of his hand, then forgotten he'd done so. Maybe it was because the rest of him was so still, immovable, while his eyes flickered from one person to another.

During a time of great festivity this stillness from a person stood out, but even that wasn't what made her stare. Maybe it was the wide stance of his legs encased in dark breeches as if he meant to stand in that spot for ever, like a tree. Something lit inside Barabal at that thought. The entirety of his form reminded her of the great oaks.

He seemed calm, yet something deeper was occurring within him. Something under the surface like a tree with roots that cut and snarled their way through impervious earth. That made her notice him. That darker, more malignant, current underneath the outwardly calm demeanour.

It was enough to give her pause, but not enough to stop her from weaving through the rest of the crowd towards him. He might be intimidating, might even have a bit of a temper, but both those traits were something she'd faced many times before.

She was a shorter than him, but her bones were thick and she was sturdy. Even if he turned truly cross with her, she'd survive it. She couldn't see anyway else to make a good impression for the Clan Graham, but she could help and be useful for that distressed woman.

26   *The Highlander's Mysterious Maiden*

Shoulders back, a few more strides, and she was entering that empty space around him. Enough for his eyes, which she now knew weren't scanning the clan, but the wide darkened fields beyond, to suddenly fall to her.

One heartbeat, two until his stature changed. His arm lowered, his chin dipped and his shoulders turned. His movements so slow, so infinitesimal it was as though the great oak noticed her. She wasn't certain that was a good thing or the fact that now she was closer she was aware of other alluring factors.

Like the fact that he was truly taller than her, yet all in some proportion that didn't make her think tree, but more like man. All man. Like a man others would go to and respect, and women would flock to. It was in the width of his shoulders, that great expanse of his chest. The very thickness of his arms and legs, as if he was born a warrior and stayed that way.

That unruly hair was lit by the fire light and held more colours of brown than she knew existed and his eyes... It was truly too dark to discern their colour. Perhaps a bluish hazel, or a grey. Too dim of light, and too many colours to know for certain. Maybe his eyes contained them all. The straightness of his nose, the full downturned curve of his lips. The squareness of his jaw, the jutting cheekbones. He was simply arresting.

Barabal slowed her steps. This oak of a man was *truly* beautiful despite his implacable stare. Possibly it was because though his lips were set, the corners of them looked as if when he smiled it cragged his entire face. She saw those same smiling lines fanning from his eyes. His jaw was almost too well defined, but the strong cords of his neck, the way his throat bobbed as if he swallowed hard because she was—she was gawking at him. What was wrong with her?

He was attractive, but that didn't mean there wasn't the possibly of a temper or a terrible disposition. He was all alone after all. There must be some reason for that. Either way, it shouldn't matter. She was needed here. She knew it and wouldn't let this man, or anyone, stand in her way.

Arranging the satchel so the bag was at her back, she marched up to the giant.

'Aren't you going to help that woman?' She pointed in the direction of the retreating horseman. 'Or will you keep standing here doing nothing?'

Chapter Three

Seoc blinked, then again, but the woman before him didn't disappear. Had he gone so far in his thoughts, he only imagined her?

You never knew on Beltane night what or who would appear. Many people from other clans travelled here to be with families, or wanderers stopped to join and rest their heads. It was a night of welcome in all ways. Some innocent and others more carnal, especially as the night progressed and all the ancient rites were conducted. When the children went to bed, but the adults did not.

It was then that the flutes gave way to the drums and the repasts away to mead and ale. That the dancing and twining of flower garlands gave away to the twining of bodies.

That time of night that seemed thin along the edges when no one knew the time and suddenly this woman revealed herself before him. She could be anybody from anywhere, or a creature from somewhere else.

Her overly mended cape, tattered dress and satchel of a type he hadn't seen in generations gave her the appearance of an ordinary woman. Albeit one he did not recognise. Though he wanted to, very much.

It was the way she imperiously walked towards him as if she didn't see any of the rest of his clan trying to gain her attention. Calan had sauntered right in her path, and she'd walked around him. Tasgall had offered her a drink, but she'd kept her head pointed straight, and ignored him.

From where she began in her walk, he didn't know, but her appearance pulled his thoughts from the shadows to the spot right in front of him.

Which was surprising. When had anything pulled his attention, stopped for one moment that nothingness? Certainly he'd been angry at Camron and Hamilton for their arrogant wager, but that anger came and went. Left him drained even more afterwards.

He'd come here tonight because he said he would help his friend, but unlike Hamilton and Murdag and Beileag who'd grinned as Camron rode off with Anna to have some words with her, he'd felt nothing. Not even satisfaction. He knew reasonably he should be pleased, but it was so faint and the pull of the shadows strong that in truth he had no idea how long he'd stood here after his friend was gone.

He didn't know until this woman stormed up to him, then hesitated before she got too close. But that hesitation… There was much to notice then because though she'd ignored Tasgall and Calan, she didn't ignore him. Her eyes pinging from one of his features to the next. Her hand wrapping itself around her satchel strap not because she was intent on keeping it on her shoulder, but as if she needed to hold on to something.

He wished it was him: he wished more she hadn't slowed her step so she'd be closer. She wasn't short, her bones were thick, as was her form. Under her frayed cape, he was denied the exactness of her curves, but it didn't stop his imagination of want.

At the now unfamiliar tightening of lust-filled heat, he paused. When had he last felt this way? Maybe she wasn't an ordinary woman after all. Maybe she was one of the fae. He

30   *The Highlander's Mysterious Maiden*

reacted to her as if she was otherworldly and she had some supernatural look about her as well.

It was in the upturned nose, the roundness of her face, the fact there was a cleft in her chin he wanted to explore. He wanted…

He wanted.

'Are you fae or a woman?' he demanded.

He swore a flush began before it vanished. Like the woman herself had made it so. Definitely fae.

'Are you drunk or a fool?' she said.

He'd had a bit to drink, but stopped long before any of it affected him. Not that he would tell the woman when she was suddenly leaning forward, her nostrils flaring as she sniffed him.

He liked her closer, wanted to see if the flush was true, so he leaned forward too.

Rearing back, she retorted. 'Are you mad?'

That was direct, so fae or woman, he'd be direct as well. 'Most probably.'

Last Beltane he'd been out of his mind with fever and pain, he hadn't believed he would live. The pain and shame hitting him so hard, there were times he hadn't wanted to. Yet here he was a year later. He'd eaten, drunk, exchanged a few words. But when he could give no more, he was left alone with the shadows in the far fields. How they had called to him.

Her eyes narrowed. 'That's no excuse, you know.'

He snapped his eyes back to hers. They were so large and dark and what he could see of her hair was the same. He cursed the night and those shadows now since they hid this woman from him. 'An excuse for what?'

'For not helping that woman.'

There was no other woman than her, but out of curiosity, he unbent his torso and looked around. No one but his clan

Nicole Locke 31

members, no one as riveting as this creature who leaned into his space when most people avoided him now.

'What woman?' he said.

She looked at him as if he truly was mad. 'The one thrown into a sack and taken away against her wishes.'

Ah. She talked of Anna, who'd been trapped by Camron. 'It wasn't against her wishes.'

'She was screaming and hitting that man, I would most definitely say it was against something.'

Last night, Camron had arranged a secret meeting to address his unfortunate pursuit of Anna. Everyone knew of Camron's love for her, but over the last several weeks since Camron confessed that terrible wager to him, Seoc realised that Anna loved Camron just as fiercely back. She was too stubborn and hurt to vocalise it.

So between them all, including her sister, Murdag, Beileag and Hamilton, Camron had devised a plan to surround Anna tonight to get her to talk, to not run. To not let more time pass between them.

Seoc knew they would find their love together. And so, as a friend should, he'd joined the circle. Standing. Saying nothing. Feeling nothing. Then patient, tender, reasonable Camron threw a bread sack over Anna's head and rode off with her. As far as any of them was concerned, Camron should have done it years ago.

'It wasn't against her true wishes,' he corrected.

The woman huffed. 'I saw what I saw.'

Maybe Anna wasn't the only stubborn one. And yet... 'If you saw what you saw, then why aren't you helping her?'

The woman's eyes widened, her plump bottom lip pulled in, but then she cocked her hip and the demanding light to her eyes turned to pure fire. 'You were nearest. Probably be-

32 *The Highlander's Mysterious Maiden*

fore she was even placed on that horse. Are you saying you could do nothing?'

He liked her fire, but that bit of discomfiture and vulnerability when he pointed out she could have helped Anna was intriguing. Almost recognisable.

If he wasn't already alert to her charms, to the pull she had on him, he was now. Lust. Intrigue. What was happening to him? This feeling was more than simple distraction. None of it made sense when he shouldn't be interested at all. She'd done nothing but yell, blame, and point her finger at him. Yet, he wanted to throw a sack over her head and ride off with her.

'I didn't do nothing, I stood as I wanted to.'

If anything her expression turned disappointed. 'I should go then.'

'Because I stood?'

She eyed him from his toes to his head and in between. As if she was weighing him up at an auction. It made his heart beat that bit faster and he had the urge to grin. Her gaze fixed on his lips and he couldn't catch his breath.

She stepped back. 'I've got things to do.'

He needed to know with whom. 'Are you staying somewhere?'

Another tip up of her chin, another stare as if she dared him. 'Here.'

With whom? His heart hammered the incessant question. He wanted to know who was the fortunate family to have such a woman visiting. 'You just arrived?'

At her quick nod, he looked around, but no one came to greet her and he offered no shout out to find whomever she was to visit.

He didn't want to be without her company. And if he'd learnt anything from Camron and his gathering Anna in his arms to ride off with her, it was that he needed to seize the moment. He had no bread sack, only himself. Broken with his soul too quiet inside him, but not when he was with her.

Not when she was with him. How long would it last? He didn't hope for a for ever, but he was alive with her now and he wanted it. Wanted her.

How could he keep her here? He took a step closer. 'That's good.'

She hiked her satchel again and he was rewarded with her cape falling to the side. His mouth went dry and a certain prickling began in his hands, a heat in his veins, a feral possessiveness riveting his very bones.

With her cape brushed away from her body, what he'd only guessed at before was now truth. Her form would be a handful, even for him. Desire relentlessly pounded through him. Why now did he feel, why her? He didn't care. Or rather he did, but now wasn't the time to ask and answer questions.

He simply had to seize this moment in any way she would allow.

'Do you require food or drink?'

'What?'

'You've travelled and you might need refreshments,' he said. 'I could fetch you some.'

'Won't you help them?' she said.

Camron and Anna didn't need their help. 'They're long gone now.'

She looked over her shoulder and frowned.

Ah, she carried a tender heart being so concerned for his friends. 'And even if so, I'm telling you, lass, that it's a good thing.'

Her expression eased and his shoulders straightened at the accomplishment. He was conversing and feeling and all with someone new. It was sudden after being numb for so long he felt drunk with it. But with her frown fading and her shoulders easing, all because of a few words he said, he wanted to shout to the night sky. He, after all this time, had helped ease someone else's burden?

He wanted to do it again. Jogging to his skein and mug, he poured a healthy dose of his mead. On this perfect night of all nights, he wanted to share his best metheglin batch yet. He knew after all these months the herbs had flavoured the honey to perfection.

Walking back over, he thrust the goblet in front of her. 'Here, try this.'

She narrowly eyed the goblet, then him. 'What's this?'

'Mead.'

She licked her lips.

Ah, she was thirsty. First he could provide comfort and now sustenance. His chest bowed up.

'You said you weren't drinking,' she said.

'That's because it was waiting for you,' he said.

Her eyes shot to his and stayed. Studied him as though he'd have answers for her. He didn't.

She took the goblet, drank deep and smacked her lips. 'I can see.'

'See what?' he said almost breathlessly as he watched her mouth.

'Why you weren't drinking it—it could be improved, no?' she said.

Seoc stilled. Waited. She'd insulted his mead, yet he had no reaction to it. Only to her tongue which ran across her lips to taste his drink.

Madness certainly, but he didn't care. He could blame it on the drums, on Beltane, on the last horrifying year. Or he could believe it was this woman who'd arrived just in time to save him. No, that was madness.

No one could save him, no one would want to, but she stayed and stared at him. She poked and bothered him and he felt more alive than he ever had.

And…he couldn't think. This close he relished her height and the way the thin cape whipped around her legs in the light breeze. He loved the tightness of the satchel's strap now she'd reversed it and the way it cut right between her ample breasts.

He loved the way she looked at him as if she was as fascinated with him as he was with her.

Would she want this, he didn't know. She had come to upbraid him. But she'd arrived on Beltane. Beltane, not any other night, and Beltane was known for celebrating freedom and life. She'd arrived tonight and it was for a reason.

Taking the cup from her, he set it down. Then grabbed her hand and was rewarded with the widening of her greenish-brown eyes, but she didn't pull back. Not even when he fully wrapped his hand completely around the softness of hers.

'What are you doing?' she said.

He didn't know.

'What's happening here?' she said, her voice indignant and abrupt. But he felt her slight tremble ease and already her hand warmed in his. Had she been cold and trembling this entire time? Maybe he'd fix that with her, too.

Who was she? These little bits of vulnerability so quickly hidden he knew were a trained reaction. From her marching to him, then hesitating. From her cutting her blush short to this direct tone of voice, all hiding that slight tremble, the coolness of her fingers.

She was faking her bluster. And if that didn't speak deeply to something in him, he didn't know what else would. He'd been faking everything since Dunbar, but he wasn't faking this. He wanted her and, by God, before this night was through, he'd have her.

36   *The Highlander's Mysterious Maiden*

'Come with me,' he said. His voice already roughened; his body already strung tight.

'Where?' she said. 'Is it to find help for that woman?'

Oh, that did it. Still holding her hand, he walked towards the only place he knew there'd be privacy. The shadowy fields.

She dug in her heels. 'What are you doing?'

'Taking you,' he said.

'To go fix the mead?'

Still no reaction inside him for her insulting his mead. He'd have to see about that later. But her words stopped him. That stopped him because she truly didn't act as though she knew what he was about. Maybe he was the only one affected, maybe this whole thing towards her was one-sided. Maybe...

Cradling her face with his free hand and not letting her go with the other, he bent until his lips almost touched hers.

'No, for this.'

Chapter Four

She was exhausted. Confused. It was Beltane and the night with all its merriment had gone to her head. She was hungry, thirsty as well. Worried over travelling from one clan to the other, then arriving too late to be useful.

Those were the reasons Barabal held still as the man stood close to her. He dipped his torso, his warm breath brushed between them. Smelling of parsley and ale. Of him. And his words. Three simple words in that voice of his that sent exhilarating shivers up her spine.

Her weariness *had* to be the reason she simply stood there. It couldn't be because the hand cradling her cheek was a kind of tender touch she'd never known before.

It couldn't be because the nearness of him radiated a type of warmth not even fire could create. A fire flamed and flared and beckoned, and something of that was here in the space between her and this man. But there was more; an unexpected tension that kept her tethered, that kept her *still*.

Nothing kept her still. Why was she standing still? 'What are you doing?'

'I'd like to kiss you, and I want your permission,' he said.

She'd never been kissed in her life. No one had ever looked at her in any romantic way. Certainly not the way he was looking at her, all imposing and intense. Why would some

38   *The Highlander's Mysterious Maiden*

random man, no, *this* man, the only man she had ever found remotely attractive, want to kiss her?

'Why?'

He hummed. Yet it didn't sound as if he avoided an answer, but he had to think about it. Which should have felt insulting, but instead made her more aware of the other things about him. Like his deep rumbling voice which rolled warmth through her from her ears to the soles of her feet and everywhere in between.

Perhaps he would hum again if she asked more questions.

'Why did you have me drink the mead, then?'

He huffed and she felt his warm breath. 'Because I wanted you to taste it.'

His voice, if possible had gone huskier, his eyes full-blown dark. His calloused fingertips against her temple and jaw were so hot, it felt as if tendrils of fire arced from his simple touch.

'Which I did,' she said.

His eyes dropped to her lips, stayed there. 'Now I ask for a taste.'

That made no sense, the cup and skein were out of reach. 'You set the mead down.'

Another hum, quick this time like a rumble. A slight flutter of his fingertips against her cheek while his other hand tightened around hers. As though he wanted to hold her there longer. As though he knew she'd leave at any moment, and he didn't want that.

His lips quirked; his eyes roamed her face as if he'd never seen her before. 'You talk of the cup?'

'The cup of terrible mead.'

Almost a smile then, his eyes lighter, happy or close to it. It drew her in. How could it not? A man who stood apart from festivities, from all joyousness, whose gaze went far past flower garlands and looked to the unlit fields, now had eyes that sparkled.

At her.

Almost laughed.

At her.

The thought was like a sluice of ice over her heart. 'Is this some kind of joke?'

He blinked and the happy light dimmed in his eyes.

'Should I be looking over my shoulder because a great sack is coming my way?' she continued.

This wasn't some serendipitous attraction. He appealed to her, but how could she believe for a moment he might be attracted back? She'd been travelling for over a day. Her clothes were mud spattered, her hair in disarray. The satchel strap chafed the skin on her shoulder and neck.

She wasn't some fae from a tale as he'd accused her of. No, she was a big-boned, big, curved woman whom he'd tricked into drinking bad mead and believing he wanted to kiss her.

Until that smirking mouth gave away his jest on her. Ashamed, embarrassed, Barabal stepped back.

The awe-inspiring man held still for one fraction of a second as if what she had said stunned him.

He dropped his hand and straightened. His entire countenance changed in the tiniest of increments and she tracked the effect of her words on him. She'd lost the warmth from his hand, the scent of ale-scented leather when he dropped his touch. But all the other heightened senses disappeared as well.

The light in his eyes fully dimmed, his gaze grew distant. The softness of his lips tightened. He'd drawn in and up; he was no longer a man offering her food and drink, giving her curious smiles and a yearning tension.

He'd turned into that forbidding dark tree with twisted

40   The Highlander's Mysterious Maiden

roots. The one that stood all alone in near shadows and didn't race to rescue any maidens or offer kisses.

This imposing Graham clansman didn't offer her anything at all. Not one welcoming gesture in any of his features or countenance.

Not because she'd caught him at some game to make her a fool, but because what she had said offended him.

Barabal clutched her satchel strap.

She might as well not bother to unpack. She didn't know how she would continue on in the dead of night through unknown land. She didn't even know how to get through the tightly packed crowds celebrating Beltane. And if she skirted around, she'd likely interrupt some tryst, or be trapped by a drunken man who wouldn't listen to her refusal. Like— No, she wouldn't think of that time.

There was only this man here whose gaze was already over her shoulder and whose withdrawal brought only loss when she shouldn't feel any loss at all. She'd just met him.

He was the one who'd demanded kisses when he had no right, when he didn't even ask her name. Now he acted injured and insulted, when it was she who was. This had to be a trick, an elaborate one. She refused to have it.

'Are you to answer me? I did wonder if you had a terrible disposition after you didn't help that woman and now you play a jest on me?'

Never looking at her, he answered, 'Maybe it is a jest. For how could this be true?'

Gone was the intense stare, the voice that rumbled through her. Everything was distant, his question said more to himself than to her. He'd left, but she didn't know where he'd gone. 'What do you mean?'

'It's Beltane, isn't it? Only Beltane and nothing more.' Then without looking at her at all, he walked off.

Nicole Locke 41

Many people had turned their back on her when she talked. At first, Barabal had attempted to curb her tongue. But then she'd learnt that no one paid her any heed. In fact, all her instructions were made as suggestions, which made her feel as though she could not be of any assistance. So now she disregarded the finer points of conversations to state her point.

But this man had dismissed her and wandered off as if she wasn't standing there. As though he had a shroud across his eyes.

And what did she do, but watch him? Even if she wanted to call out, she didn't know his name.

She didn't want to. He'd played some cruel jest on her, one she didn't understand, but maybe that was the Graham way. Maybe hoisting women over their shoulders against their will and pretending kisses was their custom.

Except, he'd asked her permission to kiss.

Had he? No one wanted her and definitely not right upon meeting her. She must have inhaled too much smoke from the bonfires on her way over. Maybe she truly was hungry and a bit weak. It couldn't possibly have been that mead; it was too weak for any effect.

Looking about the crowd now, she could see that it had thinned out and those who were left were having far too good of a time to ask for any help.

Barabal clutched her satchel strap and moved the bag back to her front.

Now what was she to do? Even though it was easy to find that strange man who'd asked to kiss her before, he had disappeared.

'Oh, I missed him.'

Barabal turned.

A beautiful woman with long dark hair, wearing a far-too-

42 *The Highlander's Mysterious Maiden*

thin chemise and what looked like a gown thrown over her arm, looked curiously at her.

'Who?' Barabal wanted to ask why she was undressed, but it was Beltane, so it didn't need explanation. But a stunning half-undressed woman who was completely alone was curious.

'Seoc.' The woman stretched an arm up. 'A man about this tall and he places his hand upon his chest?'

Oh. This woman knew the man she'd just met, the man who'd said he wanted to kiss her and then walked away. She knew his name and how he hovered his hand. Knew him enough to ask for him, half-undressed as though she needed her gown mended or didn't want to waste any time when she finally was with this Seoc.

'I'm Murdag, by the way.' The woman smiled.

'Barabal,' she replied.

Huffing, the woman shifted the gown from one arm to the next. Frowned, then looked sheepishly back up. 'This must appear odd to you, but I went to the stables first and taking this off was necessary.'

Because, obviously, she wanted to meet Seoc for a tryst in the barn and desired no delay. 'You were to meet Seoc in the barn?'

Murdag laughed. 'Oh, that's funny. That man never cared for horses and lately his loathing has only worsened.'

'So it's you who likes horses?'

The woman blinked. 'I adore horses, one in particular, no matter how troublesome he can get.'

So Seoc didn't like horses, but Murdag went to meet him in the stables first and when he didn't show up, she went out to find him and drag him back. Barabal did not like this woman at all. Only because she was selfish with her trysts,

Nicole Locke 43

not anything to do with the fact her laugh was beautiful and she was half-naked, looking for Seoc.

'I so wish he'd adore me back,' Murdag said.

Half-undressed, no man could resist her. Obviously, Seoc had come to his senses and remembered he was to meet her so he could…adore her back. 'Maybe you should return to the barn.'

'Oh, I couldn't.' Murdag's brows drew down. 'I'm down to my underclothing and if I return there, I'll end up naked.'

Barabal did not need that picture. She didn't. What she needed to do was leave. But it was her first night here and she shouldn't be rude because that wouldn't make a nice impression. So she said the only polite thing she could under the circumstances. 'He probably won't mind.'

'No, he wouldn't.' Murdag snorted. 'He'd probably be glad to have every bit of my clothing to himself. You know he's ruined most of my gowns. It's why I take them off before even entering the stables. He nips and pulls and there it is: another gown ruined.'

Barabal could see that. Seoc staring intently, those hands of his, that strength. The way his lips looked when it seemed he was about to kiss her. He'd looked hungry enough to tear her clothing off too.

But he hadn't. She'd said a few words and he realised she wasn't this slender, ethereal creature before her and walked away. Which is what Barabal wanted to do because what was she to say now? 'You could tell him.'

'I talk to him all the time—you know how stubborn they can get,' Murdag said.

Barabal wouldn't know. No man had ever come close to wanting a conversation with her, let alone getting under her clothing. If they were stubborn at all it was in the obstinate way they wouldn't listen to her instructions. But not stub-

44   *The Highlander's Mysterious Maiden*

born in any way with trysts, and desire, and lust and tearing off clothing.

Murdag chuckled low. 'But it would be nice, wouldn't it, if horses could listen?'

'Horses?' Barabal choked.

'Not that I haven't thought it before with the stubborn creatures, or when they're hurting and they pleadingly look at you to make it better.'

They'd been talking about horses and not men naked in barn stalls, hay stuck in their hair. Barabal gaped, tried to cover it up, blinked her way back into composure. Usually, always, she was able to hide her reactions. When she was much younger, she'd trained herself to conceal her reactions. It was safer that way.

But this time she didn't do it quickly enough.

Murdag tilted her head, her expression easing to an understanding that had Barabal turning bright red. So red she knew not even the night's darkness could cover her embarrassment.

'All this time I've been standing before you in my chemise and mentioning Frenzy nipping at my clothes.' Murdag grinned. 'And you thought I wasn't talking of a horse, but of Seoc. Interesting.'

No, it wasn't. Closing off any reaction, even a blink that might give her away, Barabal kept her eyes steady on the woman whose eyes were filling with recognition and whose full lips looked as though they'd grin with glee at any moment. 'Who's Seoc?'

'The man who was talking to you like I am now...except much closer to you than me.' Murdag pointed. 'Isn't that his mead?'

Barabal looked to the skein and goblet still on the grass near her feet. So this Seoc walked off without his skein? How lazy. 'His mead?'

Nicole Locke 45

'Yes, his,' Murdag said. 'Didn't he tell you he makes it?'

If someone insulted something she'd worked hard on, she'd advise them right away why they were wrong and she was right. And this Seoc hadn't said anything at all, not even his name.

'No, he didn't,' Barabal said without a moment's hesitation. This was not the impression she wanted to make. Not at all. Never.

'And yet he was—' Murdag's expression turned almost intrigued, calculating. 'You know I haven't seen him like that with anyone ever.'

'Offering people bad mead?'

'You didn't like it.' Eyes wide, Murdag laughed. 'Please tell me you told him that. I can't wait to tell Beileag and Anna of this.'

Was the Graham Clan so close they told each other everything? 'There's nothing to tell.'

Murdag grinned. 'Oh, but there is and, if so, you have no idea how utterly pleasing it is you came here.'

Who was this woman who was undressed and talked of Seoc as though she knew him well when Barabal knew nothing at all?

She would have to travel the night to another clan's land unless she could redeem herself. Unless... 'If this Frenzy nips, you shouldn't stand so close to him.'

Murdag snorted. 'If you knew me, you wouldn't say that.'

But she didn't know her even though Murdag was wide eyed, staring at her as if she could see into her very soul and read all her thoughts. It was unnerving how closely she was staring at her as though she was an answer to a question.

Hadn't Seoc stared at her so intensely, too?

No, she had to be mistaken on that. Some Beltane madness coming over her because of the fire's smoke.

It had only been a jest he'd played on her. Maybe this woman played a jest, too, but until she knew, until she could find a home for herself, Barabal would try to cooperate.

Silly hope again? Perhaps, but she was also exhausted in her heart and her feet.

'Are the teeth all right?' she said.

'Frenzy's or mine?' Murdag vigorously rubbed her finger over her teeth. 'Did some of herbs from the mead get stuck in my teeth? I swear Seoc put extra greens in there this time. Don't you think he did? How embarrassing. I'm glad you told me of it else I'd be running around talking to everyone with a piece of green stuck there.'

Did this slender, beautiful woman think she was flawed? Even if Murdag's entire mouth was covered with foul-smelling rotting food, Barabal didn't think anyone would notice.

And the mead had the almost right amount of herbs, it was merely missing a few things like more honey or fruit at the beginning. Something to give it that upfront kick before the palate was enticed by all the flavour.

But then all the words Murdag had said sunk in. Was she trying to trick her into saying something of the herbs in Seoc's mead? Barabal couldn't shake the idea that Murdag played some game with her as well, or at least wanted her to blurt some truth or answer when she didn't even know what the question was.

Murdag suddenly rushed forward and bared her teeth. 'Did I get it all?'

Barabal blinked.

Murdag stepped back. 'Sorry, I tend to be a little more forward.'

It wasn't that. It was that someone had asked such a question of her. Usually it was more orders or facts, not something so personal.

'Yours are fine. I meant the horse's teeth,' she corrected. 'If there is no issue with them, or sores anywhere, then place your hands on either side of his muzzle and rub.'

'Can't imagine Frenzy would like that.'

'He won't, but he'll know his mouth is also bothering you. It might help with his nipping if you do it quick enough after he tears another hole in your gown.'

'That's brilliant. I should have known to do that.' The woman tilted her head. 'I believe we will be great friends.'

Was this entire clan mad? She'd never had a man who wanted to kiss her or anyone offering to be her friend. Her offer couldn't be true and she intended to test that.

'I have no time for friends.'

'Did you tell Seoc that?' Murdag said. 'Because something of the way he was leaning towards you didn't imply he would believe you any more than I do.'

She should never have been late to arrive here. Everything was wrong. Her days weren't like this.

'Shy, are you? Where are you from, Barabal?'

She wouldn't answer that. 'Why do you need to know?'

Murdag's brows creased. 'I wanted to know if you're visiting someone, some family we need to find, or if I can help you find a place to stay or work?'

Why did the fact she had no family still sting? The last thing she needed was this woman to help her find employment. Not even an hour here and she'd already be in someone's debt. Then as had happened so many times before the insinuating remarks would happen and she'd be run off as some beggar who couldn't pull her own weight. 'I'm not visiting, and I don't need you to find me anyone.'

Murdag smirked. 'Stubborn, too. Oh, this is going to be

48   *The Highlander's Mysterious Maiden*

fun. I'll leave, then, and perhaps see you in the morning. Tell Seoc I'm happy for him.'

Gripping the strap of her bag over her shoulder, Barabal watched the strange woman walk away. The Graham Clan was large enough not see her in the morning, or to be friends.

Or to tell this Seoc who wanted to kiss her anything. From now on, she'd avoid that man if she could.

She needed to prove herself first. And maybe, some time, she'd like a man to kiss her, but not when it was some Beltane folly.

Now what, though? The crowd had disappeared. There was still lots of laughter and much talk. But the musicians had taken their instruments and the people around the fires were diminishing as families and lovers took their leave.

She looked behind her in case someone else decided to surprise her with conversation or hurtful questions. Nothing but trees.

It had to be late. Truly late. Maybe late enough that'd it be almost morning. If she knew nothing else, then early morning was when baking and food needed to be prepared. After a night at Beltane, the cook or baker would need extra hands.

But she didn't want to go to the kitchens. She never wanted to go to the kitchens, so who else would be awake? Somewhere to keep her busy so she wouldn't have to think of this strange night and she had no place to go to any more.

Some place she could be accepted, left alone, or, better yet, listened to and appreciated.

Barabal snorted. Hope again. When would she ever learn?

Chapter Five

'Something is wrong with your brother.' Seoc strode over to Camron. It was the day after Beltane, the day after he'd felt for the first time in over a year and the first time he was rejected at anything in longer than that.

That stung.

Perhaps that's why when last night he'd walked away from the most beautiful woman he'd ever met and run into Murdag, he'd agreed to imbibing in all too much ale. He hadn't asked why his friend needed more drink, but then she hadn't asked him either. He'd appreciated it until she began to talk of her strange encounter with this woman called Barabal and wondered what he thought of her.

What had he thought of the woman who'd appeared out of the gloam and into his life?

By then he'd had twice as much ale as Murdag and thanked his stars he was twice as large. He should have remembered that though Hamilton was the usual suspect for games, they'd all played tricks on each other a time or two and this was Murdag's time.

He hadn't answered Murdag right away because he only had one thought and that was her name: Barabal.

Could it be any more perfect? It was a name that conjured curves he wanted to lose himself in for the rest of his life and

50   *The Highlander's Mysterious Maiden*

a sharp tongue that piqued his curiosity to unholy means on how she came about those words of hers.

Barabal. A name she'd given to Murdag, but not to him.

If he could feel any worse after her rejection, that did it. Though Murdag revealed their entire conversation and asked him about his side of matters, he reeled too much. So instead of answering his long-time friend, he'd walked away into those shadows and wandered all night.

Only to see Hamilton quietly conversing with the scouts recently returned with news of the English. Their bodies' positions and low murmured words immediately made him alert.

So he'd kept an eye on his friend and come to the conclusion that as badly off as he was, it wasn't as bad as Hamilton, who was as troubled as Seoc had ever seen him. But Hamilton didn't want to talk and Seoc couldn't find Beileag to see if she knew what was wrong with the happier twin. Thus, he came to Camron.

'What has Hamilton done now?' Camron said.

'First, can I say I'm surprised to see you alone this day after you whisked Anna away? I'd think after the years of waiting you wouldn't emerge from a bed for years.'

Camron grinned. 'Anna and I just returned. I thought we'd rest, but Murdag arrived asking for help on finding shelter.'

'For a horse?'

'For a woman just arrived.'

Everything in Seoc seized. 'Who?'

'I didn't ask for I was not invited to help; thus, here I am.' Camron chuckled. 'Tell me of Hamilton.'

Damn Hamilton, Seoc needed more on where Anna was headed because he knew the home they searched for was for Barabal. All night he'd walked, the numbness, the familiar desolation in his chest fighting with that finite interaction with that force of a woman. If he forgot her, if he even let slip away any of what they'd shared, he'd fear he'd fall into an abyss no one could reach.

'But I want to know what—'

'Brother first,' Camron said.

Seoc exhaled roughly. Camron's concern for his twin was justified. Still, the strength to talk of him now was slightly draining. He was a bucket filled with life-giving water, but there was a hole somewhere and he couldn't hold on to the water no matter how much he wanted to.

'Seoc?' Camron said.

'Tired only, my friend. I think the night is catching up with me.' Even now his thoughts drifted. 'It's not so much what Hamilton has done, it's what he hasn't done. No pranks or jests or even bawdy songs sung badly on Beltane. He's suffering.'

'You believe it's because of his wanting Beileag?'

'I know it is,' he said. 'It's clear they carry feelings for each other, so what is he doing?'

'Perhaps trying to undo the harm of that wager I made,' Camron said. 'About which you're still cross with me, no doubt.'

He was angry at both of them. 'Not cross. It may have helped you gain Anna's hand, but how can Hamilton gain Beileag if he pursued Murdag first?'

Camron snorted. 'Not as though Murdag gave him a chance.'

Seoc shuddered. 'Don't know what he was thinking about with Murdag, she has all those horses.'

'Is she any less comely than Beileag?' Camron said.

Seoc never thought about it before. 'I don't know what he thought to accomplish by ignoring Beileag last night.'

'Hamilton ignored Beileag?' Camron said.

'You were a bit occupied,' Seoc said. 'But while you were wooing Anna, with her throwing petals at you, Hamilton and Beileag stood like enemies forced in the same room.'

52   *The Highlander's Mysterious Maiden*

Camron frowned. 'I've been blind.'

'We all have,' Seoc said. 'But I believe it's more than Beileag that troubles your brother.'

'Tell me.'

So Seoc told him of how he'd spied Hamilton furtively talking with other scouts. How he'd avoided Seoc all day and how he'd seemed distracted.

'We've had meetings with council, what more information do you think he seeks?'

'I don't know, but it can't be good. Travel to Stirling in September is early enough for my comfort. I want the summer.'

Camron stepped back. 'All right, tell me what occurred last night while I was away with Anna.'

'I told you, I drank with Murdag, then walked.'

'Where?'

'The fields.'

Camron frowned and Seoc braced himself for more questions. More asking of why he did what he did. He didn't know why he sought the shadows and all the murky bits of night. No matter how much he thought he could reach them, they were always that bit further away. Last night was different, though. Instead of his thoughts spinning to nothingness, he dreamt of a woman whose soft cheek and scent kept him from his darkest thoughts.

Camron was right to believe something had occurred, but he was loath to talk about any of it. Because it could only be Beltane madness. He prayed that it wasn't.

'What are you up to today?' Camron said.

Seoc exhaled. 'I need to be off to the cellars.'

'A night after Beltane and you haven't checked your supply, man? You are slipping.' A pall fell over Camron's face. 'I apologise, my friend.'

Because last Beltane Seoc hadn't checked his supplies ei-

Nicole Locke 53

ther. There were others who knew how to make the favourite classic mead. Others who could check the supplies after anything ran out after such a grand celebration. Just because he was best at it didn't mean he was essential. His sword arm had been essential.

Now he was chasing shadows. Yet Barabal hadn't looked at him with pity. Disdain, certainly. Pique and confusion, absolutely. Then that moment when he'd touched her round cheek, when he'd brushed the tip of his thumb along the cleft in her chin, then he'd seen something else. Desire had flushed and warmed those cheeks, had darkened her impossibly dark eyes.

Desire for him. And as she stared, as she took in all of him, none of that wavered and he would have given his favourite recipe to know what she had been thinking. Because he would have sworn it wasn't what she actually said.

And he would have gladly made her all the mead she'd want for years, if he knew what she'd been feeling because he had felt too much. The flush of her skin, that pointed edge of her chin, the warmth of her breath.

That had been the sweetest of all. She couldn't breathe naturally, the one tell-tale sign she'd been as affected as him. She never did answer if she was fae or a woman.

He believed her to be both. There he'd been, staring in the shadows, wondering when he'd be nothing more than utter numbness and nothingness, when she'd suddenly materialised...

He looked to Camron, whose expression looked both grim and patient. He'd wandered again. What had they'd been talking off?

Ah...him, and his injuries, and how he'd never be allowed to forget either by his scars or his friends. 'Not an insult to have friends who care.'

Camron gave a short nod. 'If I remembered differently, at the time you didn't care much for the attention.'

54   *The Highlander's Mysterious Maiden*

Once he'd been transferred from the travois to an actual bed, he'd slung his fists so often at Camron and Hamilton's jaws he was surprised they weren't permanently marred. 'Don't be standing too close to a man half out of his mind with fever.'

Camron's expression shut completely.

Because they both knew he'd swung his fists more times after the fevers and the healing than he did when he was in that weakened condition.

'You mentioned my brother was out of sorts?' Camron said. 'Could there be anyone else?'

Hamilton and himself apparently, but he wouldn't be confessing to anything.

'Everyone will seem out of sorts to your good fortune. I don't need to ask how your night went. You're so happy, you're glowing.'

Camron regained his grin. 'Men don't glow.'

'How do you think I found you so easily?' he said. 'And how is Anna?'

'Glowing.' The corner of Camron's lips quirked. 'She's agreed to marry and we talked of everything.'

He had to ask. 'Maclean as well?'

'That man will cease his haunting.'

That time in their lives still brought him regret, but if Anna was eased and if his friend was married, it could not be better news.

'I am truly happy for you both.' He was only burdened and saddened for himself. For one blinding moment his life had changed last night. Or he'd thought it had.

Blind was the right word for him. Beltane madness, yet Barabal, a woman who did not tell him her name, still lightened his dark thoughts.

Camron tilted his head. 'You are well?'

Could his childhood friend tell he'd been completely al-

Nicole Locke 55

'tered by an encounter that was so brief it should have been inconsequential, but he still reeled from it?

'As well as too much drink would leave me. I'd worry more about Murdag.'

Camron frowned. 'She looked well enough when she interrupted Anna's sleep.'

Ah, yes, because of Barabal needing lodging. So the woman who'd turned his life upside down had stayed. But where and why?

Seoc wanted to ask Camron, but at his softened expression, he knew his friend was thinking of his love again. It was as if all the years of wanting and separation had healed overnight between them.

Seoc would never know a love like theirs. Not if he stayed numb. But then he hadn't exactly been numb last night, had he? His reaction to the stranger had to be his imagination, but still he could not shake her from his thoughts.

'At least she was dressed this morning,' Camron said.

'Who?' Seoc said.

'Murdag—you haven't noticed?'

'Noticed what?'

'Apparently she's often been running around in her chemise.'

His friend implied Murdag went without her clothing more than once? 'Often? When?'

Camron chuckled. 'Just last night, my friend.'

'She should not do that.'

'Because?' Camron said.

Seoc turned his full attention to Camron, who did not hide his enquiring expression. Did this fool think he was interested in Murdag? 'She is like a sister to me.'

Camron sighed. 'I guess that answers matters. Anna always wondered if anything would blossom between you, but since you don't notice when she's half-naked, I would guess there is nothing there.'

Murdag was beautiful and full of life. Something he didn't know if he ever was. 'She likes horses too much.'

Camron snorted. 'Should have known that'd be a deterrent. Although, that being said, if she's a sister to us, maybe we should say something about the chemise thing she's doing lately.'

'You can. Last time she was displeased with me I had to clean the stables.' Seoc fake-shuddered.

'Was that humour I hear?' Camron asked again.

Seoc schooled his expression. 'Only truth.'

'Are you certain you're well?'

Why did he keep asking that? Did he glow? He'd felt something last night and he couldn't let it go. It probably showed, but he wouldn't talk about it with Murdag when she asked and he wouldn't with Camron. It was humbling enough the way it had ended. A denied kiss and she hadn't shared her name.

'I'd worry more about you after using the word blossomed.' Seoc forced a chuckle, felt the pull in his chest and everything light vanished. 'You now sound like a matchmaker.'

Camron huffed. 'I longed for one woman all my life, fates preserve anyone in need of my matchmaking skills.'

'But you picked the right one. Your average is fairly good.'

'Fairly? It's unequalled,' Camron's grin dropped. 'But I wonder about Murdag. Has she seemed more reckless or restless since we returned?'

'I haven't noticed.' What more had he lost since Dunbar?

'You observed my brother well enough,' Camron said.

Only because, in the hope to avoid everyone, Seoc often skirted the edges of their homes and Hamilton had been doing the same. 'Not as much as I'd like. I believe he's making decisions without us.'

Camron frowned. 'I always wished he'd set aside his careless ways, but not if he suffers.'

'He's not you.'

'And why would he want to be?' Camron said. 'But regretfully, I believe he struggles with it.'

'Because you're twins and should be the same?'

Camron shook his head. 'Because there any many changes ahead of us and he wants to hold on to what is here.'

Even if Seoc wanted to hold on to their old way of life, his had been torn from him by a sword's edge. He couldn't remember those carefree days enough to bring them back. If he felt anything at all, he'd envy Hamilton's passion. 'Many changes.'

Camron clapped him on the shoulder. 'Look, my friend, things haven't been so poorly between us and the English.'

Seoc knew why Camron was vague in his words when he truly should have said between the Scots and English since Dunbar. Since the forces of the Comyns had been bested by Surrey and King Balliol surrendered to King Edward. Camron never wanted to talk of Dunbar to Seoc. Which was just as well; Seoc never mentioned either. What was the point when they had all been there? Still, Seoc looked away so Camron couldn't see his eyes dim. He had had no hope since Dunbar.

Camron cleared his throat. 'Andrew Moray and Wallace have been giving them a good fight up north, haven't they? It's only a matter of time till they make their way south and we join them.'

He wasn't the same man he was at Dunbar, not in body or in heart. Swinging his gaze back, he answered, 'So we're off to war with little training. Tell me how that's better?'

'You think I have trained like I did before? I have been pursuing Anna.' Camron said. 'And you at your weakest is another man's fortitude.'

He had been as strong as he'd ever been at Dunbar, and

58   *The Highlander's Mysterious Maiden*

still he'd failed. Camron might believe he had strength, but Seoc knew differently. It wasn't merely his sword he needed to get used to, but his heart. Since he had nothing inside of him, he knew any fight left in him was gone.

Still, it did not matter since they'd all been called to Stirling. His only choice was to rally and march alongside his friends with whatever was left of himself and protect them. 'My weak is weak,' he said.

Camron arched his brow. 'Well then, the day isn't over. We can begin now.'

'Shouldn't you be seeing to Anna?'

'I've already seen to Anna.' Camron smiled.

Seoc would have to get used to his friend's happiness. 'And Hamilton?'

Camron paused a beat. 'Word will spread that we train, and Hamilton will come to us.'

The reasoning was sound, but Seoc was loath to pick up a sword. Over the last year as they'd scouted the neighbouring clans, he'd been forced to hold it a time or two. But if anyone noticed his lack of using it, it wasn't mentioned.

He didn't know if he could block even the most basic of moves.

When Camron rubbed his forehead, Seoc jumped on the tell. 'Perhaps the night has caught up to you?'

Camron lowered his hand. 'I'm not tired, plus don't you want to enact your revenge?'

'For what?'

'You weren't pleased on the wager made to gain Anna's hand.'

No, he hadn't been, but that outburst he'd made, that rage at the thought his friends took advantage of their one chance at love succumbed, as everything had, to nothingness.

The thought he couldn't hold on to his convictions weighed heavy in his chest. 'It was a bad decision that turned out well.'

Camron's brows creased before he gave a jaunty tilt to his head. 'So no revenge.'

Revenge would have taken some interest and Seoc felt none. Still, he answered with something that might quell Camron's studying gaze. 'Are you craving a poorly flavoured mead so badly you taunt me?'

'Isn't that what you've been feeding us already all these years? How can that possibly be any revenge?'

Seoc huffed. 'Now you are giving me ideas. Maybe a bit of poison mixed in to rid myself of your bad jests.'

'You won't get rid of me. Not when Anna is searching for beds and rooms for Beltane visitors and will be looking for a new bed for us as well.'

'Don't want to sleep under her parents' roof?' Seoc said.

'More aptly I don't want to sleep next to Murdag since Anna shares her room,' Camron said. 'That woman snores.'

Seoc didn't need to ask why Camron knew this. Since they were young, Murdag shared every private moment. So many times, he and the others wished she wouldn't be so vocal about everything.

'Are there any homes empty or partially built?' Seoc said.

'I'll look into that,' Camron said. 'So, happily so, there's no rest for me. We can train, then I'll help. There is time.'

Seoc had never seen his friend so content or filled with more purpose. Camron was correct that Moray and Wallace and their wins up north could be enough to turn the tides in their favour. He didn't want to think, now that his friend had a true marriage and a true future, that what they fought for could be lost.

If he could do something to prevent that, then he would. 'Then we train.'

Chapter Six

A low chuckle and a melodious squeal woke Barabal from a restless sleep. She opened her eyes in time to see a scampering half-naked woman clasping the hand of a completely naked man, who was happily loping behind her.

It was a sight that would have woken anyone. But it wasn't the complete lack of privacy that startled Barabal. It was the fact she'd fallen asleep and was currently slumped against some tree.

Rubbing her eyes, Barabal adjusted until she was fully seated against the roughened bark. Her satchel was still at her side, but her clothes were soaked through from the wet ground. It was full daylight. And by the look of the sun's direction, it was well past noon.

On a groan, she stood and brushed off her cape and gown. She was covered in leaves and mud and the breeze against her wet clothes made her shiver.

Barabal didn't know how she'd got here. She'd wandered around the fields for a long while after Murdag left her. To occupy her hands and stop her intrusive thoughts on a certain Highlander, she'd picked up strewn goblets, clothing, platters broken and intact and anything else that didn't belong. As best she could, she made various piles for others.

It wasn't much, but perhaps some man could find their

braies again. Although if they belonged to the man who'd gleefully followed the woman, it might be hours yet until he was concerned with any bits of clothing.

When and why had she decided this tree was the spot to rest? She couldn't remember. Exhaustion must have overcome her.

Perhaps it was best to start all over again with a new day. There was certain to be further tidying up needing to be done and her extra hands might be welcomed. In fact—

'You must be Barabal.'

Barabal swung around. A woman with long black hair, blue eyes and a glow about her that reminded Barabal of happiness stood behind her.

Was the entirety of the Graham Clan insistent on walking up behind people? And why couldn't she hear them when she was always diligent? Always. Her life depended on it.

'Why must I be?' she asked.

The woman gave an odd smile. 'I suppose you don't have to be, but my sister, Murdag, has been looking for a woman named Barabal. When she couldn't find her, she asked for my help. I thought perhaps you might be her since you bear an uncanny likeness to her description.'

Now what was she to reply to that—pretend she wasn't who she was? There would be no purpose to say otherwise. As embarrassing as it was because the rest of her appearance was as dishevelled as her clothing, she answered, 'I never required her to look for me.'

'It's best not to require Murdag to do anything,' the woman said. 'I believe she said you were interesting. And once you know my sister, you'll realise she never lets anything go once she's thinks you're a friend.'

Not everyone she had met in her travels had been cruel and callous. There were many who attempted to befriend

62   *The Highlander's Mysterious Maiden*

her or at least offer some courtesy. But no one, not since her mother, had been interested about her.

'That's the most ridiculous thing I've ever heard,' she said.

Her remark only resulted in a quirk to the beautiful woman's lips. 'That may be true—I can't think of the last time my sister asked me for help. In fact, she goes out of her way to avoid me to be honest. You can't believe the times we argue.'

Something like wistfulness stabbed at Barabal's heart. Fool. She had no use for an arguing sister. And was this woman purposefully misunderstanding what she was saying?

'So then why are you here?'

'Because if you intend to stay, and given that it's past noon I'll surmise you will at least for another day, then you'll need a place to sleep. Unless you like sleeping in the forest?'

Leaves stuck to her; shame filled Barabal. It seemed impossible for her to make any useful impression. 'What fool wants to sleep in the forest?'

'Exactly. I have a place for you, if you like.' Smiling, the woman pivoted and briskly walked away. Barabal snatched up her satchel and followed.

She put the strap over her head. 'Are you taking me in?'

The woman shook her head. 'I've been occupied trying to find our own home.'

Was the woman new here as well? That made no sense. But if she asked questions, then that often invited the other person to ask questions of her. And she didn't want that.

'Won't you ask me where, then?' The woman slowed her pace—that serene smile never left her expression. Could someone be that happy?

Barabal shrugged. 'A corner in the stables or a spare rug in someone's house is fine with me.'

The woman lost her serene expression, and her brows drew down. 'That is… We have better accommodations for visitors.'

She didn't want to be a visitor, but she'd have to prove herself first and that would mean not being greedy. 'I have no requirements.'

'None at all?'

There was one. 'Is it near any kitchens?'

'The kitchens are only near the manor house. If that's all you require, then this will be easy. You must be exhausted from your travelling from…?' The woman trailed her words.

She wanted to make this her home, she needn't lie, but still she averted her eyes as they continued to walk. 'From the Buchanan Clan.'

'So you're a Buchanan.'

'That's where I came from.'

She thought the woman would push, but when she didn't Barabal didn't feel relief. Not until she said, 'Well, we all come from somewhere. This has always been my home, and now it will always be my home, as soon as I can find a new house.'

Why now? Barabal again held her tongue as they continued their steady pace. Occasionally the woman at her side was greeted, some asked about her sister, or a man named Camron.

When that happened, the woman would blush and a contented look would enter her eyes. Was Camron her husband or intended?

'You don't ask many questions, Barabal. You haven't even asked for my name.'

The polite thing would be for this sister of Murdag's to offer it, but since she didn't, Barabal believed she'd been too rude to have earned it. 'Is it important?'

The woman hummed. 'My sister mentioned you might be shy. I'm Anna.'

The Graham women were odd. Instead of simpering away

64 **The Highlander's Mysterious Maiden**

at her abruptness, or preferably returning a few caustic words in return, Anna kept her glow of happiness and her determined walk.

Instead of taking charge the way she usually did, Barabal indebted herself by following this woman so she could accept lodgings she hadn't earned. Next, she knew she'd be asking for somebody to feed and clothe her. Or wasting time by asking about people's lives. Perhaps she—

'Here we are.' Anna waved a hand to a house with a small door which immediately swung open. A woman, younger than her, and carrying a bucket of clothes, walked out.

'Oh, Mary, I'm glad we caught you before you went to the creek,' Anna said.

The woman hiked the bucket on to her hip. 'I'm surprised to see you here today, Anna, since you seemed well and truly caught last night. Did you enjoy getting what you always wanted, but don't deserve?'

Barabal watched Anna's face flush even as a steely glint entered her blue eyes. 'No more surprised than I am to see you having all the time to wash your clothes today. After all your efforts last night. I may be caught, but it seems as though someone got away.'

The woman's back stiffened and something inside Barabal, which had been fumbling along, righted itself. She might not be comfortable with happy Anna, and certainly not with her forward sister Murdag, who pretended to be worried for her. But Barabal recognised the sound of a jealous, unkind woman and these were the kind of enemies she knew how to put in their place.

With a false smile, the woman added, 'It's quite a tale you and Camron revealed in front of the entire clan. One that I'm certain is to be repeated for years to come.'

Anna's smile was brief. 'Oh, good. I don't want last night

Nicole Locke 65

to be forgotten and I'll gladly regale anyone who asks on all the happy details. But for now, this is Barabal and she needs a place to stay while she travels. Last I remember, this home has a spare bed.'

Mary's eyes swung to her and lost their venom. With a smile that would have been convincing had Barabal not seen the exchange between the women, Mary replied, 'Always glad to have new people and there is a bed available here, if you like.'

'As long as it's not next to yours,' Barabal said. At the woman's tightened expression, Barabal added, 'Because I don't want to crowd you and make you move any of your things.'

Mary pursed her lips, but Barabal kept her expression guileless, until the woman stepped aside. 'No inconvenience at all since the bed's not near mine. Sorry to not show you myself, I must be on my way.'

When Mary was out of earshot, Anna huffed. 'I apologise. My sister warned me about bitter feelings. I ignored a good man for a long time and the other women noticed and resented it.'

'Camron declared his feelings a bit unusually last night,' Anna continued. 'Fortunately, he waited for my stubborn self to recognise him for the man he is and accept him. Don't know what's to happen to me in the future if I smell bread and flowers again.'

Barabal gaped. This woman was the one carried off last night?

Anna laughed. 'Too much? I believe my sister's enthusiasm has got me a bit forward as well.'

Now that she stood closer to Anna, she could see the woman's gown was as rumpled as her own. As if she'd spent the night in the fields, but instead of alone, she'd spent it with a man.

66   *The Highlander's Mysterious Maiden*

An image of Seoc's entranced expression flickered before her and Barabal shook it off. He'd only jested he wanted her. The moment she gave him any resistance he'd wandered off for the lovely Murdag.

Who was Anna's sister, apparently. She truly needed this day done. 'I find being overly friendly a waste of everyone's time.'

Anna's glowing expression dimmed, but only a bit. 'Not a gossiper or question asker, I see.'

'Would my lack of questions affect gaining a bed?' Barabal asked.

'Direct again. Now I know why my sister likes you.' Laughing, Anna waved her towards the door.

Opening it, Barabal stepped into the dimly lit one room with several beds, a table between each, and two women who sat on one bed, their heads bowed together as they whispered.

When they saw her and Anna enter, they abruptly stood and gave wide smiles. Maybe they were genuine, but Barabal didn't care. If Mary came from this room, she was determined to believe that all of them were horrible.

'I'm Barabal,' she announced. 'I intend to live here.'

The dark-haired one's expression crumpled. 'That would be your bed, then. Next to mine.'

Barabal eyed the bed, which was piled with items. Did they think she would sleep on top of their clothing?

The other woman, with light-coloured hair, continued, 'Welcome, Barabal. I'm Joan, I hope you like it here.'

Four beds and now four women. A few items around for comfort, but not much, and that included storage. It was meagre, but cosy and unusual. 'What is this place?'

'We requested this home to be built when we had nowhere else to go,' Joan said. 'My parents died, and my brother and his family took their home. I didn't want to live there and Eunice here comes from the Murray Clan.'

So they had no place, just like her, and the Graham Clan built somewhere for them to live. Barabal wasn't softened by Joan's words, however. They'd whispered between themselves and Mary treated Anna poorly.

Anyway, Barabal didn't have time for friends until she found she was accepted as useful in a clan, and she truly didn't have time for people who were inconsiderate.

She dropped her satchel beside the bed. 'Well? How am I to sleep on top of all this?'

Eunice gave off a little sound before she scooped up the items from the bed, dropped half of them, then dropped all of them trying to gather the ones already on the floor.

Barabal watched the woman struggle grabbing the stockings, linens and other bits to place them on the opposite bed. Eunice wouldn't have to struggle so much if there was a bit of organisation around here.

'And are there no hooks on the walls to hang our cloaks?'

Joan shook her head. 'There's been no time for—'

'I saw you sitting on the bed and conversing in the middle of the day. That seems time enough to get some hooks on the walls for clothes.' She looked around. 'At least Mary intended to do washing, though it's late for that in the day, isn't it? How will it have time to dry?'

Eunice gave another sound as she placed some trinkets on another's bed.

'Maybe she needs help in her tasks?' Barabal arched her brow when they weren't getting her hint. 'I believe that moment to help Mary is now, don't you?'

Eunice straightened and Joan's expression tightened. 'If you believe—'

68 *The Highlander's Mysterious Maiden*

'Honestly, do I have to do everything around here?' Huffing, she took off her cloak and threw it on the bed.

Sharing an expression, the two women hurried past her and out the door.

Barabal half expected Anna to either throw her hospitality away, or scurry off like the others. Instead the woman, who was as uncannily beautiful as her sister, looked as if she might burst into laughter.

'This place will do,' Barabal said.

'You should know when Eunice is apart from the others, she's not so terrible.' Anna looked like she wanted to grin. 'I can see why Seoc noticed you.'

Did these women have nothing better to do than make up stories, and what did she care for Eunice? 'Seoc did not notice me.'

'Then you went up to him first?' Anna said. 'I think my sister might be right about you.'

She refused to make any more comments.

Keeping her grin, Anna pointed to the walls. 'I'll see to those hooks and maybe some more blankets. Can you think of anything else you need?'

Though she was loath to ask, she'd lost half a day and couldn't waste any more of it. 'A place to work?'

'Kitchens need—'

'Anywhere but there,' she blurted and kicked herself for being so obvious. She was absolutely useful in the kitchen. Her sauces were unparalleled and something she created to find comfort, but working with people in the kitchen was something she avoided, for it caused a nightmare she'd like to forget.

'Are you certain, because Cook could use a hand with food preparation. Most of the men have returned and it's as though they haven't had a true meal in years.'

Nicole Locke 69

Where had they returned from? If this was some intrigue like at the Buchanan Clan, she wanted no part of it. 'You wouldn't want me in the kitchens.'

'Then no kitchens.' Anna tilted her head. 'By any chance do you know anything about carpentry?'

Raising her chin, she answered, 'I know little of carpentry. I know how to sweep and know not to get in the way. I'm strong enough to hold a stout dowel or two and if there's work elsewhere that needs doing, I'm just as good as the next person to carry whatever's needed.'

'That should do. The mill is one of the largest buildings over that direction, you should try there. There is time still today.' Anna yawned. 'Final meal should be in three or four hours from now. I believe my lack of sleep is catching up to me so I might not be there, but Murdag will.'

'Can I not get a meal if someone won't escort me?'

Anna slowly shook her head as if she'd said something funny instead of half the truth. It had happened to her before. 'I believe you can eat anything you want. Especially ask for anything that requires more herbs than usual. And welcome, Barabal; I mean that truly.'

Did she? 'I was born a Colquhoun.'

Anna's eyes startled wide and Barabal wished she could take back that bit of honesty.

'Oh, I was just there myself. Maybe in our travels we missed each other,' Anna said.

Had this woman meant to sound so remiss? Not wanting more confusing emotions thrown her way, Barabal frowned.

'Well, we're not missing each other now. I look forward to more of our talks, tell Seoc hello when you see him.'

'I won't—' Barabal started, but the strange woman stretched her arms above her head and walked out of sight.

70   *The Highlander's Mysterious Maiden*

There was something odd about the two sisters that wasn't easily dismissed.

But then who could she dismiss from the Graham Clan? Certainly not Seoc, the man who had jested he wanted a kiss. He couldn't be true either, could he?

There had been so many people in her life with just as many temperaments she had to puzzle through to be offered a place to sleep or a piece of bread. So many ways to greet simply so she wasn't run off from a clan the moment she arrived. She thought she knew how to interpret others.

But she could solve no one's intentions here. Murdag offering friendship, Anna welcoming her. And Seoc...

Barabal exhaled slowly. These people didn't know her enough to offer any such friendship or anything else. The things Seoc had said to her were a jest on his part. That was proven when he'd walked away in the direction of Murdag.

It was best she ignored these strange people, and focused on this little building that was to be her home. Even without hooks, it was better than some places she had stayed.

Did she dare unpack?

The others looked as though they had, their personal items, as meagre as her own, placed in baskets under the little tables by their beds. She didn't need much. Shoes mostly right now. Maybe she'd go to the cordwainer's first for work. People always needed shoes.

With that thought, but not knowing in what direction to go, she headed out. A few people smiled or stared, but mostly she was ignored. On the path she'd chosen a small crowd had gathered, but there was space to go around them so she didn't think any of it, until the cheers rose above her thoughts.

Then she noticed the crowd very much, but more specifically, the men in the centre of that crowd. Had she gone to the lists? Again, she meant to walk around, but her eyes snagged on the large man in the centre and her feet stopped until her thoughts could catch up.

It was Seoc, but not the man who'd stood alone at night on Beltane. He was just as large, deep rich brown hair just as messy, his form, the features of his face, all the same. But nothing else was. Breeches, boots, no tunic. Uncovered was the strength anybody glancing at him would see. A slight sheen on his golden skin, brown earth caught along one shoulder and across his cheek.

He was in a half-crouch, sword in hand, his entire being engaged until his muscles were taut and in sharp relief, and she was struck in awe.

Can I kiss you?

This was the man, this beast, this hulking silhouette, who'd asked permission to kiss her? He was too primal, too predatory.

The sword he held was formidable, yet the handle looked laughably small in his sizeable hand. His wrists twirled the steel as though it was no more than a will-o'-the-wisp.

A laugh not of joy, but of a darker victory. His opponent grunted, but then grinned. 'Come at me, then,' he jibed.

Spine straightened, Seoc rolled his immense shoulders.

Barabal's breath caught. He was magnificent in his stature. How had those massive hands felt tender against her cheek?

Muscles bunched as he lunged and swung. A clang of steel rang out and hit somewhere in her middle. She vibrated with the reverberation.

He wasn't handsome, but there was a beauty in the majesty of the toughened lines of his sharp cheekbones, something feral in the jut of his jawline.

A shout, something primal, as he charged forward. His hair falling in line behind him, his feet showing speed far quicker than anyone could expect.

72   The Highlander's Mysterious Maiden

Something equally primitive rushed inside her.

The man facing him feinted to the left. Another taunt said that she couldn't decipher and their position changed.

His eyes were on his opponent, but he faced her squarely and she admired all his form. As he bared his teeth, Seoc's muscles tensed, his strength held back by his will, by his mastery.

A powerful awareness shot through her. Nothing she'd ever felt before, but knew what it was: desire. She squeezed her knees together as lust ripped through her. She'd seen others fall prey to the emotions, but she was plummeting.

She couldn't catch her breath. Felt her lips part in one weak pant. This is what she'd felt last night. When he'd almost had her in his arms.

He clasped his sword in both hands now, raised it and then she saw it…like the hand of God had torn his chest in two only to smash it back together. All the bones and muscles intact and perfectly formed, merely a scar like a shallow cavern remaining.

That scar wrapped across his chest, and along one of his sides, yet he fought like that? She could see there was a tightness, a constriction that limited the ease of the fight in him. But it made him no less formidable a warrior.

For he had lived through such an agony that had cracked him in two. Barabal locked her now shaking knees.

On Beltane she had been riveted by his presence. Felt his great oak tree strength. Understood that something within him was snarled just underneath his façade. Was this scar part of it?

She'd thought him magnificent before, now a palpable *need* beset her. Feet still, knees locked, yet her body leaned towards him as he and his opponent continued their training.

The man he fought danced on his feet, lowered his sword and gave a wide opening that Seoc took and rushed forward.

Until the man swung his fist and connected with his nose. A blunt crack and a huff of pain before Seoc darted back.

'God's ale, Camron,' he spat.

The man laughed as Seoc wiped his bloodied nose.

'Maybe you do need more practice.'

Perhaps it was the pause in their training, a lull in their taunts, but Seoc's spine stiffened, his muscles gone taut before his head jerked and his gaze snapped to hers.

His grey eyes blew hot. His muscles tightened and flexed as he tossed his sword to the confused man at his side.

Barabal pinched her gown up. Her feet suddenly able to move, she swung and hurried the other way. She had no time for whatever he was about. At least that was the lie she told herself.

Chapter Seven

His day was shot with a continuing malaise of too much ale, Beltane festivities and the woman who'd rejected him, so Seoc reluctantly raised his sword and faced his long-time friend. But from the first arc of his sword, he cursed the agreement. His scar pulled and his skin stretched. The tightness constricted the natural flow and sweep of his arms. His reach wasn't quite what it was. He had to advance more than he liked, a move that in the short term wouldn't matter, but over time, would exhaust reserves best left to staying alive. So, too, he had to deflect more often.

He found no pleasure in the squash of wet earth at their feet, the smell of leather, steel, the savoury scent of allium coming from the gardens.

Not even the solid punch of Camron's fist against his nose conjured a gleeful grin as it would have in the past. There were only a few men who dared reach past the hilt of his sword, let alone get past his guard. It was too dangerous, but Camron, an experienced swordsman, knew him well. Before Dunbar, he would have been prepared for a simple punch, or been pleased to have been bested.

Now, however, he simply absorbed the throbbing pain of it. When Camron waited, most likely for him returning a swing or exchanging taunts, Seoc slumped. His own grin falling, Camron stepped back, his expression turning serious.

Seoc tried to rally some semblance of camaraderie except he felt nothing and, though his nose stung, the numbness that continually haunted him descended.

He was about to cede the entire day until he heard that feminine gasp and every fibre of his being tracked it until he was rewarded by a transfixed Barabal.

Something in her widened eyes and blush alerted him to the very physical truth: she admired what she saw.

Without thought, he gave a bark of warning to Camron before he tossed his sword to his friend to pursue a woman whose startled gaze warded off the numbness he felt.

But he lost her.

Maybe he'd tarried with his words to Camron, who looked pleased on his calling off their training. Or maybe he'd wasted moments attempting to tidy his bloodied nose and mud-caked breeches. He certainly took his eyes off Barabal when he picked his tunic and pulled it over his head. Because she hadn't been far from him when he spotted her and yet she was nowhere to be seen.

Where the hell could she be?

He wiped sweat from his brow and cursed when his hand came away with a streak of mud. Damn Camron for flinging it when Seoc had forced him into a puddle. Camron might have mud on his ass, but he had it over his face.

He was in no shape to pursue the woman from last night, but the widening of her eyes and that feminine gasp knocked reason from him. He felt a certain alertness at her reaction to him. Something essential, like taking a breath for the first time.

She might have rejected him last night, but he was compelled to talk to her.

After months of nothingness, he'd be a fool not to pursue it.

76   *The Highlander's Mysterious Maiden*

Rounding the pen of pigs and children drawing with sticks in the mud, he almost ploughed into one of his clanswomen.

He stepped back, while Joan's hands raised. Neither one of them hurt, he apologised to move on.

When she didn't step around him, he looked down. 'You can knock into me any time.' Joan smiled.

Still looking over her head and trying to hide his impatience, he said, 'I'd likely hurt you.'

'Even better.' Her smile turned seductive. 'It looks as though you trained hard. Back at my house I have some water and linen to clean blood and mud splatter.'

What did he care for that? Seoc ran his sleeve roughly over his face. 'You didn't see Barabal run this way, did you?'

Joan's smile fell. 'I did, but luckily she didn't see me.'

That snapped his gaze to the tiny woman, who seemed mollified by his sudden attention because she straightened and her eyes became earnest. As though she had to tell a story.

He had no time for this.

'Do you know Mary, Eunice, and I allowed that woman to stay with us and she demanded we make changes and hasten our laundry?'

'Truly?'

Whatever was in his expression emboldened her because Joan placed her hand on his arm. Now he had no complaint with his fellow clanswomen, but he'd seen a time or two when those three weren't exactly kind, so he'd never much cared for their company.

And he truly didn't care she was touching him. But she had seen Barabal's direction, and he needed all the help he could get.

Joan nodded as if she told a terrible secret. 'You should have heard her cruel words to poor Mary after she kindly warned Anna that her Beltane foolishness will surely follow her for ever.'

'Foolishness?' he said. Maybe he was capable of feeling again, because something a bit like anger was burning along his thoughts.

'Oh, yes, that embarrassing moment for her when Camron threw her over his head—'

'And declared her his for all the clan to see,' he interrupted. 'I was there and heartened for my friends.'

Joan clamped her lips shut, but didn't stop touching him, so he added, 'And I've heard Mary talk to Anna, so don't pretend her warning was kind.'

Joan slid her hand away. 'But—'

'Where did Barabal go?'

Joan sniffed and stepped out of his path. 'Towards the tanner's.'

There were multiple buildings between here and there, but it did alter his direction. But not by much. His home wasn't that large. He'd find her.

After his talk with Joan he was further determined to find the woman who'd captured some piece of him.

She'd put Mary, Joan and Eunice in their place? Good for her. Those three were known to manipulate.

He wished he'd been there to hear Barabal instruct them in manners and industry. Maybe Eunice would wake up to Joan's ways, and not follow so much.

And yet…shame tinted his utter buoyancy because Anna wouldn't have to constantly defend herself against those three if, years ago, he hadn't brought the Maclean to Graham land.

After Alan Maclean betrayed her, some people had turned on Anna for giving her heart so freely. Mary, who had had her eye on Camron, often battered Anna down.

And Barabal on her first day here had defended his

78   *The Highlander's Mysterious Maiden*

friend? He hastened his stride and glanced around every corner. Could Barabal have actually gone to the tanner's? He shuddered to think. But then he wasn't impeccably dressed himself. If he had to get a bit of squashed—

'Exactly.'

One word, just one. But it was distinct enough he stopped mid-stride.

'I'm not asking for new leather now or taking yours, cordwainer.' Barabal's voice continued. 'I'm asking for some used leather to cobble together so I can show you what I can do to boots.'

A low murmur which belonged to Ol' Bal. Seoc could only imagine what that bad-tempered cordwainer retorted.

'Of course I know what I'm doing,' she said. 'I just explained that I know the difference between a cordwainer and cobbler now, didn't I? You know, some mint might help with your hearing.'

Another pause and this time Seoc carefully stepped forward to see if he could spot the woman who eluded him.

'Well, I know that mint helps,' she said. 'Now where can I find some?'

Another few words from Bal, his ancient voice getting louder, but Seoc didn't pay any mind to him because he could now see Barabal. Her back was to him, but the double doors were open and he could appreciate the jaunty tip of her head and well-rounded bottom.

He wiped one palm down his leg to give his hands something to do other than grab her to bring her towards him.

'What do you mean you don't know where it is?' Barabal said. 'You live here, don't you?'

Another pause and words he couldn't make out. He couldn't see Bal, which meant he couldn't see him either. He didn't want this interesting conversation to end.

Nicole Locke 79

'Well, you should ask your wife about where things are, maybe she could teach you the skill. It's helpful.'

More words from Bal and this time it was a string of them.

'No worries at all, I'll pick some myself.'

A short pause.

'But even if you think I should take my time,' Barabal continued. 'I want you to know I won't, I'm quite efficient and my stitching is superior, you'll see. Don't touch that piece there and I'll show you. I'll be back.'

Seoc couldn't believe his ears and when Barabal emerged from the cordwainer's shop, he couldn't believe his eyes.

For he was right to follow her, to pursue her, to be intrigued by her. If possible, she was more beautiful than when the Beltane fires highlighted her dark hair and the moon's light revealed the cleft in her chin.

For now he could appreciate the pink tone to her round cheeks, the dark framing of her eyelashes to her dark eyes. And bless the sunlight for she'd warmed enough to not wear that monstrous cape that hid the bounty of her curves. Oh, her dress was mud-splattered and leaves seemed crushed along the hem, but she was here before him and he wasn't wrong.

She was like the last ember in the darkest of fires.

'What do you want?' She frowned.

You, he almost blurted. Swallowed hard on that word. Had he lost all control of himself, but then being near her, he wanted to lose that control. To talk to her of anything. What was it about her?

She put her hands on her hips. 'Are you here to run me off?'

Her tone was acerbic, but there was that delicate flash in her eyes. That little light of vulnerability she covered up so skilfully, he couldn't believe it to be true.

He might not have known her any time at all, but he'd

80   *The Highlander's Mysterious Maiden*

talked to Murdag and now to Joan, and if he wasn't riveted to absolutely every nuance of her expression, he would have said this woman ate cold iron to break her fast. So when she showed him something so delicate, so fragile, as a little uncertainty, it was like a gift. One he wanted to know with all his heart and vanquish whatever demon had put it there in this remarkable woman's life.

Too soon. All of it, yet he didn't want to stop whatever this feeling was. 'Run you off?'

'Out of the Graham Clan,' she said.

She sounded so certain he would do so it broke his heart, if he had one. 'No one's to run you off, Barabal.'

'You know my name.'

Because Murdag had told him, else he'd have asked for it. 'And you know mine because you asked about it?'

Oh, he liked that flush on those cheeks of hers. 'Some woman told me. Now let me pass.'

How could he coax her to say his name? 'You need some mint.'

'Did you overhear me talking to the cordwainer?'

'Difficult not to overhear when the door was open.'

She scoffed. 'Then you know I won't tarry to gather some mint for the cordwainer first. It truly helps with hearing. Maybe I could make him understand my use.'

She sounded so resolute, he hated to tell her the truth of it. 'Ol' Bal will never offer you any position. Balfour hasn't had an apprentice in all the years I've known him, even though his hands are as tied up as his long laces. Grahams often go to either Stewart's or Buchanan's cobbler to get our boots if we need them quick. Otherwise, it's a wait.'

She frowned. 'My stitching is sound, and I can even make decorative double stitching to look like flowers. He'll take me.'

She was a marvel if she was that skilled, but still he shook his head.

Her shoulders slumped. 'So you are to run me off.'

Again, she repeated this as though it'd happened to her before. 'Why would I run you off?'

'Because I haven't found a useful occupation yet.'

'You arrived last night; it wouldn't matter to me if you found one months from now.'

'But you aren't the leader here, so I don't see how your opinion matters.'

Now that stung. Not his pride, but the fact he'd lost the Graham leader, and his son was imprisoned by the English king. She was new to the Graham Clan, but did she know that? He waited for the heavy darkness to beckon him again.

Maybe him seeking any chance of happiness was hopeless for him. Maybe he'd always be reminded of his weaknesses.

'True.' He stepped to the side. 'I shall let you pass, then.'

She frowned. 'Why did you follow me and wait outside the cordwainer's?

Because he'd wanted to see her in sunlight. Wanted to ask if she'd changed her mind about him after last night. He thought maybe she had since she'd watched him as he trained with Camron. But he'd be a fool to say any of that. He sounded like a fool in his own head with these thoughts. No one could tumble this fast.

Except he'd been surrounded by muffled numbness for so long, was it any wonder that a sharp-tongued, opinionated and beautiful woman didn't at the least fascinate him?

But she didn't want anything to do with him. She had rejected him last night, run away from him today and she hadn't sought his name, but was merely told it.

He needed to make an excuse for his behaviour. 'I was

82   *The Highlander's Mysterious Maiden*

not standing and waiting for you, but I was on my way to the cellars.'

'Someone order you to get drink?'

'I wanted to inspect the ale and mead.'

She looked him over and he tried not to straighten his shoulders. And, despite the residing emptiness that threatened still to overwhelm him, it was heartening to have a woman of her bone strength and height looking at him. 'Does this clan not have alewives or do you think them not good enough?'

If she talked this way to Joan, he could see hard feelings ahead for all involved. 'Do you get in arguments?'

'All the time, but that's no reason to ignore my question.'

Her question… If one took it personally, it would be offensive, but there was something offended in her tone. As if she was ready to defend those alewives should he disparage them. Now that merited thought. 'Aye, there are alewives and they're more than good enough.'

She narrowed her eyes, assessed him again. 'Then are you shirking your other duties by running off and hiding in the cellars?'

Why was he always one step behind this woman's thoughts? He told one lie, but now was in too deep to remedy it. 'My brew is in that cellar and I wish to study it.'

'You came from the lists.'

'Now I'm off to the cellars.'

Eyes narrowing, she looked him up and down. 'Like that?'

With her eyes, not completely dark but a beautiful greenish-brown, on him, taking in everything and not cringing from the remembrance of the angry gash across his chest? Absolutely.

'Do you believe the casks care for my appearance?' he said. 'I only mean to check the fermenting.'

Nicole Locke   83

She waved her arm around. 'Like that you'll muddy the brew.'

He still had mud on his face? He'd throw dung at Camron next time they trained. Or... 'Do you have some linens by your bed to clean me up?'

'Why would we do that?' She pointed to her own cheek. 'Use your sleeve there.'

He had, but he tried again. 'Is it gone?'

Her eyes roamed his features, and he was hoping the mud wouldn't be gone so she'd have to help him.

But she gave a curt nod, and he couldn't cover his disappointment. 'You know of ale-making?'

She shrugged. 'Of course.'

'And cobbling?'

'I already said that, didn't I?' She turned one way, then the other. 'Do the cellars have dried herbs?'

'They do.'

'And are they near the gardens?' At his nod she continued, 'Fresh would be better. You'll take me.'

'Take you where?'

'Towards the cellars. I don't have time to get lost.' And with one firm step towards him, she took his sleeve and tugged. And just like that, any thoughts of wallowing in his dark thoughts disappeared. When he took one step in the direction she moved him, she let go and he felt that loss. But it wasn't enough to walk away. Now he stayed because he wanted more.

With a curt nod, Barabal strode forward. 'Even if this Balfour won't take me on, and he'd be a fool not to, it doesn't mean he doesn't need some good strong mint in his life.'

'Bal can be as bad-tempered as a dormant urchin.'

'I know what's best.'

How did she know, and should he tell her they were headed

84   *The Highlander's Mysterious Maiden*

in the wrong direction? If he did, any conversation with her would be too short and he needed more time with her. Oh, he was not foolish enough to believe this woman could solve all his problems, but everything in him knew she was more than a distraction and that was enough.

'His hands are terribly gnarled. Has no one helped him?'

Making certain he kept his stride short, they continued to walk in the wrong direction. 'Many have tried, but I don't believe anyone has lasted as long as you did by his tables.'

She gave a slight smile. 'Then all's not lost for him.'

Did she have hope? 'People believe he bumped off the last cobbler.'

'Dormant urchins aren't usually so bloodthirsty. And he's a cordwainer,' she corrected. 'Cobblers cobble what's there, but a cordwainer begins from new leather.'

When he saw the little jaunt to her step as she corrected him, he felt almost something. To smile? To hope? And he would have sworn she jested.

She pointed. 'The forest is right there, perhaps I can return to him quicker if I pick herbs myself.'

The forest and glades surrounding them were full of herbs, but then she'd be gone that much quicker. 'There are more reasonable places to find work.'

'I won't do the kitchens.'

She blurted that so fast he knew he'd ask her later about it. Right now she wasn't running, despite the mud, blood and sweat of his countenance. 'There's beekeeping or foraging.'

She pursed her lips and looked down.

He did as well and noticed her worn shoes peaking beneath her skirts. What a pompous fool he was. This woman arrived to his clan last night. She was no doubt tired and needed supplies, and here he was trying and failing to woo her. 'But you're correct when you believe the forest foraging could be quicker.'

She glanced up to him, then back to the line of trees. God's honey, he would lose this chance to talk to her. 'However, I don't know if everybody's done with the forest yet.'

'What could possibly be done with a forest?' she said.

'It was Beltane last night and people would have used the cover of trees.'

'To sleep? It's past midday now, everyone should be awake,' she said. 'And if you're trying to skirt around telling me people are tumbling about naked, please save your breath. I saw all that mere hours ago.'

Barabal watching or being invited to watch was more than intriguing. Merely the thought sent desire slipping through his veins and he adjusted his walk to cover his reaction.

'Further I'm not a child, I've had my menses and you know I have breasts because you keep staring at them.'

He stumbled.

'Something wrong with your leg?'

'No,' he said. But he stopped, he had to. And it wasn't because she'd mentioned him staring at his breasts. In fairness to him, he noticed all of her. Though intrigue and desire licked at him on the thought of what she'd witnessed in the forest, her mentioning her magnificent breasts was enough to cause him a third leg.

'You aren't well. Why don't you stay here?' she said as if he hadn't contradicted her. 'It doesn't matter if I find the herbs in the garden or in the forest. I'll find them.'

What could he say to keep her here?

She peered closer at him which made it all the worse since he tracked the little space between him and her curves. Between him and her nose or those enchanting freckles. At the sunlight making more of them across her cheeks.

86   *The Highlander's Mysterious Maiden*

At her lips softly pursed, plumping them until he knew he'd die if he didn't taste them.

'Are you certain you're well?'

He blinked. 'More than.'

'I don't believe so, you looked quite stunned. Perhaps the blow to your nose was worse than you thought. When I get to the gardens and gather some mint, we'll get you some mugwort as well. I don't believe you're quite right in the head.'

He chuckled, winced. Her gaze fell to his raised hand. The one that almost rubbed at his chest to ease the pain there.

'Did you recently take ill with throat and chest?' she said.

'No.' But her noticing his discomfort had the effect of cooling his lust.

'I'll get some for that, too,' she said. 'A few herbs like chickweed and honey will help.'

She wouldn't let him refuse. 'You get in many arguments, don't you?'

'Always,' she said. 'But that's only because people are either ignorant or too stubborn to know what's good for them. Are you one of them?'

He didn't know if he was one of them…but around her he was something. He wanted that something. 'You have healer knowledge.'

'Of course,' she said.

Defending those she barely knew, determined to help the cordwainer who scared half the clan, and with enough knowledge to be a sage. Why would anyone run her off? Though he could barely lift his sword the way he wanted to and the emptiness where his warrior heart should be was all but extinguished, he wished to defend her.

'Barabal, why did you have to travel here?'

Chapter Eight

Why did Seoc not ask from where she came, but why she was here? It was so much more painful a question. Why did she have to travel? Why did she keep feeling lost?

'Why ask me questions that do not matter? Are we not to get you to the cellars and me to the herbs? I need to be of use to the cobbler and, if not him, somewhere else if we do not laze about.'

His brow drew down and though he tilted his head to watch her for more than a few steps, she did not turn her head to him.

Maybe it would be best to veer towards the forest to pick the herbs on her own, but surely, they were getting close to the gardens. She might not know her way here yet, but she expected to see the chapel which had to be as large as the Laird's manor overlooking the glen. But the village laid on land that was not flat and not easy to navigate.

Having a guide allowed her not to run in circles, something she was grateful for, and maybe should say, but he was walking to the cellars anyway, so he was not put out.

'My mother was an alewife,' he began. 'One of the best. It was as though she knew when barley needed to be used and the ripest moment to stop one fermentation process to another.

'It wasn't only my family who thought she was the best;

she was admired by the whole clan. Much to my father's chagrin, I followed her in her tasks more than his. I even tried to emulate her in her process.'

Barabal couldn't remember anyone telling her a story of their lives. She sat around tables, interacted with good families, but this…listening to this man's voice, the easy way he walked beside her as if he had nothing to do but talk to her never happened.

Yet when had she listened in turn? She could fool herself she and Seoc walked towards a destination so there was purpose to what they did and perhaps that made this easier for her to listen to him. But she couldn't fool herself into believing this moment wasn't unusual in her life.

This was the man who'd teased her for a kiss on Beltane. Who'd left her to pursue another woman. Yet still he talked. Why? It was a poignant story and there was no point. He'd go to his cellars and she to the garden and there'd be no reason to interact after this.

He'd made clear he didn't truly want her in any capacity. He'd seen her gawking at him, but he wasn't pursuing her. He was merely travelling the same way she was. It was only some game he played with her. And though she might be attracted to him, she'd been convenient for one of his jests.

Yet she couldn't ignore what he told her. 'Your mother's gone, isn't she?'

'Many years now,' he said. 'My father and I miss her. When it became certain we'd never taste brew like hers again, I began to learn in truth much to the gratefulness of my friends.'

'Why would they be grateful?'

'Because while I followed her in her tasks, I was too young to know the proper way to make any of it. Camron, who I trained with, and his brother Hamilton would be required to try my latest attempt.'

Nicole Locke 89

She imagined what he'd be like as a child with his friends. 'What happened?'

'Once I made some ale with macerated grass.'

'With honey or barley?'

'I was but five and it was mashed grass.'

She laughed. 'Why did they drink it?'

He smirked. 'When you know them, you'll know they never back down from wager or dares.'

She sobered at that. He said it so easily, as though friendships were a given. She had never thought such a thing. Not once, but she did wonder whether her brothers had such an easy life since they were allowed to stay on Colquhoun land and were surrounded by people who remembered their parents and happier times.

She'd like happier times, easy friendships. Something in her chest fluttered at the thought of having that here with the Graham Clan. After all, Murdag had just blurted the word at her as though they would truly be friends. And maybe if she had some friendships she could stay here. But that had to be false hope again that— She glanced at the man who was glancing at her.

How lost in dark thoughts had she gone? She gave him a smile, and his eyes, some mesmerising mix between grey and blue, dropped to her lips and stayed. She expected to receive some jest about kisses, or maybe a retort on her rudeness. Instead, his blueish-grey eyes lifted and softened to something like understanding.

Barabal glanced away. How far had they come since the cordwainer's? It seemed as though they were surrounded by houses now. Many people walked around them and they gathered some looks, mostly friendly, so nothing was out of place. Perhaps the Graham Clan village was circular built and Seoc took them through a short cut.

90   *The Highlander's Mysterious Maiden*

Her not paying attention to their surroundings wouldn't do when she had to return to the cordwainer's. 'Perhaps—'

'When I was tiny,' he began at the same time.

Snorting, Barabal swung her gaze back to Seoc.

Something like amusement flashed in his face. 'I was tiny.'

'For your mother's sake I hope so, but somehow I doubt it lasted long.'

'My mother carried me well and when you meet my father, you will see he why he calls me little.'

There could be no one larger than him and she'd never meet his father. Nor would she know friendships like he did. And everything in Graham land was odd.

Odd because it felt easy. Like this walk. Like Anna needing defending from that Mary. She didn't know these people and yet everything she did was as if she did. Maybe it was her years of studying everyone. Maybe friendships and connections were like practice and she'd finally come to that point.

'My mother called me little as well,' he said. Then he grew quiet. Too quiet and he turned his head from her like she did when she wanted to avoid anyone getting too close.

His comment should have been humorous. No one would call Seoc small, but he said it so wistfully, something pulled right out of her chest. Something like truth.

'I travelled here last night from Buchanan land where I lived for the past year. They never called me small or big, though. Maybe if they had, I'd have stayed?'

She thought he would chuckle at her attempt at humour, or appreciate that, instead of pushing him away, she had actually answered his original question. Instead he grew quiet and they walked several moments before she saw him open his mouth and shake his head. Then he flexed his hand before he dropped it.

'They did not like you?' he finally worded.

Ah. And this was why she pushed people away. Why she had no use for them other than to be useful herself. Because they'd ask questions and prod until she revealed something of herself. Then it would be for nought. She'd leave because it was time, or mostly, they would be too horrified to talk to her again.

But he'd told her of his mother and a few personal words in exchange was fair, wasn't it? 'They were kind enough.'

'Then why?'

When he fully turned to her until it would be rude to not turn towards him, it was as though the world fell away from them. She didn't know who slowed their steps first, or who stopped.

All she knew was they were suddenly placed away from the bustle of the clan doing their chores and no one glanced at them or tried to interrupt with greetings.

It was just them.

And it was as though her eyes couldn't help but take in all his features, with more details, once again. Like the waves of his hair carried much darker strands and his eyes weren't grey, but highlighted with blue. She wondered, too, if his nose had been broken before for he ignored it even now that it looked a bit swollen, as did his upper lip. And even the bruise along his cheek where surely Camron's fist must have grazed didn't cause a wince of movement.

No, that came from the steady rise and fall of his chest and his hand that flexed and raised just that bit. As though he wanted to press it to his chest again, or maybe touch her.

Though he simply stood there patiently, she felt his question. Oh, she could ignore it, and say she had to get on with her tasks and to not be bothered, but she couldn't shake wanting to tell him. And it wasn't because the answer would be something safe like telling him she wanted to help the Gra-

92   *The Highlander's Mysterious Maiden*

ham's with Beltane. That was the lie she had told herself when she left the Buchanans. She wanted to tell him the truth.

'It was my time,' she said.

A long pause. 'Has there been other times?'

He wanted to know if she'd left other clans. Too many, too much darkness and loss. Too personal to reveal. He'd lost a parent and missed them, but it wasn't the same as being rejected as she was first by her brothers, then her clan. Then by so many others since.

Even last night she was rejected when this man walked away after asking for a kiss. Yet now they shared conversation, and she revealed something of herself. Like there was some connection between them. As if the great oak tree swayed towards her, and she wanted to embrace him back. If she looked down, would those snarled roots of his be wrapping around her own ankles?

Too much. And none of it could be true. Not his sincerity, or the fact while they were in the middle of the village it was only them, and he saw only her. It was a ridiculous feeling and one that would serve her no purpose, just like hope.

She craned her neck to look around them. 'We must be close by now to the gardens.'

A slight tick in his jaw. 'They are by the chapel.'

'Where is the chapel?'

His eyes still on hers, the light of them darker, he pointed in the opposite direction of where they were.

Everything in her paused. 'Why did you take me in this direction?'

His brows creasing, he said, 'You tugged my sleeve this way and we began to walk.'

But he knew where she'd wanted to go. Overheard every word exchanged between her and the cordwainer. Knew more because she'd specifically told him where she wanted to go.

He knew she'd promised she'd be efficient and would return shortly. And this man, this great big oak of a man, whom she'd even offered to help with more herbs, delayed her. On purpose.

Paling in horror, she pivoted to go the way he pointed.

'Why didn't you laugh?'

'Why are you walking with me?'

'If it was a jest, it was funny.'

She eyed him then and, though her eyes glared at him with utter disdain, he liked them on him too much to care.

'Funny,' she fumed. 'Is this even the way to the chapel or are you continuing your humour?'

The flush of colour on his cheeks incensed her further.

'It is the right way.'

'How would I know? You've already proven yourself to be a liar,' she said. 'I believe I'll ask a few people along the way.'

He kept pace with her a bit longer. She tried to lengthen her stride, but he kept up with her even so. It only made her angrier. 'Leave me alone. Go the other way. Never talk to me again. You have wasted my time and, worse, the cordwainer's.'

He'd made her look like a useless fool on her first day with a clan she wanted to make a strong impression on.

He grabbed her arm, held still. They stopped and he let go. 'Wait—let me explain.'

'I will not wait for you. You are a terrible being.' Barabal lifted her skirts and hurried off in the correct direction.

Chapter Nine

Where was everyone? Needing a distraction, Seoc strode from one side of his village to another. It been more than a week since the Beltane celebration and he'd ruined any chances of winning Barabal's favour.

He'd done nothing but throw himself into clan affairs. The council had met several times since the rumours were confirmed that Lord Andrew Moray in the north and William Wallace in the south would successfully combine their forces. This went far beyond the raids since Wallace had centred his operations in Ettrick Forest. They were fast controlling most of Scotland beyond Stirling. A fact that wasn't missed by the English king.

If messages were true, they would indeed convene around Stirling before September.

There was a part of him that hoped the rumours and messages weren't true. But weeks had gone by since they'd returned to Graham land and the scouts only confirmed what they all dreaded. Another battle would soon occur.

A battle, even a potentially successful one, wasn't enough for Seoc. It wouldn't bring back their Laird, Patrick or release, Patrick's son, David, who was still held prisoner since Dunbar.

Amid the incoming reports of war, the clan built Camron and Anna a new home for their life together. Mostly completed, it was a residence his friends often disappeared into whenever they got the chance. He couldn't be happier for them.

He was simply glad he and Camron had time to train together. However, no matter the hours spent, he couldn't get past the restrictiveness across his chest, the tight pull under his arm. As the week progressed, it had only got worse and everything pained him.

It would have helped if Camron's brother, Hamilton, had been around. That bastard had fled the clan on a fool's journey to join the other Scots readying to gather at Stirling. Had he been captured and tortured by the English along the way?

Camron and Anna were concerned with the news, but it wasn't surprising. Hamilton had done reckless acts in the past, but him riding towards Stirling went beyond jests. Especially since Beileag had ridden after him. Both of them had been gone for days now and everyone had to wait for their return. There was nothing to be done. A search party could alert the English.

He needed a distraction else he'd descend to ruminating on Barabal's ignoring him. So of his closest friends, the only person he could tell of his chest pain would be Murdag, who was in the stables.

Seoc shuddered. Damn horses, the beasts were barely controllable on the calmest of walks. In war or battle— No he wouldn't think of that time. Of Sir Patrick's ride towards the English instead of away. Their Laird called for a retreat at the same time he charged forward. It was a nightmare of a memory he couldn't break himself from.

A stomp of hooves, a woman's voice. The strong smell of hay and horse. The pain in his chest worsened. Maybe he should walk away and return to his cellar.

96   *The Highlander's Mysterious Maiden*

'Stop your pacing and enter already, Seoc,' Murdag cried out. 'You're making it worse with Frenzy.'

Bracing himself, Seoc stepped into the stables. 'What's happening here?'

Murdag, with horse brush in hand, jumped. The horse swung its head and nipped her gown.

Murdag pushed the horse's nose and stepped away from the great beast. 'I can't get Frenzy to stop ruining my gowns. Have to take the things off or else I'd be sewing all day instead of mucking out stalls.'

'Only you would believe cleaning floors of dung is better than sewing a few holes in linen. But at least that explains why you've been walking around in your underclothes.'

'Only at night when it's dark,' She narrowed her eyes.

'With firelight around you,' Seoc pointed out. 'We've all been wondering if you'd gone mad.'

'You've talked of my state of dress no doubt with humourless Camron.'

'Reluctantly.'

Murdag grinned. 'You'll know I've lost my mind when I wear those underclothes backwards.'

Seoc imagined it. 'I don't believe we'll know even then. But no doubt you'll tell us.'

'If I go mad, I'll be certain to share every detail of it.' Murdag laughed. A sound that should appeal, but there was a jaggedness to it.

Was Murdag not happy, and what more had he not observed since Dunbar? 'What's happening with you, Murdag?'

'I'm just me, taking care of the horses and practically living in the barn as usual.'

'Is there something wrong with the horses, other than a penchant for clothing?'

Nicole Locke 97

Something like wistfulness flashed in her blue eyes. 'Don't they look well?'

'I'm trying not to look at the beasts,' he answered. 'Are you taking them out enough?'

'As much as I can.'

Her smile didn't reach her eyes. 'You're not riding far, are you?'

'Have you seen Barabal today?'

Seoc knew when the subject was changed. 'Why do you mention her?'

'Barabal gave me a tip to stop him biting my clothes, but it didn't work.' Murdag laid her hand on her horse's flank. 'You know the whole clan saw you walking Barabal around.'

Seoc knew they'd caught the eyes of many. It wasn't because of him, but that Barabal was beautiful and walked with such fierce determination.

'She didn't appear to be the lost sort of person, or one to ask directions,' Murdag said with a coaxing tone that rankled.

'She's nothing of the type.'

'But you two walked in circles as though you were solving all of Scotland's problems.'

He crossed his arms. 'Were you following us?'

She shrugged. 'I had to divert attention from the spectacle you created.'

They were only conversing. 'I've talked before.'

'You've never talked like that with any woman. You haven't talked to any woman like you did the night of Beltane.'

'She's comely.'

Murdag bit her lip. 'I think it's something else.'

This was a distraction he could do without. 'Have you been spying and gossiping?'

'She's been here a little past sennight, she's managed to

98   *The Highlander's Mysterious Maiden*

either anger, frustrate, or frighten most of the clan. Ol' Bal is practically hiding in his hut. Anna, Beileag and I adore her.'

Because of the clan or because of how he reacted to her? 'Ol' Bal never comes out anyway.'

'And Hamilton is terrified of her.'

There would be a reason for that. 'What did Hamilton do?'

'None of his usual jests, something quite tame for him, actually, and now he's nigh on terrified of her.'

Because he hurt her somehow. 'You will tell me.'

'I believe it might be safer for me when Hamilton gives his more humorous account.'

He knew what Murdag meant when she said safe. He'd seen it often enough. Hadn't that sharp wit of hers put Joan in her place? Hadn't she seen Barabal insist the cordwainer drink her mint teas? Or those times she marched from one place after another offering her advice and help, only to be refused.

He tried to keep himself occupied, but Barabal was new to the clan and noticeable. Or maybe he couldn't take his notice of her away. He could admit he didn't like that slump in her shoulders before she tried to hide it. And he hated he'd hurt her.

Because he had lied to her, and not out of kindness, but for selfish reasons.

'She's got a heart to her.'

'Anna, Beileag, and I are well aware of her heart, but that's not why I was diverting attention.'

His gaze snapped to hers. Grinning, Murdag continued, 'I had to divert attention because she kept smiling at *you.*'

If he had a heart, if he had anything inside him at all, he'd feel that barb. But all he felt was that heavy numbness close in on him and he looked to his feet. Breathed deep. Fought it and knew he'd lose again.

Nicole Locke 99

He'd come to Murdag and these cursed stables for distractions when none could be found. But it seemed his troubles found him even here.

'She hasn't smiled at you since that day, which means… what did you do?'

'I gave her the wrong directions,' he said.

Murdag stopped brushing. 'What?'

He looked back at her. 'She wanted to go the chapel gardens, and I walked her towards the manor, somewhat.'

'Oh, you didn't!' Murdag laughed and shook her head.

'I did.' He warmed. If Murdag laughed, perhaps he had been thinking too much about this. Maybe Barabal could laugh or shake it off.

Murdag sobered when he didn't change his expression. 'Oh, no, you truly didn't.'

What could he say? He shrugged.

Murdag closed Frenzy's stall. 'Seoc, she'll believe you played her for a fool.'

'Anyone who knows her would know that's false.' He'd never met a more intelligent woman in all his life.

'But people don't know her and it was her first week.' Murdag hung the brush on the opposite wall, sunk her hands in a pail of water and wiped them clean with a linen. 'She might believe you played a trick on her.'

He shifted against the barn wall. Had he done what Camron and Hamilton did with their wager? He didn't have love with Barabal, but he had something. Had she thought he made fun of her?

'Ah. That may be where her ire came from, then.' He winced and this time he didn't try to cover rubbing his side.

'Have you been hurting this entire time? Why didn't you tell me?' She came to his side and lifted his tunic. 'I might have some—'

100   The Highlander's Mysterious Maiden

A gasp had them both turning towards the doors where Barabal stood.

'I'll come back.' She spun and was already out the door.

'Go after her,' Murdag said.

Racing out the doors, he just saw Barabal swish around a corner. She was by no means a small woman and every lengthened step, no doubt to be quicker and more efficient, swayed her hips in a way that called to everything in him. And because he felt anything at all, he obeyed that call.

A couple more strides and he was by her side again. 'Let me explain.'

'No need to explain.'

'Then why were you there?'

'I wasn't there to find you, if that's what you asked. I came to the stables to find some work to do.' She pulled up abruptly. 'Why are you even walking with me? I obviously interrupted something.'

'You didn't interrupt anything.'

'It wasn't work,' she said. 'Why are you standing so close to me?'

Because when she stopped, he did, too, and this near to her was exactly where his body wanted to be.

'You didn't interrupt anything. Hamilton or Camron could have joined us in the stable when you arrived.'

Her brow creased. 'I don't need to know the peculiarities of the Graham Clan. Murdag can be there for you or whoever else. It matters not to me.'

He tried and faltered in understanding all she meant.

'I'm going over all the words Murdag and I said—do you believe you heard intimate words between us? Is that why you left?' he said.

Barabal spluttered, her loss of words lighting something

inside him. Maybe she was jealous. Maybe she felt something for him.

'Murdag's like a sister to me. I have no feelings towards any woman here, save perhaps for one.' He said the words, knowing he was giving himself away. It was too soon to have such feelings, but he couldn't ignore them. When she startled, looked hurt and glowered, he knew he'd made it worse.

'I saw you with Murdag in the stables; I saw you follow her on Beltane when you couldn't have your way with me,' she said through clenched teeth. 'I don't need to know what goes on in your clan, or especially with you and your...your feelings towards a woman. I don't even know why you're explaining matters to me.'

Seoc staggered. He hadn't made it worse with his confession, he'd made it all better.

Barabal waved her hand. 'Why are you smiling? Stop bothering me and be done.'

Everything about this woman held back his darker thoughts. Her beauty, her fierceness because she believed he liked Murdag. All he wanted was to put his hands right on those mouthwatering hips of hers and squeeze his palms in that enticing extra bit of roundness and kiss her. Kiss her until neither of them could stop.

He wanted her and if her reaction that he was interested in anyone but her was true, then there was a chance she wanted him, too.

'My God, lass, you've giving a man hope.'

'How dare you,' she bit out.

Because of her he dared. 'Barabal—'

'You talk of hope as if it's something good. Oh, for a life so fortunate as to—' She started, stopped. Pulled herself in, then pivoted to walk away.

He gaped at the woman who was already far too many

102   *The Highlander's Mysterious Maiden*

steps away from him. This time, he wouldn't let her leave. He'd had a week of her walking away and couldn't face it again. All week when he wasn't lost in his darker empty thoughts, he obsessed over how he'd lost Barabal's attention. Now he had her full attention and she was furious with him.

'What is so wrong with hope?' It was all he wanted to find again since Dunbar. With the battle ahead, he felt none.

'Useless, empty emotion that gets nothing done and makes everything worse.'

That he'd never believe. His thoughts were often full of shame and remorse, or he felt nothing at all. But he remembered hope. And here, with her, with her watching him, with that startled gasp she made and her possessiveness because Murdag was touching him, he was dizzy with possibilities.

'I walked with you in circles to spend time with you,' he said.

She stopped again, but didn't turn to face him. 'I saw you look at me on the lists and when you ran away, I followed you. I wasn't going to the cellars. When I heard your voice at the cordwainer's, I waited outside until you came out. I wanted time with you.'

She whirled on him. 'Time with me. You said it was for a jest?'

Shame filled him. 'I was a fool to do so. My friends play many jests, it sometimes eases awkwardness.'

'It was my first day.'

'I know.' He spoke the truth. But he wanted her to know him, very much. Not because of that vulnerability she showed, although it called to his own wariness. He recognised that now. How many times had he covered up his weaknesses not to recognise when another did it? And it wasn't only because he didn't feel dead inside by being near her. It was her and her doggedness. Her strength. It shone.

What had this woman done to him in a week? He felt like he did before the losses in his life. Before he made so many mistakes.

'And Murdag?' she said faintly.

She wanted to know why Murdag stood so close to him, why she touched him, why she offered to 'take care of him'. But it was a story he didn't want to tell anyone, not with so many prying eyes and ears.

'Friends since childhood,' he said. 'We can talk somewhere else. I'd like you to know something.'

She crossed her arms. 'I haven't got enough work done today.'

With hope showing him the way, he couldn't accept her denial. 'You watched me. When I fought with Camron in the lists you noticed when my tunic was off—'

She made some choked sound.

'So I followed you and waited,' he continued to fumble.

She opened her mouth, closed it. 'You talk of my...'

'Seeing me,' he helped. Then wondered because she had been at a distance and he'd been facing Camron more than her. Maybe she hadn't seen his scar. 'You did see me?'

She looked around her wildly. 'I did.'

'Then we talk of that,' he said.

'You want to talk of me seeing you.'

'Immediately.'

Face flaming, she blurted, 'Where is this somewhere else you want to go?'

'Place.'

'The private place you want to go,' she hissed.

'Under the alehouse—'

She was suddenly walking before him and all he had to do, all he wanted to do, was follow.

Chapter Ten

Mortified, Barabal followed Seoc to the alehouse, which was blessedly empty, then down the long narrow steps. Each step brought cooler, darker air despite Seoc lighting sconces along the way.

She'd expected cold, dank. What she didn't expect was a treasure house.

'It's large,' she said.

Seoc almost grinned. 'This isn't the only chamber. Notice how it is cooler, but not truly cold? Down those additional stairs are more chambers where we keep the large casks for ale and mead and those smaller alcoves over there for other sundries.'

She'd seen crypts or undercrofts this large, but then they were usually under a substantial chapel or castle, not an alehouse.

'The chapel and the manor have their own as well,' he added.

Under these vaulted ceilings casks lined the partly bricked and stone walls. The aged oak, spilled brew and ale scents were masked only by a pungency that certainly was cheese wafting from another chamber. Above their heads, great vines of dried herbs hung and some already dropped to the floor so they walked on thyme. Nothing of the outside permeated here.

'I told you my mother was an alewife,' he said. 'She wasn't a small woman and neither was her mother, and so on. They slowly expanded the rooms. It goes far beyond the house above, which is why the ceilings are smaller along the walls where the alehouse sits and the rest is good for me to stand.' He looked to the ceilings. 'I've spent years of my life here.'

His expression and voice were warm as he took comfort from this cellar his mother had built. 'You have places to sit.'

He gave her a look. 'Doesn't mean they don't get their work done.'

She wanted to shy away from how well he knew her. 'There's an advantage to it, is all I meant.'

When he tilted his head as if he wanted to ask her what advantage, she turned away. If he didn't understand the need for places to think about things like how to improve on sauces, he probably wouldn't understand her explaining it.

For her that need had been met by the little alcoves in the kitchens. At night, despite the occasional mouse, there was something comforting about the smells of the day, the absolute quiet after all the noise. When she learnt her skill there, she'd thought the kitchens and alcoves with all their usefulness were where she was meant to be.

Until that one night when she wasn't alone with only the mice, and she never wanted to enter a kitchen again.

But this place, these thick walls and ceiling were like being in one giant cosy alcove. It was empty during the day, and she suspected it would be again at night. She could come here any time. Perhaps after this embarrassing conversation she could remain here a bit until the redness of her cheeks disappeared.

He looked around like she did. 'We can talk here about the lists when—'

'We don't have to talk of it,' she blurted. 'You already

106 **The Highlander's Mysterious Maiden**

apologised about the walking in circles. It's all settled, why bring up the lists?'

His brow creased. 'But I want to talk of it, it's why we're here. This is a place I often go. It's quiet and I can think.'

Her heart leapt. He did understand about a place of his own. Oh, she wished she didn't know she had that connection with him. It made her think of things like hope, and friends and family. Which was all too much hope since the true reason he'd brought her here was to mortify her. 'Why would you believe I want to say anything about it? You saw what I did, but I left afterwards. You don't have to be smug about it. You could have left well enough alone.'

'Because...' he began, then stopped. 'What do you mean: what you did? What did you believe you were doing near the lists while you watched the fight?'

'You know what I did,' she said. 'But why you keep harping on about my watching you and seemingly wanting details, too, is another matter. But you clearly won't let this go. So say your words. Just know, you'll be leaving this cellar before me, and I never want to talk to you again.'

'That's what you did?' The light in his eyes brightened and he almost smiled. 'You watched *me*?'

Why was he acting as though it made him happy? On a curse, she swirled around, fully prepared to storm the stairs again. She didn't need to be insulted any more.

'Wait!' He cursed before adding, 'Please.'

She stilled, but didn't turn around.

'You have a habit of running from me.'

She had a habit of avoiding being embarrassed in front of him. She looked over her shoulder. 'Say more gloating words to me then.'

'Gloating?' One of his hands lifted, like he would touch his chest again. Did his chest pain him, or was it a habit? Now she knew the scar was there, his movement intrigued, but not enough to ever ask it of him. At least not when he intended to humiliate her because she thought him stunningly handsome.

'If you believe I'm gloating, I'm concerned I can't say what I want either. Though I dearly want to.'

His voice held that distant sound he made right before he walked off for Murdag's company. Murdag who had wrapped around his side, lifted his tunic, and said she'd take care of him.

Why did that thought hurt? He'd already showed his true self when she'd refused his kiss, then he went for another. She'd tried to avoid him all week despite him suddenly appearing everywhere.

Except this time, she'd followed him, and he was looking at her with longing, but that had to be the dimness of the chamber despite the blazing sconces. 'Then why are we here?'

He pulled in a short breath. 'Your reactions were pleasing, lass, more than you can know. Give me a space to enjoy them and to figure out how to proceed.'

All she told him was her humiliation by her gawking at him. 'You're not nice.'

'That's because you believe I'm gloating.' Grey eyes crinkled as though he knew a secret. 'While you are more lovely than I have words for.'

Lies. She placed her foot on the step.

'I don't want to talk of gloating.'

'But aren't you?'

His breath hitched. 'Perhaps, but not why you believe. Please know, Murdag and I are close enough she knows of a grave matter I've only told a handful of people. And now I want to tell you. Because you saw me on the lists, you know most of it already.'

Barabal refused to look at him. Perhaps he did want to

108   *The Highlander's Mysterious Maiden*

talk of something important and not her foolish admiration. If so, it was almost worse.

Why did the people of this clan continually offer help or ask questions of where she was from, or share matters of their own life with her? All the kindness in the world never meant she could stay with any of the past clans. Her own family had forsaken her.

'Barabal?' he said.

'I know nothing of your secrets or your life. Say what you must and be done with it,' she said. Maybe if he hurried with her humiliation, he could return to a willing Murdag. Friends or not, she truly shouldn't care. So, she found him fascinating, and a part of her wondered what it would be like to kiss him. But love wasn't meant for her. Not until she belonged somewhere.

Seoc gave a long exhale, but it didn't sound as if he was irritated at her abruptness, more as though he was thinking about what to say. She took her foot off the stair, but didn't turn around.

'It's about my weakness.'

She saw no weaknesses. Was he teasing to get her to confess her admiration of his strength and form? The way his back rippled with every swing of his sword, the cords and lengthening of his thighs with every thrust? Was she to blurt out about wanting to touch the bulges of muscles over his shoulders? Because she did.

'The scar across my chest I earned over a year ago and it pains me, but I don't give in to it,' he continued. 'Today, however, I broke because the increased training aggravated it. I went to Murdag for her easing tincture.'

She couldn't have been hearing him correctly. He tortured her on her inability to turn away from gazing at him, he meant to tease her on her obvious attraction to him and he wanted to talk about something insignificant first?

She turned. 'Your scar.'

'You saw it when I was in the lists,' he said. 'I never talk of it. Not since the incident.'

She stared at this man, stared so hard, she took in all his perfection and imperfections. How his grey eyes held so many colours, and his jaw looked as though it ached to be touched. There was a softness in his lower lip and his nose was just a bit too big, but still fit him. Even here he was larger than life, yet this cellar, this cramped space, fit him, too.

She stared because if he was sincere, he wanted to talk of his scar paining him and how he had sought help from his friend, Murdag. That he didn't want to discuss her gaping at him and humiliate her. Then maybe he was sincere before, too, when he called her lovely or confessed he liked her company.

Could he actually *like* her? She'd tried to avoid him this week, but she'd seen him none the less. Not only because he was striking in all manners a man should be, but also in that mysterious way that was just his. That oak tree with the dark snarled roots underneath. How he'd interact with others, then get this faraway look in his eyes.

Now they watched each other and he wanted to talk of his scar? Something she saw, but meant little when it was healed, yet there was a wariness to his eyes that dulled. Did she cause this wariness because she hadn't yet replied to him?

Why did she care? She purposely pushed people away until she could be useful so they didn't throw her away again. Why was everything with this clan so different?

He sighed, closed his eyes. 'The scar's too much. Why would you want to talk of it?'

She didn't. This clan was constantly sharing with each

110   The Highlander's Mysterious Maiden

other, but whatever caused that harsh carving was significant and she was shaking simply because he looked at her and said he wanted to spend time with her. She needed to talk of something else.

'What does Murdag give you for the scar?'

He turned to her again. 'Widow's bark.'

'On your skin?'

He pressed his hand on his chest. 'It's for the pain.'

'I know that.' She waved her hand. 'I meant for the rest, such as tears in the skin.'

He frowned. 'We put some linen to bind it.'

'Is it bleeding now?' she said, alarmed.

'Not anymore.' At her nod, he added, 'But it feels as though it does. When that happens we bind it and it makes it feel better for a bit.'

If they bound it, it would support whatever damage happened, but unless everything was done correctly when he was healing, that binding could make it worse.

'Is it tight and you can't move?' she said. 'I noticed with your sword—'

'You noticed my sword?'

Her face heated because it wasn't his sword she'd noticed. 'You raise your left arm higher than your right. The binding you say you do will support weaknesses, and will feel better, but it won't make you stronger. While that healed, you should have been doing everything but binding it.'

He gawked and her cheeks grew warm.

'How do you know this?'

She knew because she watched the rippling of those arrows of muscles at his waist. 'I have eyes.'

'No, I mean how do you know about the healing?'

That was safer to talk of. 'I learnt it along the way.'

'The way to where?'

Nicole Locke 111

She was wrong when she thought talking of his arms was safer. Nothing was safe when she kept blurting truths to him. Better to keep to the subject. 'Did anyone give you salve?'

He sighed. 'In the beginning—'

She shook her head. 'Afterward, while the scar was forming.'

'I might not have been an easy patient.' He rubbed across his chest and turned away.

No patient was easy. 'It might be too late to help you. But if you're not a fool, you'll let me.'

'Let you what?'

'Do you have good oil, like seed or nut? Herbs? Linens?'

His brow creased. 'All around us.'

Barabal examined the shelves. There was even a bench he could sit on to make the process easier. Did she dare? Of course. It was the right thing to do. She couldn't believe no one had done this already.

'You sit there,' she ordered. The cellar was well stocked and organised. She took some linens, set them in a metal bowl, and poured water over them. She rearranged a table and some boxes until the bowl was against a lit wall sconce to make it hot.

'That won't catch fire?'

'They're soaked in water for steam and heat. We won't be here long enough for it to dry and catch.'

She gathered the mortar, pestle and herbs next.

'Now what are you doing?'

'Same as before. I'm helping you,' she said as she crushed the mint, chamomile, and looked for lavender. 'That's why you brought me here, isn't it?'

Never taking his eyes from her, he sat and clenched his hands between his splayed knees. 'It is now.'

Ignoring his cryptic words, she poured the oil on top of

112   *The Highlander's Mysterious Maiden*

the herbs, then took the liquid to a sconce and held it there. Maybe he didn't bring her here for help, but he'd gone to Murdag for it, who only ever gave him willow bark. She had something else.

'You'll burn your hands,' he said.

'I only need it warmed. The herbs are dried and it's better for them this way,' she said. 'Why is your tunic on? This can't be applied over your clothing.'

He eyed the mixture she gently turned.

'If you believe I'll harm you, you can leave. This is better than willow bark for pain relief. But if you don't want any help, I have better things to do—'

'Like mending shoes, stable work, and looming?'

She thought she'd avoided his attention this week, but he'd noticed her failing to gain other positions in the clan. 'I have other skills as well and maybe you should increase your own instead of gossiping about others.'

There was a crinkling around his eyes as if she pleased him. 'Oh, you believe I merely talked of you, do you?'

His disarming expression zinged right from her toes to her—

A prick of fire on her fingertips and she jerked away. 'Your distracting will only delay your healing.'

'So, you're a healer, too,' he whispered against her ear, as he disengaged her fingers from the heated mortar.

His chest to her back, his arms on either side of her—how had he moved so fast?

Facing the flame, she was surrounded by the man who held her hand and inspected the tips of her stinging fingers. His hands were hardened and coarse, his touch gentle and warm as was his breath that fanned over her head. Against the sharp bite the fire had left against her fingertips, she felt the brush of his chest against her back, his heavy arms around her waist. Gentle, everything so gentle, but it didn't feel gentle as great waves of some craving overcame her.

'You could have harmed yourself,' he rasped mostly against the tips of her fingers as he pressed a firm thumb into her palm which splayed them. But the slight burn from the flame was nothing to what he was igniting in her body at such a simple touch. He was holding her hand; he was almost embracing her. He smelled good, like sunshine against stone. It was addictive and she leaned back…until she realised what she was doing.

Grabbing the mortar from him, she jerked out of his arms. 'I'm not harmed.'

Almost reluctantly he lowered his hands. She was already several steps away from him when he turned. Expression blank, but his eyes roved from her hands to her feet and back up again. 'I'm sorry, I didn't mean to startle you.'

He hadn't startled her, she'd startled herself. And she wasn't about to explain any of that to him. 'I'm not a healer either. I've learnt some skills from one who was kind enough to teach me. But a true healer needs years for their craft.'

'Why did you quit?'

Horrified at such a word, she blurted, 'I left.'

'To by chance arrive at another clan in the middle of the night?'

How was he guessing any of this? 'These questions aren't pertinent.'

His expression and posture eased. 'So you quit, are not a healer and don't know any more about healing than I do.'

What was this conversation? 'How could you come to that conclusion?'

He fully straightened, a light to his eyes again. 'Well, you should know I never used a mortar before.'

114   *The Highlander's Mysterious Maiden*

She narrowed her eyes at him. 'You mix metheglins, which require herbs.'

'But I never made them into mush.'

'That would explain why your meads are terrible. You need to break the herbs to release their aromas.'

He chuckled. 'Are you saying you know more about mead making than I?'

'I wouldn't know that,' she retorted.

He did grin then, a roguish one, and she had that same feeling of wanting to lean into him. To see what that grin meant while he again had his arms around her.

'Mashing the herbs makes them impossible to separate from the brew, it's best to bundle them,' he said. 'The rest of the savoury aromas I leave to the kitchens.'

She didn't want to talk of kitchens. 'Are you arguing that I can or can't heal you? This conversation has taken so long, I have to rewarm the contents.'

'Barabal, I'm only jesting with—'

'Either sit or let me be on my way.'

His earnest expression fell. She had done that to him. She'd done that to most people who tried to be kind to her. At first, she'd attempted some sort of friendship when she was younger, but they never lasted, and it became pointless to try. People needed to accept her or not. It was up to her to find that place to be useful, but she'd been searching for so long and was getting tired.

Maybe that's why she kept watching this man, why she talked to him when he could provide her nothing and she wasn't useful to him. Maybe that's why she wanted to lean against him, just lean into that strength and his faraway looks. To feel his roots hold her strong. His scar was horrific, but she wasn't surprised by it. He was a survivor. His roots ran deep, held him firm.

She never stayed in any place long enough to grow any roots.

A muscle ticked in his jaw. So many insults he probably wanted to voice before he walked those stairs and away from her like so many before him.

Except he didn't. Instead, he tilted his head and studied her some more. Then more until an almost smile reached his lips. Her gaze fell from his eyes to those lips, especially when they curved a bit more.

She blushed. What was wrong with her? If he kept watching her as he did, he'd probably see her wants and desires. Her vulnerabilities and her shame. Could it get any worse?

'I didn't offend you, did I?' he said. 'You're flustered.'

'I'm not flustered, I'm trying to be efficient. Now tell me where I can set this down.' Maybe there was a table in another chamber. That way she could be useful and escape this conversation. Because staring at Seoc and becoming flustered couldn't be good.

'There's a little table against that wall.' He indicated with his chin.

How had she missed that? She set the mortar on the little table, then picked it all up and set it beside the bench. Slowly, he eyed it, then her. She wasn't so naive to believe he didn't see the slight tremble in her hands.

'Now why would you be flustered?' Pointing at the mortar, and the bench, Seoc said, 'Barabal, is this your way of getting to spend more time with me?'

She grabbed the mortar. 'This will never work.'

'Even if I cooperate?' He reached behind his head and pulled off his tunic. Threw it on another bench and sat on the one before her. Then he grew quiet.

Maybe that was because she was staring at him again and it wasn't for some scar across his chest. It was because of

116   The Highlander's Mysterious Maiden

those shoulders, the bulge of his arms. The ripples of muscles along his stomach.

Pivoting, she turned to the flame again.

'Don't burn your fingers,' he murmured.

'I didn't burn them the first time.' It wasn't her fingertips she was worried about.

'So what's this to do? My injury's been stitched, burned, bound and salved. People made honeyed mixes until I was sick of the smell of it.'

'A healed wound like that means you suffered, but the fact you don't like a smell won't make me pity you. Your scar has been healed by any means necessary. It obviously saved your life,' she said. 'As for what I'll do…'

He raised his brow, but she couldn't answer because she only just realised what she truly offered. This wasn't about handing him the oil, she intended to work the warmed oil to ease the muscles. She'd have to touch him and not only once.

What was she thinking? 'This was a mistake.'

'What is?' he said. 'I don't want your pity.

She sighed. She hated when people wasted her time and now she'd delayed him from his duties because of a bit of fluster. 'Your wound is healed, but the muscles around it healed wrong.'

'Healed wrong? I have no open wounds. How can some oil make them as before?'

'It's not the oil, it's the easing of the wound.' She shook her head. 'I know this sounds mad, but applying this heat and doing stretches sometimes eases injuries.'

He reached for the mortar. 'Tell me what to do.'

'Not you.' She held it out of reach. 'Someone else has to prepare it, rub it into the flesh, then lay heated linens.'

He paused. 'Someone?'

'*I* have to do it.' Although how when she was trembling and

Nicole Locke 117

trapped by her need to belong, to be useful? Trapped because this man called to her simply by being silent. By giving her glimpses of humour and charm, of sensitivity and steadfast roots no matter how much adversity.

His pause was even longer before he added, 'For how long?'

'Weeks, months? Every day.' Multiple times if it was bad, but she wouldn't tell him that. It was an effort to tell him this much. Mostly because of his expression which sort of lost its edges.

'You're to touch me, to rub oil into my flesh,' he deadpanned. 'And you'll do it every day.'

When he put it like that and said it as he did, all low and incredulous, she knew she couldn't possibly. 'This was a mistake. You don't have time for this.'

He startled to sudden awareness and his eyes pierced hers. 'You say you can help me and you won't?'

'I didn't say that.'

'So you won't waste that oil and herbs and simply walk away?'

He couldn't have known what those words would do to her. He couldn't. Of course she wouldn't walk away if she could be of use to someone. And never, not once would she waste resources.

She must do this as she'd said she would. It would be no different than when she and Rhona had eased Morna's newly healed broken leg. Thinking of little Morna and the relief she'd felt, Barabal felt purpose again. But when she walked closer to Seoc he seemed larger. And she didn't mean that because she was comparing him to a young girl. It was him.

And the acres of bared skin. The hard jut of his shoulders, the ridges of muscles that tensed and flexed. It was a man before her, not a child, or a woman or anyone else but Seoc.

Seoc, who'd stopped her footsteps on Beltane night and made her unsure of everything she'd done since. It was him. Always him. She couldn't even close her eyes and pretend he was someone else. Another step, unsure now, as his knowing eyes remained locked on her.

He wasn't the same. This wasn't the same.

She scooped her unsteady fingers through the warmed oil. Had he bespelled her? Perhaps it was the quiet of this place, far underground while the rest of the clan walked above. Maybe this place was magic. How else did this cellar with its arches and benches accommodate such a man as he? How else could the flickering scones highlight his bronzed skin with such utter masculine beauty?

Twirling her fingertips through the oil, watching the herbs turning and turning, it felt safer to look at her own hands than the man with his vast, heavy, weighted stare.

'Barabal,' he said, his voice low. 'Look at me.'

She slid her gaze to his. His eyes were the colour of the dead of night without the cold. Instead, they burned hot. He dropped his gaze to her mouth, pulled in his bottom lip and licked it before going back to hers.

'Are you hating this?' she blurted.

His eyes flashed. 'What?'

Why did she say that? 'You said you hated the smell of honey and herbs. Does the oil affect you as well?'

He tightened his lower lip. 'I'm distracted by something else.'

Was he in pain and she was denying him any relief because she was standing here gawking? But he didn't say that and he stared just as hard. What was happening here? What was this tangible thing between them? Nothing could be happening between them. 'Arms at your side.'

When he did, she took that scoop of warmed oil and laid

it on the top part of his scar. Before the oil could escape her hold, she dug her fingertips in and pressed until she could feel the curve and knot underneath his skin.

He sucked in a breath.

'Does that hurt?'

His eyes flashed to hers. 'What are you doing?'

If she could concentrate on the muscle's movement and not the man, simply find the places where the curves were unnatural, maybe this was possible.

'Lay back.'

Seoc blinked.

She sighed in impatience. If she had to have a conversation about this, she'd lose herself again. She felt odd enough with him as it was, any delay would make it worse. It was best to get on with the work, until there was nothing between them again.

'The bench is wide and sturdy enough to support you, isn't it?' she said.

'It's used more for a low table than anything else.'

'Then lay back.'

Head tilted in curiosity, he did as she asked. All the while, he kept his perplexed heavy-lidded gaze on hers. When he settled, he laid his hands on his stomach.

She looked at the way he was situated. The bench was large, but not overly, yet it was his size that could impede her access to him. 'Put your arms above your head.'

His brows drew in sharply. 'You want my arms above my head?'

When she nodded, he did just that and held his hands together. 'Like this?'

It should have made him less threatening. Less everything. Instead, his vastness was on full display for her viewing. And that was all she could do: view. The gnarled slash scar glared

120   The Highlander's Mysterious Maiden

against the male perfection, but it was of no importance to the rugged planes of his torso, the thick strength of his legs. The sheer perfection of his face. He was everything and her eyes were desperate to see him all at once.

'Lass, whatever it is you want to do, get on with it. I'm barely holding on.'

His scar pained him, and she was dithering.

Trying and failing to ignore the man watching her, she focused on the scar and the bunched muscles at the top. She poured the oil in her hands, rubbed them, which released the lavender scent. Darting her eyes to his, she said, 'Tell me if anything hurts.'

The moment she laid her hands on his side the corporeal sensation was almost painful. Not for him if his silence was an indicator, though when her fingertips began to unfurl against his side, his muscles locked before he released a slow breath. When she glanced up and he gave a curt nod, she continued to flatten her palm.

Underneath her now almost tingling hand, she felt the puckered ridges of the healed scar. But she was aware of how insignificant that ridge was to the rest of him. From the heat of his skin, a warmth infused from the sun, his scent of stones and man. How nothing gave as she pressed the oil into the unforgiving strength of his flank. He was warrior through and through.

Another breath from him that suddenly raised his chest and slowly lowered it. Fascinated, she watched her hand crest with him. 'I have to knead the muscles here,' she said. 'It will apply more pressure.'

His agreeing hum cut short when she laid one hand on the other and forced the muscles around the scar to realign. She felt him tense, relax, his breath shortening. Knowing there was considerable time since he'd healed this unnatural way, she'd pressed hard.

'Am I hurting you?' she said.

A heavy pause before he grunted, 'Continue.'

So she did, working from the thin, ragged edge that went just under his arm down towards his centre. She moved in small brisk movements. The scar was deepest and wider the further it carved along his torso. If she could ease this bit, he'd get some relief.

But the longer she worked, nothing eased. Not the way his muscles felt under her fingertips or the pebbling of his skin. And his reaction echoed something in her own tightening body.

Gooseflesh beginning from her hand still touching him. Shivers that rippled up and across her breasts making the tips tight nubs until she pinched her arms inward in a vain attempt for relief.

She ached. And this only from the barest of touching his side. The worst of his scar was slashed across his lower torso where his muscles rippled in waves and her fingers would have to comb through the smattering of hairs above and along that line of hair arrowing under his belly button.

What would happen if she flattened her entire palm to touch him, her fingertips brushing the brown tight points of his nipples? What would happen to her breath, her heart, the waves of heat fluttering through her now if she continued to the band of his waistline? It would be overwhelming.

She felt overwhelmed.

'Barabal—' he said, his one utterance of her name said so carefully, her entire being trembled. If he commanded her to look up at him, she didn't dare.

What was this? Her shortness of breath, her skin flushed, she could feel the light sheen of sweat prickling her lower

122   *The Highlander's Mysterious Maiden*

back. Her heart pounding, her mouth dry. She craved more. He was partially clothed, they barely touched, but she felt utterly lust-filled and naked before him.

'Please, lass, look at me,' he said, his voice no more than a rumble.

Not a command, but a request to raise her eyes. Palms flattened for balance against him, feeling the rapid rise of his breath that matched her own, she dared to pull her gaze to his. The tension between them exploded. What was this, what was this, what was this…?

When her gaze locked with his, she knew. It was anticipation. 'Do you want to claim that kiss?'

Chapter Eleven

Flat on his back, gripping the edges of the bench behind him so he'd stayed still under her touch, Seoc barely heard Barabal's question.

But his body reacted. Before his thoughts caught up, he'd shoved himself up on that bench, widened his legs and grabbed her hips before either of them was prepared.

He couldn't ever be prepared. Strung tighter than he thought a man could be, his gaze roamed her pleasing length, darted across every feature of her captivating face.

For days he'd craved that kiss, needed the press of her generous curves against him. Desired nothing more than the cant of her hips rubbing until they both succumbed to pleasure. He didn't care if they were fully dressed, didn't care if he made a mess in his breeches as a result. He wanted that kiss.

The urge to touch, nibble and taste her plump lips nigh overwhelmed, but now he had heard her question, he needed to answer it. And he didn't want to do that like some brute.

Because he'd been too forward before, too demanding. On Beltane she'd woken something in him, and he'd charged forward. Clumsily he'd chased the startling sensation of her presence, and he'd scared her away.

Or rather irritated Barabal away and ever since she'd run

124   *The Highlander's Mysterious Maiden*

or hid. But no more. He heard that gasp, saw that flared hurt in her eyes when she'd thought he wanted Murdag.

He'd confessed to his continual vulnerability, and she'd offered to help. Everything in him demanded he devour her, but he needed to do the opposite to keep her by his side.

And now he held still, she'd stayed. She'd asked the question and watched him like some curious fae. He wanted to roar in triumph.

'Do I want to claim that kiss? More than life itself,' he said.

Her eyes dropped to his lips, then swung back to his. The merest darting of her tongue against her lower lip caused him to tighten his grip on her hips. At her shifting, he released the tension of that grip, but didn't let go.

Slow, he warned himself as he gauged the heat in her eyes, the slight tremble, the temptation that was all her. He could almost sense her want and soon he would taste it.

'Come here,' he growled.

He was rewarded with her stepping between his widened legs. She was close, but every fibre of him yearned for closer yet. 'Is this permission, my Barabal? Do you agree to a kiss?'

A furrow between her brows. 'Of course I'm giving you permission, didn't I just ask you?'

By God's ale, she was heady. 'I'll kiss you then and kiss you hard. Do you know what it means when a man wants to touch as much as I do?'

Her expression drew tight, her eyes heated, but not in desire, in frustration. 'It's a press of our lips is all. Something to—'

She'd stopped that sentence, that thought, when he very much wanted her to give voice to it. To admit what was happening between them.

'You believe our kiss will release this addictive mix between us,' he said, failing to hide the disbelief from his tone.

Nicole Locke 125

'I'm barely dressed before you lass, and you asked me to lay on my back and reach my hands above my hand. To expose myself to your healing ministrations.'

Her body startled at his words. 'I didn't ask you to *expose* yourself.'

He almost grinned. 'No, but that's what you got. And I've been gripping the bench so hard, I'm surprised it didn't crack under my palms.'

'I didn't tell you to grip.'

'But you didn't give me permission to touch and when you were slicking your hands about to lay them on me, bent over, so I'm longing for your ample breasts to brush my arm, my side, my anything, you can wager the only way for me to stay still was to hold myself down.'

'You weren't—' She looked to the bench where he'd lain.

Was the flutter of her lids an indication she was imagining him? Seoc took in a shuddering breath to steady himself.

'While you pressed and prodded. While your fingertips dug, were you not watching what the rest of me was doing?' he continued. 'Do you know how soft your hands are, how capable and how much I've thought of the barest of touches from you? Instead, you laid them on my side and raised gooseflesh and shivers. When you placed one warmed hand on my body, did you not feel the arch of my shoulders, the strain in my breeches as though I was some untried lad?'

Her gaze skidded back to him, that dart of her tongue now a pretty slide across her lower lip. He felt that slide, *everywhere*.

'Now my hands are free and gripping you and all I want is that kiss, but, Barabal, lass, I need you to take that extra step.'

She narrowed her eyes. 'I'm right here.'

A year of numbness, of wondering if there was any point to the weeks of agony, the months now of grief. Of second-

126   *The Highlander's Mysterious Maiden*

guessing every day whether he'd ever listen to another full conversation or be awake enough to laugh freely again. Wondering, begging the heavy darkness to lift.

But now with her ordering and flashes of vulnerability and strength carrying her on, Barabal had forced him to feel. It was irresistible and glorious how she asked him to kiss her, then stubbornly stood still to make him move. All he wanted was to be aware and she made him feel alive.

Gripping her skirts, he yanked her to him, their height even, but not their strength. Her hands flying forward to his shoulders to stop him or to find balance were no match.

Falling into his arms and still he did not press his mouth to hers. Not until her own hands were fisting against his skin and she dug an elbow into his rib. On purpose or not he didn't care. He loved every pain she'd give him. All because she was *right here*.

'You want to kiss me. Then do it,' she said. 'Why are you wasting—?'

Desire tightening every sinew so his breath barely sawed out of his lungs, he cupped Barabal's nape, snaked his arm around her waist and pulled her fully to him.

One breath, that's all he allowed before he captured her lips in a bruising kiss. At Barabal's surprised gasp, he flicked his tongue between. She tasted so sweet, so addictive. So *necessary*. Cradling her hips between his, he angled his head, to plunder, to slide his tongue over hers.

At her first needful moan, his heart stuttered. At the submissive give of her body against his, at the soft press of her breasts, the pebbling of her nipples, he echoed her hunger with his own groan.

He wished for nothing more than for her to be as bared as him. One more demanding press of his lips against hers. One flick of his tongue to taste her startled desire. One to simply ease the need to consume her, then he gentled.

Nibbled and tasted along her plump bottom lip. Nipped her upper. Delighted in the short pants of her breaths against his, the answering delicate flicks of her tongue, as if she, too, couldn't stand the distance now. On a hum he pressed their lips again and his tongue delved. This time, her lips eagerly matched his, making him harden until it pained him. Lust overwhelmed and he became nothing but want and need and he again pulled away.

Just a little, just enough, and was rewarded with a perplexed and vulnerable Barabal. Only a flash, but lingering longer than she'd ever allowed with him before.

For him to see the soft side of her was a precious gift. He knew she didn't trust him or anyone fully. It came across with every wary look and abrasive word, but like this when her eyes were wide, he wanted to crush her to him and hold on.

'You believe I'm wasting time?' He brushed her hair away from her face. She couldn't be more perfect for him. 'Are you ready, then?'

'Me?' She dropped her eyes.

'Yes, you.' From her first tentative touch, he knew Barabal was untried. But she was here with him and insisted on the kiss. He wanted to savour this moment, their first kiss, well. 'It isn't me. I want nothing more than a kiss with you.'

'But you only said it that once.' She raised her gaze. 'How am I to guess?'

Curt words, said softly with wonderment. It was the sweetest of agonies. To have the bounty of her, to feel the softness of her cheek under his thumb, the ample curve of her bottom. To know he couldn't, shouldn't, take this further. But still wanting something more.

When her fists on his shoulders unfurled and her hands

128   *The Highlander's Mysterious Maiden*

slid along to clasp behind his neck, he rejoiced. Then shivered when her fingertips carded through the hair at the nape. Lust rumbled through him as she leant towards him. Her darkening gaze showing him the hunger that mirrored his own.

Cradling her face, he ran his nose along the length of her neck. Underneath the dried herbs she'd crushed against her hands, then on him, she smelled of fresh air and something sweet and earthy…like roasted almonds. Another startling discovery to add to the list that was her.

'Do you know what it did to me when you ordered me to lay back so you could have access to me?' he said against her skin. 'What it meant when your eyes roamed over every inch of my body, but didn't stutter once on my scar?' He trailed kisses along her jawline up to the shell of her ear. 'You couldn't know. Even if you guessed, you couldn't.'

'Seoc,' she said.

Barabal's eyes slid shut as if she was melting from his whispered words and slight pecks of his lips behind her ear. Already half gripping her hip, he dropped his other hand to the small of her back. 'Aye, Barabal, what is it? What do you need to tell me? Is it this—intoxication between us?'

Down her neck he went, his hands becoming greedy as she swept her own across his upper back, releasing more of that damned scent.

He didn't know where his words were coming from. He'd never talked so much in his life. But here, now he felt he had to, he must. If he gave in to only the physical act, he'd take it too far too fast.

She'd need words on his intent. She needed to know what a miracle she was simply because she was here demanding he do something.

'From the first moment I saw you. The first time you made me see you, I wanted your kiss, your touch.'

'Why?' she gasped.

'Such questions you ask.' He kissed her neck, ran his lips and tongue along her collarbone. Thwarted by too many clothes he raised his head, said the rest of his words against her lips. 'If there is an answer, it's far beyond my abilities. Except for this, you simply arrived, Barabal.'

His mouth pressed down, her lips giving instantly under his. Then there was nothing but the heat and aching desire between them. A sensation that overwhelmed anything he'd felt in the past. There was no comparison. There was too much heat and urgency. How they met, how they arrived here was too tenuous. At any time, their paths might not have crossed. What were the chances of her arriving at the Graham Clan on Beltane, of him standing available to her as he watched his friends ride off like in some romance tale?

What if she had chosen some other clan to visit, or found some other man who'd love her? What if he had missed her completely and never had a chance?

She was here, now, and he *needed*. With impatient fingers, he tore at the lacing of her gown, releasing the tightness of her clothing, giving him access to more of her soft skin. His lips delved along that now bared collarbone; his hands pulled the fabric away so he could explore one rounded shoulder.

What if he had never healed or if he had died? What if he couldn't have ever experienced Barabal, her lips as hungry as his, her lusty sounds of encouragement telling him he couldn't, shouldn't stop.

He didn't want to. He wanted to rip their clothes from both of them. Free her to his touch, to his kisses, to his hardness. Spread her legs and—

On a whimper, Barabal wrenched out of his arms. The back of her hand pressed to her lips, skin flushed, her breath nothing more than hard pants.

130   *The Highlander's Mysterious Maiden*

Seeing her as affected as he, satisfaction rushed through him, but the wary surprise from her beautiful eyes cooled him.

Eyes darting around, she lowered her hand. 'What is happening?'

Everything just happened. 'I kissed you. Our first, but not our last.'

'That wasn't a kiss,' she hissed.

'Like hell it wasn't,' he growled. 'The only thing it wasn't was long enough.'

That pulled her up. She stumbled away from him, straightened, then yanked at the laces of her gown. As soon as she was done, she would run, but he wouldn't let her do that to them.

She had to know there was no turning back now for him. It was more than her making him feel something after months of darkness. It was her and her stubbornness. Her vulnerability. Usually expressed right before she said something biting. As she was about to do now.

'What are you scared of?' he said.

As she held the laces, her head snapped up. 'What?'

'There are times when your eyes widen, when you seem as if you're a fawn about to take a first step,' he said.

She gripped the laces so tightly her knuckles went white. 'What a ridiculous comparison. Do I look like some delicate creature?'

Not with her sturdy bones and heft in her hips. She was a handful in all the best possible ways. Snatching his tunic, he threw it over his head. 'Then why are you running?'

She paused again. 'We're done here.'

With those needful sounds still echoing in his head, he knew that to be a lie. Because her hands shook, she fumbled with her gown and her breath wasn't steady. The reasons could be because of desire, or she was scared. If so, he'd protect her from his own need for answers…up to a point.

When she tied the last of the laces and took that first step away from him, he asked, 'So I'm healed?'

As if sensing his ulterior motive, her eyes studied him, so he kept his expression guileless. Because he did have an ulterior motive. Or at least one he'd already announced. He wanted more kisses and, in order to get them, he needed more time with her.

'You applied that treatment, thus am I improved now?' he added.

'No.' She turned to the stairs again as if to dismiss him.

'Then how soon do we do it again?' he asked.

Without looking at him, she answered, 'We don't.'

'Then—'

On a growl, she rounded on him. 'This oil only eases my, or any healer's, way to reach the muscles to shape them back where they need to go. Except, we had distractions. The entire method was barely started, let alone finished. And someone else has to apply it, not you. But because of—this—I won't do it again.'

Oh, no, he wouldn't let her get angry at him for this. 'It was a kiss, Barabal. One you asked for.'

She flushed, but her chin raised. 'I won't ask again. And you don't ask for the oil from me.'

If he had his way, she would. Pretending to think about her words, he looked over her shoulder at the stairs and the door beyond. Then on an exaggerated shrug, he said, 'I can't think of anyone else who knows this ability. Do you?'

She looked as though she'd eaten a thousand soured bites. 'You know I don't.'

'Then I'll see you next time, won't I?' Seoc sauntered past a tense Barabal, took the stairs up the cellar and, for once, left her alone to stew in her thoughts.

But he hadn't quite exited the door when he heard her say, 'Not likely.'

Chapter Twelve

Barabal hurried her pace towards the carpentry mill. The morning chill wasn't the only reason she hurried. She simply didn't want to talk to anyone. Or see Seoc in any way.

After the cellars yesterday she scurried about like some mouse avoiding predators. Fortunately, most everyone avoided her.

Not even Mary had exchanged scathing words of gossip with her. In fact, all three of them, Eunice, Joan and Mary were unnaturally quiet as they went to sleep. Though it seemed like Joan, with increasing frowns, studied her too closely. Barabal had to turn her back to her to fall asleep.

When she woke, Barabal knew she needed to find some place where the clan could use her skills. Except, yesterday Seoc had kissed her until her head was spinning. And it still felt that way. All she had to do was think about him watching her with his deep grey eyes as he lowered that great body of his and her breath hitched, her face flushed. When he'd raised his arms above his head and lain there like some god-like feast, her body had seized with such heavy heat she felt the need to sit.

And all of that was before he grasped her nape and slanted his mouth to hers.

She pressed the back of her hand to her lips. They tingled.

Nicole Locke 133

Still. They appeared swollen. Still. And between her legs was a wanting that had never existed before. Never. She wasn't naive with no knowledge of what occurred between a man and a woman; it was simply she hadn't experienced it. Why would she? She'd only been like this with *him*.

How and why, she didn't know. They met, they talked... and somehow that made moments for kiss and touch.

He called what was between them intoxicating, which seemed apt. There was no other explanation for her behaviour other than she must have forgotten she'd drunk a jug of mead right before she begged him for a kiss.

A kiss!

Shaking herself from her thoughts, *again*, she burst into the carpentry mill. In front of her were several large tables of various lengths, whereby next to one of them, a burly older man with unruly hair meticulously carved a tiny item cradled in his hands. Next to him sat a beautiful woman peering at his work.

'Not so deep with the dowl, lighter, lighter. That's perfect.'

The man chuffed. 'It'd be perfect if I was making something for a dog to chew on, but not for my future granddaughter.'

'Father, we don't even know if I'm pregnant.'

'The way that boy looks at you, I'd say you're pregnant or almost there.'

'That boy is a man, remember? When you say it like that it makes me sound odd.'

'Can't think of him as a man, just as much as I can't think of you as a woman,' he said. 'And I truly can't think about what men and women who are married do.'

She spluttered. 'But you did.'

'I think of grandbabies.'

134   *The Highlander's Mysterious Maiden*

'This is mortifying,' she said. 'I'm gladdened I will get this embarrassing talk from you and not Mother.'

He raised his brows. 'Who do you believe is pushing me to make toys?'

The woman looked startled. 'Mother wants you to make a toy?'

He chuckled. 'Well, not this one; I could never show her this one. She's already sewing coverings for it so no harm will come to her precious grandchild. Now that I think of it, maybe I can tell her to make large enough coverings to hide whatever this will be.'

'Why don't you make a cradle? You made a good one for me.'

'So good it went to all the families who needed it,' he said. 'But that'll be back to you before the baby comes.'

'How do you know that?'

'Because I asked them,' he said. 'I want my grandchild to have the best.'

'Oh, my word, Father, I've been married for mere days.'

'I know that Hamilton was up to mischief before you went hunting for him.'

'I did not hunt him, and I thought we weren't to be talking of mischief.'

'Not talking of that, only the babies.'

Barabal couldn't stand it. This was too private of a conversation for her to listen to. The polite thing would be to step away, but if she waited, it'd be too late to find any work.

'Is this the rest-and-chat side of the mill?' she said. 'Where can I find the people who are working?'

The man looked up as the woman stood and turned. She was taller than she looked sitting down.

'The rest-and-chat side,' the man said slowly.

Barabal pointed. 'The others seem to be sawing in that room and you're in here.'

'The *rest* side?' the man repeated.

'Father, I want you to meet Barabal,' the woman said. 'Barabal, this is my father, Ivor.'

She'd never met these people in her life. 'Are introductions necessary?'

The woman's hand fluttered before she answered, 'I'm Beileag. I'm glad you waited to come in until I returned.'

'From your hunt of Hamilton,' Ivor muttered.

'I did not go hunting,' Beileag hissed.

'The boy was lost and you found him. Sounds like a hunt to me.'

Beileag rolled her eyes as her father chuckled.

'How did you know I would be here?' Barabal asked.

Beileag turned to her. 'Sorry, but Anna told me you'd be stopping by.'

This clan liked to gossip together. All of it made her uneasy, just like the conversation between Ivor and his daughter did. Clans were close, but this one seemed overly fond of each other; she didn't know how to be around that kind of emotion.

Pointing to the object between them, she said, 'What's that meant to be?'

Beileag's expression startled, but her father's turned stormy. 'Meant to be! You said I was close.'

'With the skills, Father, not the object.'

He grunted, 'When did you learn such tricky ways with words?'

'Several days ago when I married,' she retorted back.

'Knew it.' Ivor presented it to Barabal. 'It's meant to be a horse.'

Beileag placed her hand on his shoulder. 'And will be a graceful one that will run far distances.'

136   *The Highlander's Mysterious Maiden*

Barabal frowned. 'Whoever heard of wood to be graceful when the legs don't move?'

'Are you insulting my girl's opinions?' Ivor growled.

'Father, it's Barabal,' Beileag said.

Ivor looked as satisfied with that answer as she felt.

'What's that supposed to mean?' Barabal said.

Beileag's hands fluttered before she clasped them. 'You're new to here, that's all. You don't know my craft.'

'You might as well show her, Beileag,' Ivor said.

'I didn't want to take out more examples until you understood the methods.'

'But the poor girl will go mad trying to determine from my clumsy attempts on the level of your craft. It won't make me feel bad. Makes me proud you talk and listen to how the grain flows.'

Giving a little smile, Beileag, from a purse at her waist, pulled out a figurine and placed it on the table.

'You talk to your carvings?' Barabal said. And Seoc accused her of being fae or mad.

'Look and see,' Ivor said.

Barabal peered closely at it and was astonished by a beautifully detailed fox with one ear forward and the other to the side. It was remarkable in every way.

'But the legs don't move,' she said.

Beileag blinked.

Ivor's bushy brows went to his hairline. 'I don't care who she is.'

'You do. We all do for…you know who.' Beileag gave wide eyes to her father.

Frowning fiercely, Ivor turned to her. 'You have carving skills, do you?'

She had none whatsoever, but that wasn't the point. This truly was the chat-and-rest side. 'Are you head of the mill?'

Nicole Locke 137

'The head of what?'

Beileag clasped her hands again. 'Father, she wants to know who to talk to so she can help. Remember that Anna sent her.'

'Good girl that Anna; good to see her with the reasonable twin, unlike that Hamilton you've captured.'

'Hamilton is your husband?' Barabal burst out.

Beileag brightened. 'You've met him.'

Met was too kind. He'd introduced himself with the wrong name. After those surrounding him sniggered, she realised what he'd done. Oh, he'd laughed it off, but she hadn't found it humorous at all.

Ignoring Beileag, Barabal turned back to Ivor. She was here for work and, with shavings in his beard and the giant apron with pockets, he obviously spent time in the mill here.

'I can sweep and clean. I can hold materials together when joints need to be placed.'

Ivor tilted his head. 'From your expression, I believe you met Hamilton doing a bit of mischief.'

'Did he play a jest on you?' Beileag gasped. 'I feel I have to explain now.'

She wanted no explanation. Hamilton added to her public embarrassment, but it didn't compare to what Seoc had done. Though Seoc explained the reasons why he played a jest. However, she still felt discomfort at what the clan thought of her wandering around with him all that time.

Had he done it to spend more time with her? Were his blue-grey eyes truly that warm when they looked at her, his grip that tender or his kisses that desirous? The way she responded to him in kind. Feeling flushed, she shoved those thoughts away. She didn't need for these two to see her knees go weak because she somehow still felt Seoc's fingertips cradling the back of her head.

138   The Highlander's Mysterious Maiden

Voice firm, she answered, 'No explanations are needed. I'm well aware of what this clan does.'

'Oh.' Beileag's brows pinched. 'But the rest of the clan has been welcoming, I hope. I know you're new, but not everyone is as jesting as Hamilton. He means well, but sometimes he forgets consequences.'

Barabal didn't know how to take Beileag's words. Were they an apology, or a foreshadowing of what to expect? 'I have had enough of jests already. Hamilton's friend, Seoc, made me walk in circles. And on the night I arrived, Anna's husband, Camron, had a sack over her head.'

'You stand firm,' Ivor said. 'You'll end with a good man yet.'

Startled, Barabal didn't look at Ivor with his far-too-personal comment.

She did want a good man, but she expected he would appear after she found a clan who wanted her. She couldn't find love here without a home, or to find someone to love her only to be forced to move again. And she couldn't find true love on mischievous Beltane night. Certainly not with Seoc with his snarled roots and achingly distant gaze. Not him, no matter how strong he was or how much she liked his kisses. Was it foolish hope that made her think this way? Was it too much to ask that a clan wanted to keep her and she didn't have to wander for ever?

'You were here when Camron took Anna on Beltane?' Beileag said.

'Camron, Seoc, Hamilton…it doesn't matter the name, they all play jests. I don't want any part of them.'

'Please don't blame Seoc for Hamilton's mischief. I'm certain he had a reason to walk with you longer.' Beileag pursed her lips. 'We usually give better impressions than this.'

Barabal didn't care about Seoc's reasons or the Graham

Clan impressions, she cared about her own and she was telling them what she could do to be useful in carpentry. Maybe they didn't believe her. Yet could she help them if they didn't take her seriously?

'You work in carpentry,' she addressed Ivor.

The man's bushy eyebrows rose and she noticed the increased crinkles at the corners of his eyes as if he peered at projects too long.

She sighed. 'And you're the head carpenter, aren't you?'

At his low brief hum, she inwardly groaned. She needed to make a good impression with this man and instead she'd argued with his daughter and insulted her husband. She kept making mistakes with this clan. 'Why didn't you introduce yourself, then?'

Ivor opened his mouth, closed it.

Beileag snorted. 'I believe Barabal's more wanting to talk of work, Father, than of Hamilton.'

She was in agreement. 'I know how to use a scribe and compass. And—'

'However, if we're to talk of woodworking, why couldn't we discuss how the legs move?' Beileag said.

She didn't have time to talk of toys. If she wasn't given work here, she'd soon have to seek some in the kitchens. 'And I can do—'

'You've got to let me know.'

'I've done it before,' Barabal glanced at Beileag, than back to Ivor. 'Do you need anyone? When you hewn and shape, I can clean the excess.'

Beileag's gaze grew riveted. 'You must show me.'

Ivor's expression closed off, then fell. Not a shred of softening or agreeing with his daughter or with her offer of help.

'Ack, child, you know your mother won't agree to it,' Ivor began.

140   The Highlander's Mysterious Maiden

'I need to talk to your mother?' Barabal asked.

Beileag gave a small smile. 'He's talking to me, but oh, I'd like to see you, Barabal, talking to her.'

'Let's not welcome strife,' Ivor said.

Father and daughter looked at each other, a myriad of familial expressions exchanged between them. It was as if she were completely forgotten.

She was lost here before she even got a chance to prove herself. Near frantic, clutching her skirt, Barabal glanced around.

Where had she gone wrong? There was a tabletop full of shavings. Barabal picked a bin and immediately swept debris off a table and into it. When she turned, Ivor and Beileag were engaged in a whispered conversation. Had they even seen what she did?

'What did you mean when you said you knew how to make the legs move?'

'I don't know woodworking,' Barabal said. She couldn't possibly tell Beileag about her sticks she tied together when she wanted a toy of her own. She'd made it when she was barely nine years old and desperate to have a friend. She'd called it horsey because it had rotating legs, not because it was piece of craftsmanship and looked like the animal.

'Tell her,' Ivor said. 'There'll be no peace until then.'

Barabal looked to the man who had a patient expression, but his order was completely authoritarian. As though whatever warmth he dispelled to his daughter did not flow her way. Of course it wouldn't, she wasn't his daughter.

She wasn't anybody's daughter, or for that matter a sister. They'd abandoned her.

Barabal weighed the consequences of dashing out of the mill. On the one hand, she wouldn't suffer embarrassment in front of this master carver. On the other hand, it would confirm she could never find work here. And no work here meant she was one step closer to having to work in the kitchens.

On a sigh, Barabal grabbed some twine and a couple of jagged slices of wood, she bound them together until they made an X. Then looking at Beileag, she said, 'Like this.'

Ivor's brows went to his hairline again and Beileag pressed her lips.

'But with holes here and here so the twine goes through it,' Barabal added, then shrugged. 'I don't whittle.'

Beileag took the crude example.

'I thought my horse was poorly,' Ivor muttered.

'Wait, Father, I believe this movement could be done with wood.' Continuing to rotate the joints, Beileag whispered, 'This is apparent—so obvious.'

Barabal warily eyed the woman who beamed with excitement.

Clasping her wrist and quickly releasing it, Beileag shouted as she ran out of the shop, 'You can't believe what you've done.'

She watched Beileag depart and, though there were other men conversing, chopping, and making a noise in the adjacent room, in this one, Ivor bowed his head and began whittling.

No, he did more than that. She could see what he was whittling because he put the block of wood right on the table in front of her so she couldn't miss one bit of his effort.

As if he was taunting her with his whittling skills because she'd confessed to tying two sticks with string. There again, he angled his dowel, shoving his knowledge in her direction to embarrass her.

'I never said I could whittle.' Barabal lifted her chin. 'Or that I wanted to learn.'

Ivor looked up, his expression calm and completely reso-

142   *The Highlander's Mysterious Maiden*

lute. 'This place isn't for you. You don't belong here and you know it, child.'

His words swung like a thick plank to her gut. How did he know? Hurt. Angry. So entirely embarrassed she knew this moment would humiliate her for the rest of her life, she pointed her finger at him.

And because she hadn't raised her voice since she was five years old, she said low and clearly, 'Why don't you have several bins in the corners or under the tables instead of one all the way over there? Then someone could clean as they went along and not have to scuttle about like dirty rats. Honestly, do I have to make all the changes around here?'

With his rejection words bludgeoning her over and over, Barabal pivoted and wobbled out of the mill.

Chapter Thirteen

'Is it time yet?' Seoc asked.

Barabal yelped, but didn't turn from peering around the corner of the spare housing. The one he knew she was lodging in with the other women. It was midday and the other women were not near this woman who was ignoring him.

'Time for what?' she hissed.

Seoc hoped Barabal would turn. It had been days since he last spoke with her. Days when, from afar, he'd tracked his lass's less than determined stride, watched the pinched worry between her brows.

She no longer ordered people with the same force. For days he berated himself for causing the fire to dim within her. But it was she who'd determined their last words exchanged. With her '*not likely*' she'd held her own against him with as much disdain as any great emperor of lore.

'Whom are we looking for?' he added.

'We are not looking for anyone,' she said. 'And you should not be tarrying behind me.'

Seoc sighed. Her words were firm, but not the tone. He was correct—his Barabal had suffered some loss between their kiss and now. And though he longed for the day she'd soften towards him, he wanted her to do so wholeheartedly. This wasn't that time; she'd been hurt.

144   The Highlander's Mysterious Maiden

For a moment he thought to let her go. He wasn't one to bother someone when they didn't want company. Hadn't he for months been hounded by his friends and family? But something was wrong.

He couldn't shake the belief she regretted that kiss, when he could think of nothing but the sheer rightness of it. Disturbed beyond any clarity she hated their time together, last night he'd pounded his feet across the sodden fields. And all the while his thoughts were beset like some broken wheel: Dunbar, the forest, the pain, the darkness, Barabal. Dunbar, the forest, the pain, the darkness, Barabal. *Barabal.*

Firm in the knowledge the view around the corner couldn't be nearly as interesting as Barabal bending slightly to sneakily peak, he stood calmly behind her. 'You said the mixture needed to be applied multiple times and we didn't do it correctly the first time. Thus, I'm ready to begin again.'

'There will be no again.'

'It's been days and I have found no one else. And you have had days to find someone else and have returned empty as well.'

'Somone else? I haven't even tried to find someone for you.'

Seoc wanted to grin. He might not know her as well as he wanted, but everything about her called to him. Everything. And he knew her enough to know what motivated his lass. 'Are you saying you shirked your duty to find someone to help me?'

Barabal tensed and straightened. Would she turn to him then? He wanted to look at her. For days, he'd continued to train without a tunic all in the hope she'd stare at him again. If nothing else to appeal to her conscience to help him, or better yet, to her desire.

Because that day in the cellar burned through him like some fevered dream.

Back straight, still looking away, she answered, 'I didn't tell you I'd help you. Can't you go away?'

Never.

'Or get someone else to do it.' She waved behind her as if to shoo him away. 'You saw what I did.'

Why wasn't she turning? 'They won't be as good as you.'

'Nobody ever is.' On a heavy breath, Barabal turned.

'Ah, hell, lass, what happened to you?' he said.

What he couldn't see when she was bent, or maybe he was more intent on her than her appearance, was the state of her. Her dark hair looked as if a bird had rearranged her curls with their talons. There were even bits of sticks and leaves stuck between the thick strands like some odd nest.

Her gown from neck to hem was covered in mud, as though she'd slid right along the banks and almost into the water. But it was the shallow scratches along her chin and hands that concerned him.

'You've been hurt,' he said.

'Hardly harmed and even so it's nothing that concerns you. So go on with you.'

A king couldn't order him from her side. 'Not until you tell me what happened.'

'Bees happened.'

'Bees,' he said.

'It's honey-harvesting time as you know,' she said.

'The apiarist smokes cow dung to stop the stinging,' he said. 'The whole of Scotland knows and can smell it.'

She brightened. 'Exactly.'

'Let me guess, you have a better way of doing it?' At her nod, he added, 'Are you saying that for three times a year, that man has been stinking the fields for no reason?'

146 *The Highlander's Mysterious Maiden*

'That is exactly what I told him. A gentle smoke is necessary, but not the smell.'

'And he didn't listen,' he said.

'He wouldn't let me show him properly either. When we opened a skep none of the bees were happy. We had to run to the water and while he made it safely to dunk himself in the deepest part of the creek, I fell before I could get in.'

That was how she became covered in dirt. And if there was one lesson he'd learnt of bees it was you drowned yourself before being stung.

He glowered. 'He didn't let you in the water?'

'It didn't matter.' She lifted her arm to his nose. 'Smell.'

He happily did. Though he couldn't get a good whiff of roasted almonds, the hint was there under the mud and something greener. 'What's that?'

'Mallow juice,' she said. 'Bees don't care for it. When I sat up, the swarm was over his head, not mine.'

'They were after him, not you.' He wanted to grin for her. 'So you were right all along.'

Eyes wide before she turned her head. She acted as though she had never heard a bit of praise in her life. That was concerning. 'And truly not hurt?'

She held up her hands. 'Scratched is all.'

That wasn't all, but he'd give her time to tell the tale in full later. At least now he could guess why his proud lass was hiding. 'Everyone's away from your lodging.'

Barabal blinked.

'I'll keep a lookout for you and shout out if they come close,' he continued.

'Why would I care about them?'

He wouldn't fall into that trap. 'No reason.'

Her eyes, which flashed green in the sun, searched his. He was asking her to trust him. Would she?

'No jests?'

If she'd allow him to protect her, he wouldn't fail. 'None.'

'When I come out, we'll try again with you.'

Startled at her offer, all he could do was stare at her and nod. At that, she swiftly entered her little home, while he stood sentinel. He didn't know what he'd do to delay any others, but he knew he would because she trusted him.

Maybe it was but a matter of little import, but she'd placed her trust in him none the less. When she emerged wearing a new gown, but the same chemise now with wet sleeves, and her hands and face were sparkling from water as well, he blurted, 'Why?'

Walking briskly towards the cellar, she answered, 'Because I didn't help you the other day and I can.'

He followed her, but much slower. 'But—'

'You're the one who came to me. Will you accept my help or not?'

He more than accepted it, he embraced it. But he was feeling far more than simply joy at talking to her. It was the knowledge of being alone with her in the cellar again, a certainty he hadn't thoroughly thought through.

He desperately wanted time with her, and though he'd teased and pleaded for her help, he'd never thought she'd do it. Her capitulation, along with her reserved nature over the last few days, settled wrong.

When they reached the door, he brushed his hand against her arm. 'You don't need to do this.'

At that, she turned. The scratches barely visible now they were cleaned was heartening. The tension around Barabal's eyes was not.

'Please.' She raised her chin. 'Let me do this.'

At her plea, his reservations crumbled. Seoc knew nothing

148   The Highlander's Mysterious Maiden

of what troubled her, but he'd do all to repair it. With resolve, Seoc opened the door and followed her down.

Agitated, wary, watching Barabal for any sign she'd regret this, Seoc threw his tunic in a corner, then for comfort, he took off his boots as well. All the while her movements were sure, steady, but he caught her eyes on him more than once and his heart thumped hard in his chest every time.

He reacted to her. The night of Beltane should have been no different than any other. His friends were happy and he wasn't. Standing, seething with his thoughts, and Barabal simply emerged before him.

This woman wasn't his saviour, she didn't repair anything that night, but he carried on a full conversation, and that was far more than he'd had in months. And ever since, he'd been different. As if something tilted the right way inside him again.

The fact she was his every fantasy come to life, from her wayward tongue to the swish of her hips, well, that was something he couldn't think about or else he'd be in trouble again. Especially now she, with warmed mixture in hand, turned fully to him and his entire body almost leapt towards her.

'Do you want me to lay down?' he said, voice rough.

She pursed her lips. 'Maybe on your side.'

Crooking his arm beneath his head, he turned his back to her and heard her breath release.

'Can you move your other arm?' she said.

He rounded his shoulder, so his hand lay at the small of his back. When her skirts brushed against his palm, his skin pebbled.

The warmed oil hit him before her fingers did. This time he didn't feel them tremble, or hear any hitch to her breathing. This time, he willed his body to focus on whatever it was she was doing.

Nicole Locke 149

Which seemed to be a specific slide of her fingers to palm to knuckles. His body jerked and she eased the pressure.

'I'll stay here a bit,' she said. 'Stopping now that I've found one spot won't help you. So no use grumbling about it.'

He hadn't been cuffed with words so much since he was a lad. 'I didn't say a word.'

'Your silence carries complaints, then.'

Her retort had his lips twitching. When she increased the pressure he braced for the stab of pain, but it wasn't there.

'I told you it'd help,' she said.

Perhaps her digging into his skin might have physical benefit. But for him it was her trying to help him that warmed his soul. She was hurt and she was trying. As though she carried the heavy burden of hope in her every action and was gouging it into his skin to sink it to his very bones. She wasn't to the worst of his scar, only the jagged tipped edge of it, but something of her hope cracked wide open whatever was trapped in his chest.

His eyes watered, leaked and an unbeknown pain poured from him. He couldn't even wipe his face or turn it away to hide it. At least she was at his back and wouldn't notice—

'Easing any more won't help, but I can stop,' she said.

She knew. She knew and he didn't know why he had to tell her what happened, but he did. Now. Immediately. Because whatever agony this was, and whatever she did to suddenly release it, he didn't want it to end. With her hands on his pain, and her hope near blinding him, he had to let her know about that unbearable time.

'The massacre at Berwick was unimaginable. Unforgivable,' he began. 'We banded together to address it. Our Laird believed some settlement would be reached because we had the numbers.'

Barabal's hands hesitated for a moment before she began

150   *The Highlander's Mysterious Maiden*

her ministrations again, this time, on his upper back where there was no scar, but he felt the burn and relief. The easing in his body and his heart.

When she kept quiet, he continued, 'I'm not the best of storytellers. Maybe the beginning with King John Balliol is needed.'

Stuttering her hands through the oil on his back, she said, 'You don't need to say anything of Toom Tabard who was forced upon us by that bastard Edward. I'll gladly accept his lifetime abdication to France.'

So there was no love lost there between his Barabal and the English King Edward. 'But we started it all, didn't we?' he said.

'No, we didn't.'

'I always think if the Lairds hadn't banded together and secretly negotiated with France against England—'

'Why did they do it in the first place?' Barabal said. 'Because Edward was greedy and wanted everything, including our men and funds to fight against France.'

Maybe it was right to talk to Barabal about these things. Maybe now was the time when—

'We shouldn't be talking about this. Now you're all tense again and ruining my work,' she said.

Ah. He'd keep quiet and put a bung in his story. He was used to that. No one else wanted to talk of it either. His friends had been there, and any others gave him wide berth. No doubt because they'd been subjected to the horror of his healing. While he'd been in and out of his mind with fever, he'd likely embarrassed all around him with his whimpers and bellows.

A few more digs and gentle glides of her fingers. All of her touch was against his back, which gave him some privacy. He should be quiet and continue until she was finished, but his mind and body were torn. She'd released something and though he was trying to pull it back, he was failing. His eyes had stopped their torrent, but he had to blink the rest back.

What would happen when he could no longer do so? What—

'Unless you need to,' she added, softer this time. 'Talk about it, that is.'

To talk of King Edward's rage when he realised the secret negotiations. So furious, he'd marched on Berwick and killed thousands of innocent families. All of Scotland fell to their knees when they heard of the massacre, but his march on Dunbar Castle, which was close by, made it worse.

'No, I shouldn't have started. Foolish thing to begin in truth. It was quiet and I couldn't think of anything else to talk about.' He tried to laugh it off, but his voice caught in the lie.

She stilled and he felt himself pause as well, but he didn't know what to say or how to repair any of it. Talking of bees or a few little sticks in her hair she'd missed seemed even more foolish.

'No hope for it now,' she said firmly.

He agreed with that sentiment.

'You must talk of it.'

His body trembled. 'I must?'

'I've been digging into you and nothing's giving. You're so tense now, what I'm doing is wasted. And I refuse to waste my time or efforts.'

She'd listen to him? The relief at her giving him permission to talk of the horror had him openly weeping again. He cleared his throat and tried to give them both an out when he offered, 'I don't have to talk of it.'

'I insist.' She pressed on his shoulder, and he felt that sharp relief of pain stuck inside him. If his one arm wasn't trapped and the other wasn't brushing across her skirts, he

152   *The Highlander's Mysterious Maiden*

would have grabbed her hands. Grabbed them and held on… because she insisted.

Of course she did.

'We couldn't,' Seoc began. 'We couldn't let King Edward commit another massacre anywhere else. Balliol refused homage to Edward. Our hands were forced.'

'To prevent another Berwick.'

'To prevent all of Scotland becoming a Berwick,' he said, his words becoming steady. 'At Dunbar, we had a good position. Their cavalry led by Surrey had to cross a gully by Spott Burn and some of their ranks broke up. I don't know what happened then, but we ceded our position and charged downhill. Why did we charge downhill? Was it Comyn? No one has confessed.'

Not that any confession mattered. He couldn't blame anyone for keeping quiet, many men were made prisoner that day, and— What care had Barabal for burns or gullies or facts?

Yet now he was talking, it was pouring out of him. And Barabal was listening, which gave him strength to continue.

'My theory was it was the horses. Dunbar, on both sides, was all mounted men. It's a bloody affair fighting with horses. Most warriors like the tactical advantages of it. For me, I've seen the most needless injuries happen to men who fight that way. A horse throws your balance off in an attack. And if it comes down to either you or it, no matter how much loyalty and care you have for the creature, you may have to sacrifice the animal, which I could never bear,' he said. 'Sorry. This is probably too much to think about.'

'I've never been to war or battle,' she said. 'But I've seen the after-effects.'

No. Such a woman should be protected from all war, all danger since— He flinched as she dug deep.

'You can stop those thoughts right now,' she retorted. 'I'm strong, but I'll use my elbows if you keep tensing.'

He huffed to hide his smile. He could get used to her retorts and demands. 'You don't know what I thought of.'

She paused and he wanted her to guess. Simply guess so he could tell her he was thinking of her, to let her know he had feelings for her strength of will and elbows. Feelings for *her*, but she made some disgruntled sound, and the moment passed.

He cleared his throat. 'That's what happened to Patrick. Our Laird was atop of his horse, and called for a retreat. I was there to guard him. My stride long enough in any standing battle to protect him. Except, our Laird called for retreat while he charged forward.'

'And you couldn't get to him.'

His arm was going numb under him and his other one was back so far, his fingers swept along her skirts again. What would she think if he buried his fingers there, to simply hold her to him in some way as he finished the tale she'd already guessed the ending to?

His size made him a target, his skill made him a force. His entire life hadn't been easy, but it hadn't been hard either. He had never been seriously hurt before, he'd grieved with the loss of his mother, but she'd died quickly without much pain, and there were so many happy memories of them together it eased his loss.

At the first instance of strife, he'd failed. First with protecting the clan's Laird, then by protecting himself. 'I couldn't pull him back because I rode no horse.'

'You didn't retreat.'

She knew everything, it was as though she was there with him. 'I charged forward. My attention on protecting our Laird, I didn't see the man on my left.'

154   The Highlander's Mysterious Maiden

He glanced at Barabal, then away. Did he need to say more? She'd seen his scar. She could guess, but then…that's what he had everyone doing. Guessing. Trying to gauge his moods, his feelings, his loss, his pain.

With her, he didn't want that. Oh, he knew she struggled with her own past, she was far too driven otherwise, but he could wait for her to tell him. For now, he could give her his words, his feelings. She'd asked to hear his story, something no one offered to hear before, so for her he'd tell the truth… because she insisted.

Her hands continued on his back, no longer digging, but simple lying flat and warm. He liked her surety, her capabilities. The fact her bones were thick, sturdy, as though she could take on the harshest of storms.

He felt as though he was a tree on a cliff during a storm, and she held him, calmly, steadily, so he didn't blow away. It gave him the strength to continue.

'It was one sword swipe, one sure strike across my torso meant to gut me. So I could watch my intestines fall into my hands as I waited for death.'

A flutter of her fingertips was her only reaction. When they steadied again, he continued.

'It didn't happen. Maybe it was my leap and the angle of the sword that prevented his blade's depth. Instead of dying, I fell to the muddied ground, watching my Laird rush towards the fight instead of away like the rest of my clansmen.

'I don't know how they did it, but Hamilton and Camron found me, got me on some sort of stretcher and fled while dragging me behind them.'

'And Sir Patrick?' she said faintly. 'What happened to him?'

Was that tenderness in her broken voice? He didn't dare look, for this was perhaps the hardest part to tell of all, and here was his Barabal asking the difficult questions, forging on ahead in his life, demanding he show all his vulnerabilities and weaknesses. He wasn't a fool like the cordwainer and the apiarist. He wouldn't back down when she offered help.

'He was killed. Others were taken prisoner, including our Laird's son. Many people will talk of his long life and he died with honour. Still, I can't stop the burrowing thoughts of what I missed; they twist me about.'

He took his own faulty inhale, relished in the curling of her fingertips against his skin as if she, like he had wanted to, was trying to bring him closer. He wanted her closer. He wanted to tell her everything, to tell his past and show his heart. This woman had called to him from the beginning. So he faced the truth and told her the very darkest part of him.

'I wonder, ask, demand of myself what's worse. That we lost his son, perhaps never to return to his clan? Or that Sir Patrick's buried at Dunbar, and not here, where his wife grieves still.'

He had no warning. Nothing but an enormous pause that expanded out from her after his last word. Nothing, except her hands flew from his back to his exposed shoulder as she pressed the full weight of her on it and flipped him immediately on to his back.

His free arms tingled and stung, and his back protested at the slap against the hard bench.

Then he wasn't aware of anything else at all except Barabal looming over him, her wide caring eyes searching his with questions he was desperate to have the answers to.

Chapter Fourteen

Barabal's heart broke. Poignancy and yearning poured into the cracks, overtaking her until she nigh drowned in Seoc's grey eyes.

Tear tracks on one rugged cheek, bruised lips as if he pressed them tight to hold in his emotions. The rest of him was nothing but utter masculine beauty. Her hands still slick with oil slipped on his shoulder at the pressure she seemed incapable of ceasing.

This man hurt because of others in pain. Not for himself, not for his scar. Because a wife grieved, and a son was lost. Her grip tightening, Barabal couldn't let go. She needed to hold him down a moment longer. Keep him still until whatever was overwhelming her heart eased.

But the longer they stared, locked into each other's eyes, the more her heart burst and broke and stuttered until the rest of her body broke, too. Her eyes welled, her limbs trembled, and goose pimples raced down her spine.

What would she give to have someone charge forward to save her? She felt half-mad, half-sick. She held him down, but she fell into his eyes, his soul, down to the dark depths where his roots grew.

And he seemed to know it for whatever had afflicted her was just as strong with Seoc, who, on a guttural groan, grasped

Nicole Locke 157

the nape of her neck, lifted his torso and slammed his lips against hers.

She stood no chance of balance then, not when Seoc's free arm snaked around her waist and crushed her solidly against him. Not when her other hand flew out to his opposite shoulder, sprawling herself across until she had to straddle him or slide off the other side.

Not when Seoc never released their lips as he lowered himself and she followed him down. Not when he kept kissing her as if he had to or they'd both fall or fly and the way to stay here, together, was to wrap themselves around each other and hold on.

And still it wasn't enough. Not nearly close enough.

Her slick hands palmed his broad shoulders, down his torso until her fingers fluttered against his taut male nipples. His body shivered and he yanked his lips from hers. Dropping his eyes, he tugged at the laces holding her gown, loosening her gown, but tightening her desire.

She couldn't stop touching him even when his skin pebbled. She ran her fingers down the uniform ridges of his abdomen, not changing her strokes as she crossed over the scar because what did it matter? It was healed, he was alive. He grieved because others grieved. And he was here, with her.

His chest rose and fell with his cragged uneven breaths. One long pull and the laces were free. Dropping the laces beside them, he hungrily kissed her again.

But now her hands were trapped between their bodies and her arms by her clothes. He'd freed her laces, but she was bound. She became desperate to tangle herself with him, to hold him back just as fiercely. She pulled away, and her gown fell to her elbows. Her chemise barely held on one shoulder.

Eyes locked on her newly bared skin, he stilled.

'No.' She didn't want him to stop his kisses, only to free

158 *The Highlander's Mysterious Maiden*

her limbs. She tucked in her arms to free the sides of her gown and Seoc grabbed her hands. She froze.

'Wait,' he said.

No waiting. Not with her heart shattering around him, not when words would certainly make her rampant emotions too big to control, and she was snapping, *longing*, as it was. He had to know. 'I don't want to stop. I—'

'Me as well.' He released a breath and squeezed her hands in his. 'So very much. I don't know what happened.'

'You kissed me,' she said.

'I needed to, but that's not all.' His eyes searched hers, then her hair. With trembling fingers, he tugged a small stick from her hair and tossed it. 'All gone now.'

She stared at the stick he dropped to the floor. Had that been there this entire time? He...took care of her, kissed her and said he wanted to do so again. Maybe she could wait, maybe he had more words to say to her. 'What else?'

Again, he encircled her hands with both of his. 'Tell me what made you distressed these last days.'

'What?'

'I found you hiding from the other women and you've avoided others all week. You looked sad.'

His eyes were dark, his hair mussed by her fingers, a flush to his skin that probably matched her own. And he wanted her to talk. She had nothing to say. She wasn't capable of saying anything.

'We've been here too long.' She pulled away. 'We should go.'

He pulled her tighter. 'No.'

No? She waited until some sort of umbrage filled her at his denial, but nothing within her rose. Every bit of her still clung to him. 'What did you do to me?'

'That was the kissing. It's as strong as mead, lass, and a thousand times sweeter,' he said. 'Now tell me.'

That wasn't kissing. That yearning desperation wasn't mere kissing, and she wouldn't use words because he demanded she tell him of her day. But his deep voice was gentle, as though he needed to ask, but wouldn't push if she truly refused.

'You took my laces off,' she said.

His breath hitched. 'Yes.'

'If you leaned back, or released my hands, my clothing would fall.'

'And we'd be doing more than kissing, lass, which is why I'm staying right here.'

She didn't know why she was surprised by his stubbornness. He might have suffered, and he might stand in a field alone, but he had survived. 'What if I leaned back?'

He pulled his lower lip in. 'You could.'

Then what? With heat suffusing her body, she didn't want to fight him, but that didn't mean she would spill her brokenness to him. She might not be leaving the Graham Clan now, but she would soon. Ivor said she didn't belong, which meant her days here were short.

She wanted to wait a while longer until she knew where to go. With war about to start, she couldn't be careless. That was all the reason she wanted to stay, not because of this man who grieved. She might have pinned him down, but she needed to belong first. Weeks gone by with no occupation, and she still had no permanent home.

Raising her chin, she answered, 'I haven't been distressed and I was kissing you without you knowing of my day.'

'You believe kissing is all I want from you? That I don't want to know you?' He wrapped his hands fully around hers. 'Before this, before the cellar, I watched you for days.'

160   *The Highlander's Mysterious Maiden*

He had? That shouldn't have warmed her as it did. 'I was many places. Other people observed me as well.'

'Did they noticed how your eyes dimmed?'

No one saw her eyes dim. She blinked back the sudden sting in her eyes. She was right before; she couldn't withstand these words. And that was when she thought he'd wanted to confess to his suffering.

He wanted to know her suffering. How could she deny him? He'd suffered unimaginable pain and had been on the cusp of death. His roots were snarled and blackened because a son was lost and a widow grieved. Because he lost someone dear to him and blamed himself. She stood no chance to resist him.

'Why did you tell me of Sir Patrick?'

He brushed his fingers against the back of hers. 'Because you needed to hear it.'

No, she hadn't, but he'd shared it; maybe he needed her to tell him something as well. Maybe she could. For no matter what, she knew what was between them wasn't mere lust or desire.

'Ivor said I don't belong here.'

His hands tensed. 'Beileag's father?'

She gave a small nod. 'She was there, too.'

'In the mill.' His expression grew curious. 'Was Ivor working on a project? Did he grow quiet, but showed his skill?'

To rub it her face. 'I don't have any skills with woodwork.'

Hands still clasped, he pointed at her. 'There you go then.'

'There I go?'

'He was showing you his work to train you, but then however you reacted probably told him more than you'd guess.'

Was that true? 'I didn't say anything except I didn't know woodwork.'

'Did you tell him you wanted to learn?'

She shook her head.

He rubbed his hands around hers, shifted beneath her so she had no choice but to lean a bit more towards him. 'Hence him saying you don't belong in the mill. He never lets anyone learn unless they're absolutely certain. It's too arduous and dangerous a craft otherwise.'

So Ivor hadn't insulted her, hadn't told her she had no place in the Graham Clan. He'd actually been helping her learn a craft so she could stay. He'd been helping her, and she'd yelled at him to clean his scattered shavings.

'You don't belong in the mill,' he continued, unaware of her thoughts. 'Which surprises me since you seem so skilled at everything, my cobbler cordwainer lass.'

Something flickered in her chest. Something that burned a bit brighter, something she continually pushed away, but right now, she couldn't help but ask, to clarify, if it was true. Had Ivor intended to help her? 'He meant I didn't belong in carpentry and not in the Graham Clan?'

'What else?'

What else, except the same that had happened with every other clan. Or most of them anyway. Rejection. Unwanted. Sent away or forced to run.

Seoc's soft laugh cut short and Barabal realised too late she'd been staring helplessly at him. She smiled, knew it wobbled when Seoc's expression drew fierce as if another thought occurred to him. One she was certain she didn't want to talk of at all.

Not when an insistent truth was swarming her: she could stay.

Possibly. Perhaps. But those words in her head didn't squash hope resurfacing. She had no defence to ignore it. No way of burying herself in work, in hurtful memories, or ordering someone about.

162   *The Highlander's Mysterious Maiden*

She held no position in the clan, no bonds of friendship. She was no different than when she'd arrived at the Graham Clan.

Except she was, here, secured in Seoc's arms. Seoc who kissed her as if he had to, then stopped so they could talk about her. And they did all this while she was sprawled against his bared chest, straddled around his large thighs as if what they shared was common. This didn't feel common. Or at least like anything she'd known before.

'What else would he have meant, Barabal?' Seoc repeated more forcefully.

Nothing. Ivor had meant nothing at all by his words and deeds, but what she always wanted: that she was worth the time to teach, that she could belong. And here, with Seoc, with his words and his kisses, she wanted him as well. She wrenched a hand free only to lay it on top of his.

'Kiss me.' She squeezed his fingers.

'I want to do nothing else,' he said. 'But—'

She laid her fingertips on his mouth. His eyes darkened as they roved over the tip of her ear and down her jaw to her lips. She felt the truth of his want in the warmth of his body and the pounding of his heart against her trapped arms. A beat that hadn't slowed since he yanked the laces free.

She could stay. Hope hammered through her heart and insisted she acknowledged its presence. For once, she did. Darting forward, she pressed her lips to his. He startled. Then on a groan, Seoc crushed his lips fully against hers.

It was more than any of their kisses before. Because of words, because they'd delayed, she didn't know. How would she? She'd had no experience with this before, yet some instinct urged her on. And the longer they kissed, the more she rocked her hips into his, the more those cracks in her heart healed and sealed their shared words. Until, until... Cupping the side of his neck, she pressed herself against him and like some wicked siren pulled his tongue into her mouth.

He went rigid beneath her. Then like a man unleashed, he cradled her head between his palms and kissed her deeply, urgently. A rough deep press of his lips that took her breath away.

Want coursed through her. It was the heavy heat of him beneath her, the way his hips lifted between hers, the way the hard length of him pulsed through their bunched layers of clothes.

Panting out, he nipped her jawline, licked the shell of her ear. 'Barabal, what you do to me.'

She clenched her hands on his shoulders, dragged her fingertips over the back of his neck and tugged on his curls there. 'You let go of my hands.'

'I did,' he said wickedly.

'Then we're done with words?'

'We...maybe. Stop,' he said, his voice a rasp, his words barely audible between licks of his tongue and heavy breath.

She didn't want maybes or to stop. Arching back, so his kisses broke off slowly, Barabal rested her hands on his knees. Infinitesimally, one slide and slip at a time, her crushed gown, and crumpled chemise felt to her waist.

Hands frozen mid-air, Seoc gave one low masculine grunt.

She didn't know how long they'd been down here, but it was later than before. More people had come in from the fields, there were more feet above them, more chances of them getting caught.

'I don't want to leave,' she said, her voice hoarse.

'We're not going anywhere, my lass.'

Then why wasn't he doing anything? 'Seoc,' she said, but there was a whine to her voice that hadn't been there be-

164   The Highlander's Mysterious Maiden

fore. As though some of his need was leaking over to her. 'Touch me.'

He cupped her breasts in his hands, his thumbs arching over her nipples. 'You have no idea how much I've wanted to hear those words.'

Her head fell back.

Seoc caressed and stroked her breasts, sank his teeth into her neck and gave one long suck before ducking his head and repeating the same pull on one hardened tip. All the while his hands supported her breasts, which spilled over his calloused palms, and his thumbs flicked and rubbed against one nipple, then the other. One and then—

Gasping, Barabal carded her hands through his hair and tugged, hard.

He pulled up. His eyes heavy lidded and so dark she saw little grey there. 'Is it too much?'

She felt about to burst. Her heart, her body. In this cellar that was getting darker as one sconce died, and the others flickering madly, she answered, 'No, it's only—'

'Too much.'

'I can't contain,' she panted.

'Ah, you need more then.'

She wouldn't survive.

Seoc lifted himself enough to nip her lower lip between his and rolled it gently into his mouth.

'Your eyes,' he said.

'Yes,' she said, though she didn't know what he was asking.

'They're not dim.'

'No.' They were most likely fevered with hope and lust and everything she couldn't contain because she didn't have to. Ivor wanted to show her his trade, maybe someone else would as well. And this man, this incredible, brave man held her as though he didn't want to let go.

Seoc kissed her forehead, her chin, nibbled down the side of her neck. Smattered kisses down between her breasts still cupped in his large, calloused palms.

Down the soft mound of her stomach, his deft caresses skimming over her arms before capturing her hands.

'How do you...' he stated '...how do you always smell of roasted almonds?'

'What?'

His eyes lit as he took in her flushed and dampening skin, the way her breath came in hard pants.

'You're a vision,' he said. 'Lay back.'

She did.

Holding her hands secure, he beckoned, 'Further, all the way to the bench.'

Braced by his strength, she did that, too, until she was laid before him.

Not once did she think of the way her body looked, the soft rolls of her stomach, the thickness of her bones. He did not act like a man who noticed her sturdiness and wide hips, he acted like a man who wanted to consume her. When he released her hands, she put them over her head and clasped them.

His eyes, if possible, became even more heavy lidded. 'Better than my dreams.'

Gripping one thigh, then the other, he slowly opened her legs, his gaze riveted to what he revealed. She felt the dampness there, the vulnerability, the fluttering need.

Her limbs trembled; he muttered words of her beauty, of his desire for her. Rubbed his chin against the inside of her knee, kissed down one thigh, then began his kisses from the other knee down again. All while he skimmed his knuckles along the outside of her thighs in winding circles before flattening his palms, sliding them between her thighs, parting her even further so as to make space for him.

Riots of emotions tightened within her. She knew of men and women. She didn't know of this. 'What are you to do?'

'What I need to, what you want.' He kissed again, lower, skimming his lips and his tongue to her core. 'A kiss.'

And somehow, she knew what he'd do by the hoarse desperation in his voice, the way that same agony echoed in her core.

'Do you want my kiss, my Barabal lass?' Rubbing his thumbs along her skin, he set her writhing body alight.

'More than.' She clasped the sides of the bench to hold herself down.

Seoc's grey gaze tracked her movement and hummed his amused approval before he bent his head, a brush of his breath before he lathed her in one long swipe, then again. He was so big, so broad he encompassed all of her and she never wanted his touch to end.

A flush waved across her skin as she remembered he, too, had gripped this same bench. Had he felt like this? He couldn't have felt like this.

An arch of his brow, a brief kiss against her heated flesh. 'Exactly, lass. That's exactly it. Just like that, gripping tight, holding back.'

'I'm not… I can't,' she stumbled. How could he guess her thoughts? But she didn't get a chance to ask him because he ran his pointed tongue along the furls of her lips and Barabal gasped. It was the signal he must have waited for because he settled his body between her legs, then didn't let up as he teased with his tongue, his lips. Soft rhythmic kisses that coaxed, beckoned, until her hips duplicated the dance.

'Good, so good.' He hummed against her swollen flesh before he took her sweet bud into his mouth and nibbled, nipped.

Nicole Locke 167

Blew one cool bit of air against her heat, before swirling his tongue. Barabal's hips bucked. Seoc tightened his grip on her thighs, which trembled, she couldn't still them.

'Seoc?'

'That's it, lass. I can see you're almost there, feel you fluttering against my tongue. Wanting—' Deepening his carnal kiss, his tongue, Seoc's lustful groan vibrated against her fluttering wet heat.

Everything in her tightened, swelled.

'Now, Barabal,' he rasped against her spilling desire. 'Now, lass, I want to feel you.' Gripping the bench, arching her back as ripples of pleasure swelled, Barabal keened.

Chapter Fifteen

Seoc thought Barabal's touches were torture, her kisses agony, but the moment she lifted her hands, then gripped the bench beneath her, he came completely undone.

'So dear, so sweet.' He breathed against the cushion of her thigh. 'You've undone me.'

Her arms encircled his shoulders. Their weight wholly welcomed. He'd lie like that for days if she'd let him. But they were in a cellar, on a bench. And he'd practically rutted her as though he had no care for her at all. He knew he'd have a difficult time keeping his hands off her, but there were no excuses. Gripping the bench, he pushed his weight off her. Her eyes fluttered down, but didn't close. Seoc followed her downward gaze, the one fixed on his breeches.

'Ignore it,' he rasped.

'I don't want to.' Curling her hands around his forearms, she arched her back. Her arousal, still flushed from his tongue, brushed against him. It didn't matter he was clothed he trembled.

With one hand, he pinned her waist. 'Still.'

'No.'

'I'm trying not to crush you.'

'You're too far away.'

Did she think he wanted *any* separation from her? Bury-

Nicole Locke 169

ing himself inside her slick heat until they were forever entwined was all he craved. Bowing his head, but keeping his body rigid, he trailed kisses along her neck, caressed the tip of his nose along the back of her ear. When she arched her neck to give him more access, he pulled away again.

'Barabal, you're too much temptation.'

'I know what happens between a man and a woman, Seoc.' Her eyes, half-lidded with lust, mesmerised him. 'I want this.'

So did he, but his heart, too recently revealed to her, needed more from this woman. Because he cared and he wanted no doubts. Bracing himself for the answer, he said, 'You want me.'

A flare of surprise, of wariness swirled with the desire that flooded her beautiful eyes, but he held his gaze steady with hers, silently begging her to give them a chance.

Releasing his arms and lowering her gaze, she grabbed at the rest of his clothing and pulled the band at his breeches. 'Yes, I want you. I want everything.'

Heart soaring at her declaration, his body shuddered with need. He had no defence against her words or hands. He was utterly hers.

'Don't stop.' He arched his brow as he issued the challenge and relished the answering light in her eyes. There was his fierce Barabal lass. Holding himself away from her, gripping on the sides of the damn bench, he watched her tug his clothing, each jerk of her arm shifting his hips, increasing fiction until nothing but embarrassment and her curiosity held him back from spilling in his braies.

And that was before he felt her hands cupping him, a fingertip caressing along the pronounced vein. He hissed.

'It's softer than I thought,' she said.

He gritted his teeth. 'Soft?'

'You hold yourself too far away, move down,' she said.

170   *The Highlander's Mysterious Maiden*

Gripping her thighs, he parted them. Firm enough he'd know she'd pay attention, light enough to not leave marks.

'Ordering, demanding, even now.' He lowered his frame against hers, felt the softness of her breasts, her stomach, the hard peaks of her nipples, the drag of his length through her swollen folds.

Every ounce of his being awakened as she canted her hips, positioned her centre. Sweat prickled the small of his back. Still, he had to know. 'Barabal?'

Her eyes so dark in the cellar his family built, laying on a bench he'd spent years of his life toiling over. This place with this woman together overwhelmed him. He shifted them both until they were pressed against each other and it still wasn't enough.

Both her hands gripping his shoulder, her breasts quivering with each rising breath, and everything in him drew tight.

'Please, Seoc, I want this,' she said.

One thrust, sure and deep. One arch of her body beneath his, a soft, hissed moan he both treasured and grieved. He wished her no pain at all, so he held himself still. Waited. Kissed her again until he felt her hips cant, then he rocked into her again and again until her soft pleasured gasps rasped against his heated skin.

He couldn't stop. He kissed her shoulders, her breasts, her cheek. Lapped at her beads of sweat. Releasing her knee, he cupped her breast while he flicked her nipple with his thumb again.

She clung to him, her hands just as tight, just as gripping and he relished the bites of pain, the feel of her. The worn bench supported them even while he pulled her tighter, plunged harder. His body not leaving hers. Her arms flew around him, her legs clinging to him.

A hiss from his throat, as he felt himself tighten from

the force of his passion. He would spill before she found her second release.

He said words to her, encouraging, begging, demanding. Nonsensical essential utterances before he broke. She was so right, so perfect. 'Intoxicating. Heady.' *His.*

A swivel of his hips and she cried out. Another and her spasms cascaded around him. He drove in and again. Rhythm lost to a fiery craving. Shoving his hand under her bottom, lifting her tighter until her legs clutched at his waist, Seoc chased his own need within her still-fluttering walls. No secrets, only them. Only...

Crying her name, Seoc's release hit him hard, hot, sudden. Forever. Seoc gave way to the ecstasy, nearly falling on top of her before he buried his face in the curve of her neck. Breathed her in as his body trembled and hers shivered. As he caught his breath, and her hard pants eased. Utter bliss, but they couldn't stay like this. He'd crush her.

'Hold tight.' He rolled them until he lay beneath her, and she settled over him. Her face pressed into his neck, her curves spilling over him. His heart steadied, as did hers.

He swiped her chemise off the floor and laid it over her. 'Did I hurt you?'

She hummed against him, and he wrapped his arms tighter around her. He'd take her hum as satisfaction.

No regrets, yet he'd lost his mind with her. What had he been thinking, following her to the cellar?

He felt no resistance, no fight from her as she rested against him. Though he should. It was her first time, and they'd joined in a room that held meaning for him, not for her. He hadn't even a damn blanket to cover her.

'This bench is unforgiving.' He rubbed into her shoulders, her back, tried to ease any pain he might have caused her.

'I wasn't paying attention to the bench.'

172   *The Highlander's Mysterious Maiden*

He smiled, kissed the top of her head. They should leave, but he was loath to do so. Loath to let her out of his arms for even a moment to find a more comfortable location. The sounds above them were fainter now and he knew it drew late. If they were to be interrupted, it would have already happened.

But now what? This wasn't a comfortable bed, they couldn't stay the night, and there would be no carrying her into his home he shared with his father even if she'd allow it.

'I should have thought this through,' he said.

She lifted her head a bit and peered down.

'Of the location only,' he said.

Whatever she saw in his expression eased whatever was troubling her because on a huff she settled back against him.

Cradling her against him again, he brushed her hair that was strewn over his chin.

'I have no regrets of the rest, Barabal,' he said and, because he wanted there to be honesty between them, he added, 'and I hate that even for a moment you thought I did.'

She gave a long sigh. 'It's a lifetime of habit for me.'

Her confession was said so forlornly he knew she revealed some of her vulnerability.

Another moment with her he'd treasure, even if the emotion itself he wanted to slash with his sword. How did this brave resourceful woman have any rejection in her life, let alone expect it so readily? He wished it was an enemy he could fight. But her feelings weren't something he could merely charge forward and change, even if he wanted to, which he didn't. They were her feelings. It was her past and one he wanted to know, but only if she wanted to tell him.

She'd given him so much, he ached to do the same for her.

'Surely you haven't insulted everyone in your life.' He kept his voice easy, hoping she'd find the lightness he gave her.

Nicole Locke 173

'It can't be surprising if I have.'

She said it in a teasing voice, but there was a tone that reminded him of the wariness in her eyes. Where did it come from?

'What of family?'

Her beautiful face was tucked in the crook of his neck so he couldn't see her expression, though from the fact she no longer laid so easily against him, he could tell his words had made her cautious.

He wanted her open and comfortable with him again. Lightly tracing his fingertips along her exposed arm, he added, 'You do have some family, don't you? Unless you emerged fully on Beltane night.' He paused. 'Ah, I understand it now.'

'What do you understand?' she said with a bit of bite to her voice.

Her walls coming up wouldn't do. 'This is where you confess, you're fae.'

She gave a low sound of amusement. 'Would it be surprising if I did?'

She was magical to him, and he wanted to continue to tease, but he also wanted to know her. Though he started talking of family by accident, now he wanted to truly know of hers. Did they make her guarded?

'Is your father some princely ruler of a faraway realm?'

This time she huffed a bit, but he kept tracing his fingertips along her shoulders, while the other held firm around her lower back. It wasn't much, but he wanted to provide comfort in any way he could.

She had no idea what she did for him. Allowing him to talk of his time at Dunbar shouldn't have been much, but it was everything to him. That heavy knot in his chest was gone now, not even a heavy jagged fragment of pain left behind.

174   *The Highlander's Mysterious Maiden*

She'd taken his vulnerability and rid him of it simply by listening. He knew she was wary; he'd seen it that first day and it drew him. As if whatever pain he'd kept in his heart recognised hers.

'Barabal?' Everything in him, again, prompting her to give them a chance.

She drew a long heavy breath in, one that moved him as much as her. 'My parents are dead.'

He sensed she was alone. Else why would a woman enter an unknown clan in the middle of the night? But there was pain there. It was in every reluctant word she shared, every long pause, as if dreading the words he asked for.

He waited for her to continue as she did for him, but she said no more. Whereas she'd only had to ask once and he'd poured his soul to her, he should have known Barabal would be more stubborn. After all, this was a woman who made Ol' Bal drink a tincture he didn't want.

'You must miss them.'

She shifted and settled her head in the middle of his chest until he could almost catch her eyes with his. He wanted to see her eyes very much and crooked his neck until he saw the fascinating hazel sheening with tears.

His heart hitched.

Blinking, she shifted her gaze away, but didn't move off him, even when he stilled his hand and held her against him. He wanted this woman, but he never wanted to cause her pain. By words or deeds. He wasn't doing well with that vow. The damn bench was uncomfortable, and the room couldn't be much better. Because he'd taken her in a cellar.

'That chemise can't be much. You must be cold, We can—'

'I was but five years of age when they died, and I barely remember them. It's my brothers mostly I—' she stopped, cleared her throat '—I remember them the most.'

Nicole Locke 175

She had no parents, but she had brothers. Where and when was the last time she'd seen them because her tone was so empty and alone, he knew she missed them. 'Are they gone as well?'

'They were alive last I saw them.'

'When did you last see them?' he said.

She released quick breath. 'How did you know that Ivor meant my belonging in the mill versus with the Graham Clan?'

Seoc kept his hands roving against her back. He knew she'd changed the subject on purpose. She didn't want to talk of her brothers and of being apart from them. How many years since she saw them last? Simply mentioning them she sounded so forlorn. No hate in her tone, merely lost.

Barabal was fierce, demanding, but underneath she was hurt. Something grave in her past happened that made her believe he regretted their time together. Made her instinctually think Ivor's simple comment of her not belonging in the mill, meant she didn't belong in Graham clan.

It was a habit to mistrust so automatically. How long had she doubted people, or her worth?

How could she believe she didn't belong in all of the Graham Clan or with him? He felt, however, if he pressed much more, this moment would be gone.

Catching his breath, but letting his heart go to this perplexing, yet breathtaking woman, Seoc cupped the back of her head and relished Barabal snuggling so sweetly against him. She was wary, but she hadn't run. He could share some of Beileag's and Ivor's relationship with her.

'Since childhood, Beileag has been one of my closest friends. What I'm about to tell you is common knowledge among her friends, but also the clan.

'Ivor's a quiet man and most of her life he hardly interacted

176 *The Highlander's Mysterious Maiden*

with Beileag, who wanted to learn the woodworking craft. Her mother refused for her to learn, but Beileag's strong; she learnt the craft mostly on her own.'

'They didn't look estranged,' she said.

'Beileag recently confronted him,' he said. 'Ivor informed her he had been secretly teaching her all those early years when she'd sneaked into the mill. Not by words, but by showing her each tool and how he used them. She remembered her childhood and what he had done, and her perspective changed, even about her mother, who is still an unpleasant woman. But they all talk more now.'

'He used words with me. He said I didn't belong,' she said. 'He spoke.'

That was easy. 'You must have said something to show you had no passion for the mill.'

She paused. 'Perhaps—'

A loud bang of the cellar door had them both jerking apart and off the bench.

'Did you fall asleep while fermenting again?' Heavy footsteps on the stairs.

Seoc shoved the chemise in Barabal's hands and pulled her behind him.

'I'll be up,' Seoc called out.

'I'm down here now, might as well see what you've been doing…oh.'

Naked, Seoc faced his father. 'Father.'

Barabal squawked.

His father gaped. 'Son.'

'Let. Me. Get dressed.' Shoving elbows in his back, Barabal broke free from his arm. He didn't dare turn, but he hoped her rough movements were about her getting the chemise over her head.

His father slapped his hand over his eyes. 'Warn a father before you move like that, lad!'

Knowing his father hadn't seen him bared since his balls had dropped, Seoc chuckled. 'Lass, are you covered?'

'Get me my gown,' she said.

Not a chance. The moment she had that, she'd run and, since his father was staying and rocking on his heels as though he was a child about to receive a gift, he couldn't deny his father a moment of her company. He simply wished it was under better circumstances.

'Father, this is Barabal.' Reaching down, he grabbed his braies and wrapped them around himself. 'Barabal, this is Aonghus, my father.'

'Is it safe to uncover my eyes?' Aonghus said.

The light was dim, her chemise wasn't thin. And if she stayed partly behind him, she was covered enough.

'Yes,' he said.

'No,' Barabal said at the same time.

Without lowering his hand, his father cleared his throat. 'I apologise deeply, lass.'

'Stay behind me.' Over Barabal's sound of displeasure, he added, 'It's safe now, Father.'

Aonghus lowered his hand and Seoc glanced behind him. Barabal glowered at them both. Ah, he missed the sweet flush of her pleasure already.

'Get me my gown,' Barabal hissed.

It was on the other side of the bench. He knew at some point she'd grab it herself, but for now… 'No.'

Aonghus gave a rough chuckle.

Barabal rounded on his father. 'This is no laughing matter.'

Not holding his chuckle in, Aonghus said, 'Give the lad a moment while he's appeasing his father.'

Barabal's frown deepened, just at the moment Aonghus's

178   The Highlander's Mysterious Maiden

cheeks turned red. Holding up his hands, Aonghus added, 'Seoc has talked of nothing but you since your arrival and I've been wanting to meet you terribly. He's just giving me a chance to talk to you.'

Barabal lost her frown.

'So I'm keeping you here,' Seoc added.

'To meet your father,' she said. 'Without clothing.'

'You! Think of me, my dear,' Aonghus said. 'After all, you have been well shielded by him, but I saw all of my son's bits which you shook by elbowing him in the back.'

Seoc snorted.

But Barabal… Barabal laughed. Sudden and loud. At first, he and his father joined in because it was humorous and he was happy to hear her joy even at his expense. But when the moment ended and his father and he still grinned, but no longer chuckled, Barabal's cheeks mottled red from holding in her breath and sound. Her eyes, looking flustered, troubled and dismayed, watered. When he caught her eye, his expression now concerned, she pressed her hand to her mouth to still it, but her laughter burst from her in harsh hiccupping snorts.

Then as shockingly as the sound she made, she raced to grab her gown, pulled it over her head, and without lacing it up, ran past his father. Seoc reached for her, called out, but she was out the cellar door before either of them could stop her.

The door banged shut and another sconce went out. One was still lit, but for him, with the sudden departure of the woman he was falling for and her absolutely ghastly laughter, it was as quiet and heavy as a tomb.

Aonghus watched the door, as if he, too, felt the sudden loss. 'You weren't fermenting brew then.'

'Please tell me no one was wandering outside.' He wanted no harm coming to Barabal. She'd hidden before when she was covered in mud and grass—he was loath to think of the explanations she'd have to make if she was partly undressed.

'There was no one above when I came to you. It's so late, son, I worried about where you were.' Shifting suddenly, Aonghus looked to the room, his eyes tracking Seoc's discarded tunic, the oil, the remnants of his time with Barabal.

That wasn't the reason he felt guilt and shame, however. Nor was it the cause for the heaviness to descend on his heart again. No, he felt all those emotions because of the true reason his father looked for him here.

He was grown, an adult, had trained and fought. His father wasn't worried about where he was, he was worried about the state of his son. He'd tried to pretend the last year, knew he had failed in the conversations where he slipped to his own thoughts and that his friends and family had noticed.

His father had been worried about him. Worried about how dark his thoughts had become since his scar healed. What could he tell him? He had people who loved him, but he held no hope. When he woke, could talk, eat, walk, by then he didn't care.

Not until Beltane and Barabal when she'd demanded he do something. Then he noticed, but how to say all this?

'I've been here, Father. The moment Hamilton and Camron dragged me here, I was here, but I have…had…no hope.'

Aonghus tilted his head to the closed cellar door. 'And she gives you hope?'

No. She didn't, she showed it to him, then demanded he do something about it. But he felt unfaithful saying any of it to his father, especially since he hadn't told Barabal how he felt about her, about them. He needed to show her.

'Things are clearer now.'

With a soft knowing smile, Aonghus palmed out his hands. 'I can see why. She is more lovely than even you described.'

180   *The Highlander's Mysterious Maiden*

More than he could ever describe. She'd laughed, one bright bit of happiness, and it was as though…she forced herself to dim it. Why? She'd laughed, there was happiness there. He wanted a time when she wouldn't be wary around them.

'Her laughter was unexpected,' Aonghus said.

'For me, too,' he chuckled. Would she allow him to hear her true happiness?

'Truly?' Aonghus said, then nodded slowly. 'Will she be well?'

'I will do everything in my ability to make it so.'

'Perhaps I should have left,' Aonghus said. 'I thought you were here alone.'

His father wouldn't have been wrong. Since he was a lad, he'd fallen asleep here. 'I am glad you stayed.'

'You'd speak falsehoods to your own father?'

'Would have been better if you'd waited an hour or two.' Seoc pulled on his tunic.

'I am certain,' Aonghus chuckled low. 'But can't say I don't see the humour of it all.'

There was humour here and something else. Love? Perhaps, or at least the closest he ever felt for another. Seoc rubbed his forehead. Barabal hadn't run. She'd laughed, surprised herself with it. Surprised all of them. That laugh! He didn't know if that was her usual sound, oh, but if it was, he looked forward to more of it.

Aonghus looked around again. 'You were here together and alone. Certainly your pursuit is to wed? I can expect grandchildren?'

He couldn't blame his father's hope-filled tone. After all, he had talked of nothing but Barabal to his father since Beltane. 'She stormed out of here.'

'I am sorry if I caused any harm,' Aonghus said.

'No, it wasn't only that. Although her surprise gave her a reason.'

His father raised his brow. 'Something was said before?'

They were talking of family. Barabal knew of his mother and had met his father, and she was talking of her brothers. 'Perhaps, but I don't know what.'

His father placed his hands on his hips, they fell. He placed them on his hips again, they fell. 'She brought light to your eyes, Seoc. Don't think I didn't notice. You said things were clearer for you with her around. I see that.'

Seoc's eyes pricked with tears. His father truly had been worried. 'I was never in doubt of yours and the clan's care of me.'

'Ever?'

'Never.' Seoc looked to the ground. He was still raw from all he'd shared with Barabal; he wasn't prepared to talk of any more.

'She's different, Seoc. You'll fix this?' Aonghus pointed to the door. 'She laughed, but that wasn't humour. A woman that upset has other grief nipping at her heals.'

Seoc pressed his hand against his chest, where his heart was and not his scar. That wasn't where he wanted his thoughts to go any more.

She'd been wary and hurt beforehand and had fled in distress. And that wasn't because of his father, but because… because why?

When his mother died and they grieved, Seoc did the only thing he could to make it better—he took over the preparation of ale so they'd never be without his mother's recipes. Keeping his mother's memory alive brought them both comfort. They'd grieved, but they'd had each other.

Barabal's loss wasn't as simple. There was grief in Barabal's voice when she talked of her family, but also anger. His

182   *The Highlander's Mysterious Maiden*

mother had been well loved by both of them, and though missed, there was no anger or regret about the life they had shared together.

'I don't how to repair it, or what words to say. I don't even know what this is.'

'It's love,' Aonghus said.

He was beginning to believe so as well. She wasn't the answer to everything that ailed him, but she felt like his. 'It's been so quick.'

'That's how it hit me with Fionnghal. Right over the head, love.'

Seoc smirked. 'Mother actually hit you.'

'Well, that, too,' he said. 'But it took that drastic gesture to see what was before me.'

Seoc knew the story well. As a jest, his father had nicked her freshly hung herbs. When she found him, she'd batted him with some basket weave. His mother always said they'd smiled before at each other, but nothing ever came of it. Not knowing his intentions, she'd been furious he'd done the jest and for whatever reason that was what made his father notice her.

Aonghus's sigh turned into a yawn. 'Are you to stay much longer because that sconce is fading.'

Seoc glanced at it. If he could stay here all night he would, he'd done it before. 'I'll relight another.'

With a hard pat on his shoulder, his father walked out the cellar and gently closed the door. A brief glimpse of outside showed it was absolutely dark.

How many times had he stayed in the cellar until the dawn? Once fermenting, his brews needed nothing more than maintenance, but many a time he'd mixed differently to see if he could make it stronger or added different herbs to change the taste.

Nicole Locke 183

Which reminded him to ask Anna about her parsley use—whole swathes were missing from the garden lately.

He lifted the dimming sconce and carefully lit another. It wasn't much, but he'd return home soon enough. For now, he needed to think, to cherish a bit longer how Barabal had felt in his arms.

His father said she was different. He had no idea how much. But maybe he did if even in a dark cellar his father could tell he'd changed. Simply because she'd listened, they'd kissed, he'd loved her.

Maybe he could help her by repairing her grief, finding her missing brothers. But how? He didn't know where they were, or where she was from. And he knew if he asked her, she wouldn't tell him. But she'd spoken to others. Murdag, Anna and at least once she'd talked to Beileag. Maybe Barabal had let slip where she came from?

Not enough time with her, not enough for her to know his intentions, but she had to know this moment in the cellars was significant to him. He'd told her of his mother, of Dunbar, he'd cried. Surely she had to know how important she was to him?

He needed to do the same for her. So strong, resilient. Stubborn. Words weren't enough and time wasn't on their side.

Already they would be readying the drums and horses for Moray and Wallace's campaign. If he waited, he'd miss this time with Barabal, and she'd miss her brothers for even longer. That wouldn't do.

They had so brief a summer and, though he was encouraged from the reports they would prevail at Stirling, anything could happen. He needed to be quick. If he told her he would be gone, she would ask and he wanted it to be a surprise. A great one.

For the first time, he could name the feeling in his chest.

184   *The Highlander's Mysterious Maiden*

The one that was the tiniest of flickering flame when Barabal arrived. The warmth, the heat ever expanding at her words, at her touch. Those kisses… He felt the emotion, but could scarcely recognise it. But now he dared name it.

It was hope.

As soon as it was light, he'd ask Anna, Murdag, Beileag, anybody if they knew where she came from. He'd find her brothers, bring them to her and erase that loss from her eyes, that hurt from her voice. Then she'd know how much she meant to him. Something to show her his love and not only his desire.

Bring her brothers by sword or bribe, by any means. It wasn't a basket of sticks across her head as his mother had done to his father, but it would do.

Chapter Sixteen

'I didn't believe you liked the kitchens.'

On a screech, Barabal dropped the wooden spoon into the pot and spun around to face Anna, who was standing on her tiptoes and looking over Barabal's shoulder.

'She's in here?' Beileag craned her neck around the kitchen alcove's arched entrance.

'Let me see,' Murdag said, pushing Beileag before her.

Then they jostled among themselves until all three women faced her in the little abandoned alcove of the darkened kitchen, in the dead of night, when no one should have been bothering her.

Barabal had come to the kitchens after another day where not one person allowed her to assist in any clan chore. As though they knew she was running out of ways to be useful and couldn't wait for her to be gone.

But she couldn't go. There was an escalating war, and she didn't know whether she should be angry or worried. Seoc had been missing for days.

She couldn't wrap her head around what they'd shared in the cellar. Not only his kisses, his touch, but his thoughts, his feelings. When his father stomped down the stairs, it should have been horribly embarrassing. Yet, for a bright terrifying moment, she felt dropped into another world, another life,

186 **The Highlander's Mysterious Maiden**

the one she was meant to have with Seoc as a husband and family like jovial Aonghus, who teased until she laughed.

Her laugh! Horrified, she'd fled and then Seoc had disappeared—now she was in this mess.

'You should be asleep,' Barabal said.

'So should you,' Anna said.

'What are you doing in here?' Murdag looked around the little room with its anchored shelves, sturdy tables, hanging herbs and many baskets filled with supplies. It was one of many alcoves off the kitchens to provide room for preparations. A place that was partially hidden so she couldn't readily be seen.

'She's cooking,' Beileag said with almost awe in her voice.

Murdag thumbed behind her. 'That's where you cook, near the fire and barrels of water.'

'But this is where someone who loves to cook can hide if anyone pokes their heads in the kitchens looking for her,' Anna said.

Frowning, Barabal's face flamed with the accuracy of Anna's comment.

Murdag snorted. 'If so, that person probably doesn't want to actually be found.'

'She doesn't know how persistent we can be, that's all,' Beileag said.

Why would they need to be persistent with her? All week as she'd met more of the clan and offered advice, Anna, Beileag and Murdag would ask questions of her day, or if she'd eaten. It was odd and unwelcome. 'I'm here and you can leave unless you're here to tell me there's a fire in my hut.'

'See, she does care,' Beileag said. 'She's worried if anyone's hurt in a fire.'

'Didn't say I was worried about anyone.' Barabal deepened her frown.

Nicole Locke 187

'Of course she wants no harm to anyone,' Murdag replied. 'And that's not her point. She's questioning our presence.'

'I thought my point was unless there's an emergency, you shouldn't be here.'

'All this fire talk is meant to distract us,' Anna pointed out. 'Because we have a reason to be here, and she does not.'

Barabal put her hand on her hips. 'You have no reason to be here.'

'We set out to find you and you're here,' Anna said. 'Question is why.'

'Is that parsley?' Murdag swept around her and pinched a bit off the table.

'No one said it couldn't be used.'

'That's quite a bit of parsley,' Anna said. 'Have you been doing whatever this is you're doing, often?'

Beileag sighed. 'Oh, I understand. Seoc uses it for his metheglin—are you helping him with his meads?'

Murdag's eyes widened. 'So she's helping him. That's good because I heard he was worried about the sudden parsley use.'

She'd been careful leaving the cellars that night, but had someone spotted her with Seoc? 'I'm not helping him.'

Anna's lips curved. 'Seoc needs the extra herbs, which is why there is so much more of certain herbs than others. So if you're not helping him with his metheglins, it means you're hurting him.'

'I'm not—' Barabal stammered, bit her tongue, then spat out, 'I'm not doing, or having, or anything with him.'

She was here to ignore her thoughts of him. She wasn't worried for him, or hurt, or anything. She was here to chop herbs in tiny precise slices and meticulously stir finely chopped nuts over the correct heat. Precise. Even. Methodical until she couldn't think of anything else.

Certainly not the weight of his arm around the small of her

188   *The Highlander's Mysterious Maiden*

back, or his large, calloused hands at the back of her neck as he cradled her against him. Never to almost yearn for those lasting moments after their pleasure when nothing existed but the hard beat of his heart against hers. She'd never been so close to anyone like that before.

Had Seoc felt, even for an infinitesimal moment, close to her? He'd shared so much, and she'd felt some inexplainable warmth in her heart. But he was gone, she couldn't ask him and couldn't trust it.

Especially since he'd been hiding or avoiding her for days. Maybe that was best. If she did run into him, he'd probably humiliate her in front of his friends like Hamilton did. Maybe he'd call her a different name to show how unworthy she was. She'd hate him. That's what she'd do. He was mean to leave her and cruel to humiliate her in front of his father.

Oh, she wished for more herbs to chop!

'Well, you're not doing anything with Seoc now, that's true,' Beileag said.

'Not ever,' Barabal said.

'Ah,' Murdag said knowingly.

Barabal didn't like the sound of that. 'Why are you here? I don't need food, or water, or interruptions. Since there's no fire keeping us from our beds, can you all go? I'll admit, we all should be asleep and not in in the kitchens. I'll clean this and leave as quickly.'

'What's odd is you're here at all.' Anna eyed her slurries.

'You have professed numerous times to not want anything to do with the kitchens,' Beileag said. 'That's why we keep finding you in stables, mills, the dairy.'

'Yet you're in the kitchen in the dead of night where no one can see you,' Anna added. 'And given the late time, where no one forced you to come to the kitchens either.'

'So what are you doing here? Beileag said. 'And what are you preparing for tomorrow? This looks amazing.'

Anna swished around her, held her hair back, and sniffed the contents in the pot she'd been stirring. 'Oh, I love the smell of crushed parsley.'

'Is it something to break our fast?' Murdag said. 'It needs to be heated, no?'

'Have you been making this lately? Seoc truly has been asking what was happening to his parsley,' Anna said.

'I can't wait to try it,' Beileag said.

'I'm not preparing anything for anyone to eat,' Barabal said. 'We shouldn't be in the kitchens.'

Anna nibbled a chopped almond. 'Did you roast these after you cut them? How did you not burn it?'

She was finished with this banter. Turning her back, Barabal fished the wooden spoon from the pot and harshly rapped it on the rim of the pot. Her night to find comfort in her sauces was ruined, so she might as well lay awake in her bed for a few hours before sun rise. 'I'm busy.'

When she didn't hear the women leaving, Barabal swung and with dripping spoon in hand, splattered the women with the contents.

They didn't even flinch.

Ever since she'd arrived at the Graham Clan, nothing went as it should. Nothing felt like it used to. It was like the moment she'd arrived late; she couldn't quite get sure footing with the clan. As though everything she said and did, every interaction she had with people, was a little off. A little different.

Since she was abandoned by her family she'd tried to command and control her surroundings, but she couldn't seem to do that with the people here. Despite telling him to go away, Seoc had walked in circles with her. Worse, she seemingly

190   *The Highlander's Mysterious Maiden*

had no defences against Seoc's words and kisses. And these women kept offering her food and company even though—

Spinning around, she pointed at all three. 'Why didn't you run away? Everyone runs away. I've been nothing but abrupt with you and yet, here you are.'

'You believe she's not abrupt?' Murdag rolled her eyes at Anna.

Anna elbowed her in the ribs.

Murdag yowled.

Anna poked her sister again. 'That's what you get.'

'I believe you'd proved your point, Murdag,' Beileag said.

Barabal clutched her spoon tighter. What was she to do with them?

'Do you want us to run away?' Anna said. 'If so, why have you met with so many people?'

'I haven't met anyone; I've been trying to find a position here.'

'While meeting people along the way,' Murdag pointed out.

'They aren't listening to what I say,' Barabal said.

'Some listen,' Anna smiled. 'Seoc, for example.'

Barabal's face flamed. 'How do you—?'

'I told her all about the night of Beltane,' Murdag said.

'Me, too,' Beileag said.

Nothing happened on Beltane. Nothing except meeting Seoc, who'd asked for a kiss, who'd reminded her of a great oak, with roots. One she could cling to when the world batted her away. Yet when she had clung to him, he'd disappeared.

'I arrived on Beltane Eve, that's all that happened,' she said.

Murdag grinned and in a sing-song voice added, 'That's not what it looked like when I saw you two standing close, whispering low.'

'It was noisy on Beltane, no one was whispering. And we weren't standing close, he was doing nothing while you...' she pointed to Anna '...were being carted away.'

Anna tilted her head. 'You tried to help me the day you arrived?'

'I'm not helping anyone.' She could hardly help herself. 'So you're here for what? Seoc? He's not here; he's not anywhere.'

'You noticed he's gone,' Murdag said. 'Did you notice anything else about him?'

This was a trap. 'You know he's gone, so why wouldn't I realise he's gone?'

'But we're not unhappy about it,' Murdag said. 'We're not pushing away people who want to help, or who offer to share drink or food.'

'We're not hiding away and chopping so hard you have little bits of herbs, like wood shavings, all over the place,' Beileag said. 'I've seen this before.'

'Mmhmm,' Murdag agreed.

Did they spy on her? 'I'm not unhappy about it, I'm not anything,'

'It's not only Beltane,' Anna said gently. 'The other evening, you returned to your bed with a gown crookedly tied.'

'That's when we were certain you both liked each other,' Murdag said. 'We wanted you to know we're just as happy as you.'

No one saw her. No one. If she didn't say anything, they couldn't prove anything. 'Is that why you've been keeping me from my tasks this week, because you believe I like your friend? Let me tell you, I don't.'

'And you're not worried that he's gone, or hurt because he didn't say anything about it?' Murdag said.

'How do you know—?' Barabal stopped.

192   *The Highlander's Mysterious Maiden*

'You've been stirring the pot so harshly you're practically breaking the spoons I made.'

Barabal glanced at the spoon, the one with the unusual handle that fit perfectly in her hand. When she glanced back, Beileag was smirking as though she'd made a point.

She wouldn't, couldn't, like these people or Seoc. Or he couldn't like her. Else why did he leave her?

Anna sighed. 'Barabal, I have to let you know. Joan noticed you coming to bed late. She wasn't happy. She's been after Seoc since they were children.'

'But her bosoms never grew in,' Murdag snorted.

Joan saw her after the cellar. When her hair was standing on end and her lips were swollen from Seoc's kisses. Joan saw her when her gown was askew and now was spreading around gossip. Wait. 'Are you saying anyone with a big chest gets notice from him?'

Murdag huffed. 'Didn't say that well.'

'I'd say,' Anna said. 'Barabal, please be patient with us. We want to tell you something. We like that he noticed you on Beltane. We love that your gown was askew.'

'Because he likes big breasts,' she said.

Murdag slapped her forehead. Anna frowned.

'She's admitting now she was with him,' Beileag piped up.

'I did not,' Barabal said.

'In a way you did.' Anna smiled. 'Again, that doesn't matter. He's our childhood friend and a good man. He's different with you.'

'Different than the scores of other women he was with other than Joan?'

'Oh, we're truly not saying things correctly,' Anna said.

'You don't have to say anything at all. I don't want you here and you're wasting my time.' What had she to do with

Nicole Locke 193

any of them? She was here to gather her thoughts, and they'd ruined that.

'He was quiet and alone before you came, Barabal,' Beileag said. 'Now it seems as though he has someone. Not that he didn't have us, but he was far away before, but close…oh, I don't know how to talk of this.'

She was saying it all perfectly. Barabal could never shake the moment she first saw Seoc standing alone in the darkened fields staring out at nothing.

What was snarled or dark within him called to her in ways she couldn't explain and if she did, she'd refuse to talk of them to these women. 'Well, he is far away now. And can stay alone without me.'

'She *is* upset he's gone.' Murdag looked to Beileag. 'She likes him, too.'

No one liked her. 'Is this visit some jest? Like what your husband did to me?'

'That wasn't well done of him, but I believe it's hilarious you now call Hamilton different names,' Beileag said. 'That's quite clever.'

Murdag laughed. 'He's almost terrified of you now.'

'Doesn't even like to say your name,' Anna confirmed.

This was getting nowhere. 'I'll admit to nothing when it comes to Seoc. Nothing for this clan either. I came to this clan to offer help, but instead everyone tells me I can make no improvements and to go away.'

Anna rolled her lips in, but eyed Murdag.

'Father added bins to under the tables,' Beileag blurted. 'You've made an improvement there.'

Not a lot of good that did since he'd offered her no chores to do with the mill. Even though she'd rejected him and millwork. But what did it matter? She wasn't belonging anywhere.

194 *The Highlander's Mysterious Maiden*

Seoc disappearing proved that. And now she wasn't even finding comfort in the kitchens.

Anna dipped a smaller spoon into the parsley sauce.

'What are you doing?' She wanted this whole ordeal to be over.

Anna blinked a couple of times, took another taste. 'Barabal, this is stunning and it's certain to be better once warmed and poured over fish.'

Murdag swept her finger in the bowl containing a slurry of sorrel and thyme. 'This other one is good, too.'

'Of course they're good,' Barabal huffed. 'It takes days to make them taste to this depth.'

'Days?' Murdag dipped her finger in again. 'How have you been sneaking in here and hiding that?'

Why did she say that? Was she bragging now and how did they get from talking about Seoc to her sauces?

Anna made a tsking noise at Murdag. 'We'll have none left if you keep doing that.'

Shrugging, Murdag said, 'She'll make more.'

'Oh, I have to try,' Beileag said. Anna handed her the freshly filled spoon and Beileag moaned.

What was happening around her?

Waving the spotless spoon, Beileag said, 'I used to hide my talent, too.'

She wasn't hiding any talent. Barabal swung her gaze back up.

Murdag and Anna nodded. 'For years.'

Barabal had seen Beileag's astounding craftsmanship and couldn't believe it. Then she remembered Seoc's story of how her mother didn't want her to learn. Did Beileag, did these women, believe she had talent in the kitchen? She knew she was good, but as good as Beileag's creatures?

Something like joyous pride swelled in her chest before it

Nicole Locke 195

quickly collapsed as if punctured by her past. 'There's no talent here; I don't even like the kitchens. I avoid them, always.'

All three women gaped.

Barabal wanted to take back her ridiculous announcement. After all, she was here at night when no one had forced her to be here. And she knew her way around a knife, which proved this wasn't a one-time occurrence.

Then Anna's surprised expression turned sharp. 'When was that?'

'When was what?'

'How old were you when you stopped liking kitchens?' Anna said.

When. Not why. Everything in Barabal seized.

Murdag grew equally still, then in a flurry she ran out of the room.

'Oh, Barabal, why didn't you tell us?' Beileag's hands fluttered.

Tell them what? That the Macnaghten family had intentions of her marrying their spoiled, cruel boy when she was fourteen? Sneering Archie, who crept in to scare and tickle her. The one who had caught her alone in the kitchens in the middle of the day. She should have been safe.

She *was* safe; she'd made certain of that. Why talk of it now?

'I'm telling you to leave, so I can clean. I've come here because I was awake and didn't want to disturb anyone, that is all,' Barabal said. 'You three are telling stories about Seoc and simply not listening.'

'All these weeks you have been hiding your talent and forcing yourself in other crafts, when it's clear to me where you should have been all along,' Anna said. 'Bal told me what you did to his shoes, Barabal. You tried to stitch a flowered pattern on Thomas's boots?'

196   The Highlander's Mysterious Maiden

'How was I to know he had such tiny feet?' Barabal snatched the small spoon from Beileag's hands. 'I thought they were a child's.'

'I have it.' Murdag returned with two flagons of mead.

'Maybe we can sit in the other room,' Beileag said.

'For what?' Barabal pointed.

'So we can talk,' Anna took both spoons out of Barabal's hands and laid them on the table. 'No, so you can talk, and we can listen. I believe we've all been so excited about how Seoc noticed you and you him, we weren't listening very well.'

They wanted to listen to her, as though she had something they wanted to hear? As if what she'd say would be worthy? 'I don't see the point of that.'

Murdag scoffed. 'It's what friends do. Honestly, Barabal, it's as though you are Frenzy's sister. You're the most stubbornly obtuse being I've ever met.'

'Now see who's calling who obtuse.' Anna winked at Beileag, who grinned.

They wanted to be friends. 'Because you believe your friend is interested in me, though he's not.'

'Oh, he is and the whole clan knows it. But that's not the reason we're here, we're perhaps not good at showing it,' Murdag said. 'Mostly because you're truly stubborn.'

'She's stunned, that's all.' Beileag dipped her finger in another bowl and tasted that one, too.

'How can she be stunned if she hasn't had Seoc's mead yet?' Murdag shoved one flagon in Barabal's hands and waved her hands until Barabal drank a good bit.

Anna steered her to the other room where there were stools arranged in a circle next to the large table. Murdag and Beileag joined them. As though they expected her to sit on a stool next to them and talk. She dug in her heels.

Anna stopped as well. 'Murdag, pass me that mead.'

When Murdag did, Anna drank a big glug and handed it back. 'Let's sit and I'll tell you of Alan of Clan Maclean.'

Then Anna told of what happened when she was younger, and a handsome man came to their clan. He was Seoc's friend and the whole clan had welcomed him. Anna most of all. She'd given her heart and body to him, only to discover she wasn't the only woman who was waiting for his request of marriage. There were others in other clans waiting for him as well. He'd been run off and Anna lost her trust in love, until Camron showed her she could trust again by kidnapping her on Beltane.

It seemed a peculiar way to show love, but Barabal had seen Camron look at Anna with such awe, as if he couldn't quite believe his good fortune. Anna seemed equally as affectionate, so maybe it was true.

Barabal didn't know what was happening. They sat, drank one flagon, and Murdag opened the other. Hours passed, as Beileag told the story of her own life. Filled in the details of what Seoc didn't, of her mother's cruel words and how she thought her father hated her, until Hamilton encouraged her, with much jesting, to see her world differently. Now her figurines were sought after, she talked to her father, and she was more patient with her mother's ways.

Beileag had lived with feeling unloved, but now she sounded truly happy. And before she knew she'd say it, Barabal blurted, 'He scared me.'

All three women stilled, but none dismissed her statement. So, she continued, 'I was near fourteen and living with a Macnaghten family. They were generous at first. Overly protective, too, and I believed they were good.'

She glanced at the women, but none of them said anything and Murdag gently set the mostly empty second flagon down on the table.

198   *The Highlander's Mysterious Maiden*

'But they weren't,' Anna said. 'They fooled you.'

'I didn't realise it at first, or maybe they weren't so manipulative when I was younger, I don't know, but years went by.' Barabal bit her lip hard to keep from crying. 'Their generosity was conditional. Their protectiveness isolated me until all I had was them, their son and the hours and hours I spent in the kitchens.'

'You couldn't tell others?' Beileag said.

Barabal shook her head. She'd had no one then. She'd already left behind the MacFarlanes and was abandoned by the rest of her family, her brothers.

'You couldn't trust, or didn't feel as though you could trust,' Murdag added.

'Yes, but also...' How to explain feeling as if she had no more value than chopped pieces of herbs scattered on the floor. To—

'You didn't feel as though you were worthy to ask for help,' Beileag said softly.

Barabal wiped at a tear then. Beileag understood. Of course she did, because she'd kept her secret hidden even from her friends because she didn't feel worthy of her craft. And Anna knew as well because that Alan man had fooled her and this clan into thinking he was honourable. And Murdag understood her friend's and sister's heartache because she was with them for every step.

So Barabal continued, 'That, too. I didn't realise how bad it had got until I realised they thought they owned me and that I owed them. Archie, their son, was cruel, evil. He'd do things that made me uncomfortable. Never enough that if I confessed someone would step in. After all, how could I describe the gleam in his eye, or the sneer of his mouth? How could I say when he tickled me it wasn't because he was feeling brotherly to me?'

Anna grabbed her hand. 'Oh, Barabal.'

Murdag glowered. 'What did he do?'

'Archie caught me alone in the kitchens. He placed his hands on my waist, dug his fingers in.'

Beileag's hands were clasped so tight, her knuckles were white. Barabal concentrated on that to get the rest of the words out. 'Pretending he would tickle me, he rucked up my skirt. But someone came and he stepped away.'

Anna squeezed her hand. 'What did they do to him?'

Barabal shook her head. 'Nothing. He laughed and chucked me on the chin as though he was being a sibling and I went completely mute. What could I say, he hadn't done anything.'

'That's not true,' Anna said. 'We know that's not true.'

Barabal searched Anna's kind eyes for the truth of her words and could see it. It was there. She understood. Being frightened was enough. Should have been enough for someone who cared for her to help her. She'd never found that person, or people, who'd protect her.

'And you're here now,' Beileag said. 'With us, you're here with us.'

'I left the Macnaghten Clan that night.'

'In the dead of night, where no one could see you,' Murdag said.

Maybe it was a pattern of hers. 'I never returned and don't intend to.'

'Good for you,' Murdag said.

Had it been good for her because ever since she had never found a family who cared for her at all? 'I was scared, so I ran.'

'You were brave, and you did something about it,' Murdag said. 'You know how many people live not how they want to because they're scared? That they get stuck in something

200   *The Highlander's Mysterious Maiden*

and can't find their way out? You were wronged, so you took the steps needed to make it right.'

Could that be true? She knew that day changed her yet again. That her parents' death, and her brothers turning their back, then her being shipped from her cousins' to a stranger's clan made her feel abandoned. But that time with the Macnaghten made her distrustful, more direct. She pushed people away. Everyone that would allow her to push them away that is, not these three.

Murdag handed her the flagon off the table. 'Want to finish it off?'

Barabal took the vessel and tilted it up.

'So, you've stayed away from kitchens ever since.' Anna let her other hand go.

'I avoid them as long as I can.' Barabal handed the empty flagon to Murdag. She felt the familiar trembling inside her at remembering that bit of her past. But her hands were steady, her heart hadn't clenched once. Telling the story wasn't as bad as she'd expected. It was her past, but maybe she had been strong. Strong sounded better than hope, didn't it?

'With those hours and hours you spent in the kitchens, did you do it because you were avoiding the family or because you found solace there?' Beileag said.

Barabal had never looked at it that way. 'It was both, but I believe you're right. I don't mind the kitchens and the work here.'

'That's because you can make sauces that cause people to weep,' Murdag said.

Beileag grinned. 'They truly are good.'

'Once they're heated,' Anna said. 'They need to be heated.'

They did. 'Do you want me to make heated sauces?'

'Yes!' all three of the women said.

Nicole Locke 201

'During the day, in front of everyone, so they can all know of it,' Beileag added.

Stunned, a bit afraid, but also knowing that that was what Beileag had to do with her craft. 'Tomorrow, then.'

The women smiled. She was still wary, she knew that. She hadn't told them the entire story of how she'd got to Macnaghten in the first place. And though Anna's brow creased and Barabal tensed because she thought Anna might ask more of her, such as what did she do when she left the Macnaghtens. But she didn't and Barabal relaxed even more.

Heart skipping a bit in her chest, Barabal almost smiled. Maybe this friendship wasn't so terrible. Maybe people could like her for who she was even when she was direct. Maybe her foolish hope wasn't so foolish.

Murdag harrumphed. Loudly. 'Your sauces may be good, but you do give the worst advice.'

'My advice?' Barabal said flatly, not understanding what Murdag was about even though she was relieved to not be talking of Archie or other parts of her past.

'Frenzy is still nipping at my clothes.'

Anna groaned.

It took a bit for Barabal to know what Murdag meant. Ah. The night she met Murdag, she'd advised her on how to get her horse to stop nipping at her clothes. It should have worked. 'You have to be firm with him. You can't be reacting correctly.'

Murdag pulled herself straight. 'I am reacting.'

'Everyone else is, too, while she's scampering around naked.' Beileag giggled.

'I am not naked,' Murdag hissed. 'And I did it exactly like you told me to.'

As wilful as Murdag was, she knew that wasn't true. 'Frenzy knows you don't mean it. You're soft with him.'

202 *The Highlander's Mysterious Maiden*

Anna and Beileag nodded their heads as if she'd said something so wise it would be passed down for generations. It warmed her heart a bit, it also made her laugh. Just a little, just enough for a loud snort to escape before she clamped her lips tight.

Beileag's eyes got big. 'Was that a laugh?'

Anna lips twitched. 'Think she's feeling the mead yet?'

'I believe we softened *her* up,' Murdag harrumphed.

Barabal thought, perhaps, Murdag could be right. 'Well, it's not because of this mead. It's not strong enough.'

Beileag slammed her hand to her mouth and laugh choked.

Anna patted her on the back. 'Are you saying you know how to make Seoc's mead stronger?'

Barabal nodded as sagely as she could. 'Fruit will make it sweeter and stronger…better, in truth.'

'You haven't told him yet?' Murdag grinned.

Barabal shook her head.

'Told him what?' Anna asked.

'On Beltane, Barabal didn't like Seoc's mead and wouldn't drink it.'

Anna's eyes grew comically large.

Beileag wiped her hand down her front. 'Please, please, please don't tell him until we're all there.'

They wanted to spend more time with her, not only because she was good at sauces. And it didn't have to do anything with Seoc, not truly. It had to do with her and what they'd shared in their past and just now. Barabal swallowed hard, then answered, 'I will.'

They wanted her to belong, to be friends, and return to the kitchens where she could create sauces that made people weep.

They wanted her to stay. Barabal blinked the tears away. She didn't know what had happened to Seoc to make him disappear for a week. But maybe the women were correct that he liked her, and he wasn't hiding from her. Maybe he was forced to go before he had to tell anyone about it? The war was escalating. She was the one who'd left the cellars, not he. He was the one who'd kept her from getting dressed so she couldn't immediately leave and not talk to his father. And Aonghus had made it clear he'd wanted to meet her as well. As if she was important to his son.

Was she important to Seoc? When she saw him next, would he tell her what he meant by all his words? Not only what he'd told her of Dunbar, but the other words, the ones he'd whispered against her skin. Words that sounded adoring, as though he cared for her.

Perhaps, after he confessed all his truths, she'd tell him a bit more of herself. And wasn't that a sign her being here wasn't like living with the other clans? It wasn't only others acting differently until she couldn't get her footing. She was acting differently with them.

Sharing drink and a bit of her past with these women was proof of that. She didn't even tell them accidentally like she'd done that day with Anna confessing she was from Colquhoun land. No, this time she'd done it purposefully. And it had felt good.

She felt good. Lighter. Happier.

Perhaps, just maybe, she had a place to stay here at Clan Graham. She could have friends, a family and be useful. Maybe this was her home.

Chapter Seventeen

One week. One week where Seoc did not have the bliss of observing Barabal berate or cajole someone to do her bidding, or the joy to hold or kiss his lass. One week where he did not tell her why he'd left because it was important to surprise her. To not simply say he intended to do something for her, but to actually complete it.

And he had. Dugald and Evander, Barabal's two brothers, stood beside him. It had been liked he'd hoped. Barabal had let slip to Anna where her childhood home had been, and it had been no burden to travel to the Colquhoun Clan to convince them to return with him. Now they were all three freshly returned to the Graham Clan to be united with their sister.

But now they needed patience to make this special.

So while at the border, they'd stayed hidden among the trees, their horses beside them. Not that he wanted to stay hidden, but he wanted a grand surprise for her. He needed to find her in secret, not parade her brothers around the village for her to be warned before.

He wanted the surprise. The joy. When she turned, he'd see the pure happiness of her expression.

'So she's here,' Dugald said.

'And so close,' Evander added. 'Now let's be on with it.'

It wasn't the first time the brothers finished each other sentences, or mimicked their mannerisms. It was a true sentiment of how close they were as brothers.

They weren't similar at all to their sister, however. Maybe in appearance with their thick bones and dark hair, though Barabal's eyes were far more beautiful. But they didn't match her temperament or stubbornness in the slightest. They were far too at ease with themselves and the world. Their country was on the cusp of war and they still followed him, a stranger, far too willingly.

All he'd done when he'd arrived on Colquhoun land was tell them of their sister, and invite them to his clan. He'd never seen such a lack of inhibitions. He'd been slapped and hugged and shouted at. They'd run for their horses and bags immediately when he'd barely caught his breath from travelling.

He didn't even have any proof to show them and still they'd begged for him to hurry. Certainly, there were a few Colquhoun men who knew of him so his honour could be vouched for, but they could have had some reservations.

'Stay hidden until I can speak to her,' Seoc warned them.

'We know, Graham.' Dugald lowered his brow. 'You've reminded us enough.'

'If you knew what we'd suffered, you would not delay us seeing our sister's light and smiles and laughter,' Evander said.

'I must hear it again. Now.' Dugald growled. 'Already you kept us on Colquhoun land too long.'

He'd had enough of these men and their complaints. These were his future wife's brothers and soon to be his family. It wouldn't do to get in an argument with them, but these two would try anyone's patience.

'I had messages to convey to your Laird.'

'Nothing is as important as this,' Dugald said.

206   *The Highlander's Mysterious Maiden*

Rulers of countries might have something to say to that. He, a humble Scotsman, had another point, 'Nothing? Then why didn't you come to her before?'

Both drew silent.

'Can we not hurry?' Dugald said.

'Take some care, Brother, we've been down this road before,' Evander said.

'As if you're not worse than I. None came to find us before. This is different, I know it.' Dugald slammed a clenched fist to his chest.

'And if she's here, and it is as we feared?'

'How could those thoughts be true?' Dugald scoffed. 'It is a joyous day, Brother, and we will soon see our happy sister. All will be well.'

'We've been without hope for so long.' Evander wiped his face with his sleeve.

How long, Seoc wanted to ask again, but thus far, his asking questions led to vague answers or silence. There was something not true about Barabal's brothers hiding facts from him, but they were eager to see her and Barabal seemed to miss them. Perhaps they were private, or didn't trust him. No matter, eventually, he'd know. Most likely they'd tell him accidentally if he kept asking questions. Dugald and Evander carried on entire conversations in front of him. They held nothing back.

Again, nothing like his lass. They had too many feelings spilling out, too much surprise and chatter. And they thought their sister was all light and smiles? The last time he saw her, she'd been upset at his father, but laughing, too. Would she be unhappy about his return?

No, how could she when he had her brothers? He'd show her his love.

Nicole Locke 207

Dugald lowered his fist. 'Make good on your promise, Graham.'

'We won't wait for long,' Evander added.

Patting his horse, he told them again, 'Stay here, I'll bring her to you.'

It didn't take Seoc long to find Barabal standing in the largest part of the herb garden, where swathes of cut parsley were piled in a basket at her feet. The sun shone on her dark hair; it looked almost red though he knew not a strand was in there. She wasn't facing him, so he admired her generous hips and the curve of her waist accented by her gown. His heart eased at the sight of her.

He'd missed her.

What was she doing here with the parsley? One week and what changes had she wrought upon his clan? He wanted to swing her in his arms. Kiss her long and hard, then take her hand and tug her into the forest to show her his surprise.

As frustrating as her brothers were, they were family she hadn't seen. He could prove to her his worth, his ability to love her. To tell and show her his vulnerabilities and for her to know it was safe to confess her grievances to him.

But he couldn't do any of those things, for she wasn't alone with her harvested herbs. Murdag and Beileag were there as well. They were in some heated conversation he wasn't close enough to hear. It seemed urgent as Barabal shook her head, her dark plait swaying down her back.

He knew his friends weren't harming her, but he rushed none the less. When Barabal suddenly laughed, it was as startling as the last time. Beileag was waving her hands, just as Murdag, grinning wide, spouted something else. It shocked Barabal still before she clapped her hand on her mouth and released those snorting sounds again.

208   *The Highlander's Mysterious Maiden*

Beileag, grinning as hard as Murdag, turned and spotted him. She grabbed Barabal's arm, pivoting her completely so her back was to him.

He stumbled. Why would she do that? He kept walking. But Murdag made a gesture for him to stop. Were they talking of him? He paused.

Did Barabal not want to see him? As full of almost hope as he could be, he wasn't brave enough to be truly hopeful, he still had one reservation about all of this. She'd run out of that cellar, not pleased with him or his father.

But she seemed happy now, though he couldn't see her face. Had she obsessed over the beauty and connection they'd shared, his kisses, his touch, or had she regaled to his friends the last tense moments before she'd fled the cellar?

He growled. Forget Murdag and her orders, he and her brothers wanted their time with Barabal. No subtle frown and mere waves of a hand would stall him. The sooner he spoke to her and revealed her brothers, the quicker they could begin their lives together.

Moreover, it was too early to feel any hesitation when he didn't know what they spoke of; it didn't have to be about him. And their mannerisms were friendly. In his absence, it seemed his lass had opened up to his friends. Life could not be any better.

Eyes growing wider, Beileag frowned again at him; he frowned back. He wanted Barabal's smiles and laughter, too. A few more steps and he heard their voices.

'There was nothing between Seoc and I.' Barabal shook her arm free of Beileag's grasp. 'Why must you two keep harping on this?'

Seoc stopped completely. Beileag quirked a brow at him. His friends meant to get something out of Barabal for his benefit. Something like unbridled glee flitted up his spine.

Nicole Locke 209

'Ha!' Murdag said. 'On Beltane that man was one step from devouring you and you stood there as though you needed all the devouring.'

'There was no such thing,' Barabal said.

Oh, but there was. Seoc almost growled out his pleasure of that moment they'd met. When he'd first glimpsed her fire, her softness. Oh, how he'd burned for a kiss that night.

'I believe her protests mean the opposite,' Beileag said. 'You should lift the quilt on your bed before getting into it in case Joan has stuck thistles in the folds.'

Had Joan been bothering Barabal? Had she and her two followers been spreading rumours and vitriol like they'd done with Anna?

Beileag glanced at him before lowering her gaze to Barabal again. 'Joan wouldn't dare cross her now in case she won't share her sauces with the clan.'

'So true,' Murdag said. 'It's good Joan doesn't suspect your true feelings for Seoc.'

Barabal made some choking sound, and he grinned. In his absence, had his friends pressed his suit of her? Had Barabal confessed any feelings for him? He could ask for no more loyalty or joy. And what was that about sauces? Did his Barabal cook?

'I have no such feelings. You two are fools.' Harumphing, Barabal bent, grabbed the handle of the parsley-laden basket, and tucked the wicker bottom in the hitch of her waist. 'I need to return to the kitchens.'

'Are you certain that's what you *need*?' Murdag said in such a tone he knew she was needling him and Barabal. 'Don't you want to confess anything first to your friends?'

'Friends? You're nuisances is what you are. Why aren't you like Anna, who is spending time with her husband? And you—don't the horses need, I don't know, something right

210   *The Highlander's Mysterious Maiden*

now? I thought you two wanted me to make sauces today, so that's what I'm doing. It takes time, you know.'

'We wouldn't know because you've been secretly making them in the dead of night,' Beileag said slowly, loudly.

So that's why his parsley had disappeared and Barabal had been in the kitchens. He relished this story.

'Why are you shouting?' Barabal said. 'It's doing my head in after last night and anyone around us could hear what you say.'

'Oh, not just anyone.' Murdag chortled.

Grinning, Beileag nodded to him.

He strode the rest of the way. 'Only me.'

For one moment everyone froze before Barabal wildly pivoted, scattering parsley stems to the ground.

And there she was.... In his chest, his heart realigned and his entire universe became the look of joy in her eyes.

Because it was joy, one sure flaring in her greenish-brown eyes, bursting happiness and brightness right to his centre and scattering the tangled darkness there.

Stunned, he placed a hand to his chest.

Barabal's brows lowered. 'What the hell are you doing here?'

'Returning.' *To you.*

Her eyes narrowed on him and also the two women at her side. 'And how long ago did you return?'

'Not long.' He tried and failed to keep the glee from his voice.

'And you thought the best action was to lurk behind my back and loiter in the gardens instead of announcing your return to the council or your Laird?'

'Yes.' Because not even a war was as important as her. 'You look beautiful.'

Her cheeks flushed at his compliment. 'Why would I care what I look like? Beauty doesn't mend clothes any faster.'

Murdag snorted. Beileag thumped her side with the back of her hand.

'But you have beauty and efficiency—how could I resist loitering to admire that?'

Barabal spluttered, then rallied. 'Go admire somewhere else. You left.'

He had, but he had a surprise for her. As much as he loved flirting with her, her brothers awaited, and he wanted to see more of her happiness.

'And now I want you to come with me.' When she shook her head, he added. 'Not as far as I travelled. Merely to the trees behind me.'

Murdag crossed her arms. 'Where is this going?'

'Do you two have to be here?' he said.

'Absolutely,' Beileag said.

'I'm not going anywhere with you.' Barabal glanced behind him, her eyes catching before they returned to his. 'You disappeared with no word at all.'

'Because I have a surprise.'

She glanced behind him again, her brows lowering.

'Surprises!' Beileag said.

'Does she like surprises?' Murdag said. 'Don't you remember what we discussed before? Something about a fool?'

He rejoiced in their defence of his lass, even at his own expense.

'Who...who are those men?' she said faintly.

'I don't know,' Beileag said, her eyes never leaving whatever, or rather whomever, was behind him.

'Seoc?' Murdag lowered her arms.

Dammit. The brothers didn't wait in the forest. He could practically feel their impatience at the back of his neck. Never

212 *The Highlander's Mysterious Maiden*

mind. He was facing Barabal now as they approached and could revel in the joy on her face.

Except there wasn't joy, or happiness—in fact, she'd gone deathly pale.

'Is this our sister?' one of them asked.

Barabal dropped the basket at her feet. She looked as though she'd faint.

They were closer than he thought. Seoc glanced behind him. Evander was standing stunned, but Dugald looked ready to shove everyone out of the way to get to her.

'No!' Barabal said.

He swung back around. Gone was the deathly pale in her cheeks. Instead, Barabal looked like a warrior from the olden days. The ones in tales, full of wrath and vengeance.

'You have brothers?' Beileag whispered.

Something wasn't right. Neither of them recognised each other. They were all acting as though they hadn't seen each other not in months as he'd assumed, but years. And now Barabal was fuming and her brothers looked hurt.

She swung her furious gaze towards him. 'How dare you.'

'Wait,' Murdag said. 'What's going on here?'

'I thought…' Seoc stumbled with his words '…you hadn't seen them for a while. You sounded as though you missed them.'

'She did?' Evander said, his voice steadier. Hopeful. 'She missed us?'

'How could I miss something I never had?' Barabal said.

He was a fool. He'd asked several times about their relationship and the men had gone quiet or changed the subject. He was beginning to realise why he should have insisted before he told them where she resided.

'What has happened?' Murdag said.

Nicole Locke   *213*

'As though you two hadn't a play in all this,' Barabal said bitterly. 'As though you didn't know he was dragging *them* here.'

'We didn't,' Beileag said.

'You held my arm, so I couldn't see his approach.'

Beileag gaped. 'But only to—'

'Play me for a fool?' Barabal arched her brow before turning back to him.

'No fool,' Seoc said. 'Please know, I left that night you met my father to find them. To bring back a happy surprise.'

'Without telling me. Without questioning the idea?' Barabal said. 'And what excuse did they give to follow you here?'

'No excuse,' Evander said.

'So you bribed them,' she added.

It was his turn to feel deathly pale and faint. This wasn't right. This wasn't how it was supposed to be.

'We followed happily, hoping against all odds you were here,' Dugald said. 'And you are and my heart—'

'Your heart!' Barabal said. 'If I thought you had one, I'd rip it from your chest just to skewer it with a blade.'

Seoc reached out. 'Please, Barabal, if you are angry, we should talk.'

Barabal batted his hand away. 'I'm not angry at you. I'm furious and you're a fool for believing anything they said to you, Seoc of Clan Graham.'

'Barely daring to hope you were alive, we told him very little,' Dugald said. 'Do not be angry with him. Be as we are, full of joy.'

'Don't you want us?' Evander said. 'It's been too many years.'

'And why is that?' she said. 'You left with them. With me beseeching you, you left with them.'

They reared back. Seoc did the same. What had they done to hurt her?

214   *The Highlander's Mysterious Maiden*

'It is as we feared,' Dugald said.

'No, no, it cannot be,' Evander said. 'Here is our sister, long lost to us.'

'Not your sister,' Barabal spat. 'Stop calling me that. I am no relation to you.'

'And you.' She spun around and faced them all. 'I thought I understood your jests and pranks and jokes. Throw a sack over a woman's head. Make a wager to marry before the summer's end, or walk a woman in circles.

'But bringing those two here as if they're a gift when they are nothing but vile, worthless human beings is no jest. It's cruelty.'

Murdag pinched Beileag's sleeve. 'We should leave.'

'Yes, leave!' Barabal said feverishly. 'Leave m—us! Leave like everyone else.'

'Wait,' Beileag said to Murdag. 'Is there something we can do?'

'Like what? Spread more cruelty than you have already?' Barabal's voice went low, dark. 'I don't believe so.'

Beileag gasped.

'Come on, Beileag,' Murdag said. 'It's up to them. We'll talk, Barabal, when you can, I'll get a flagon—'

'As if I'd fall for anything like that again.'

'We'll let Anna know of this,' Beileag said. 'The three of us will—'

Barabal shrieked. Birds fluttered from the rock fence. 'Yes, yes, yes. Tell Anna. Anna who knew this would happen. Because it was she who told you where they were, didn't she?'

Seoc swallowed hard. 'She said you mentioned Colquhoun—'

'Don't.' Barabal slashed with her arm.

He didn't know how to say anything else. A few words, perhaps, or maybe her brothers leaving them for a bit so he could pull her aside. When she'd first turned to him, her eyes had lit with joy, and she'd chastised him on his dallying. His direct Barabal had been happy to see him.

It was only when she'd spied her brothers that her smiles fell. His bringing them here was a mistake, but he could right this. He must. Already he felt the darkness tugging at him. The long months of feeling nothing. Of being lost, but not understanding he was. They'd talk, then he'd understand why she felt betrayed. He'd send her brothers away or force them away if need be. Obviously, Barabal had told them not to do something and they hadn't listened to her. Likely they'd done something reckless or impulsive. He could see that. They'd talked between themselves all the time as if no one was about them. And hadn't they taken his words about her living with the Graham Clan with no proof? Yes. That was it and they'd hurt their sister. He'd make it better.

Beileag's hands fluttered. 'Whatever this is, Barabal, we're here for you.'

With murder in her eye, Barabal pointed her finger at his friends. 'I don't want you here for me. Ever.'

Murdag gave another tug and Beileag's eyes watered.

He could feel tears burn his own eyes. He must know what he'd done. Mere moments before, she was becoming friends with his friends. He'd envisaged his family growing by merging with hers. Her agreeing to marriage, children. They'd be surrounded by love and bounty. Now…

'Why can't I find my feet with you?'

Seeming satisfied to see the women walk away, Barabal turned to him. 'You get nothing with me.'

'Let me talk to her,' Dugald said.

Seoc shook his head. 'I need to talk to my lass.'

'Not yours,' she said. 'What did you promise them to get them to follow you? Gold, silver? Jewels? I have nothing.

216   *The Highlander's Mysterious Maiden*

Do you? Because you'll need to pay them. Or maybe you already have and this is entertainment for you all. Amusement. A grand jest.'

'Why this venom? Are you not…are you not joyous at our reunion?' Evander said.

'Where are her smiles and laughter, Graham?' Dugald said.

Seoc didn't know. As much as he searched her eyes, turned over her words and, yes, venom, he couldn't understand what he had done wrong. She looked so utterly betrayed; he didn't know what to say. So, he stood there, stunned, reeling, wishing for his laughing lass back.

'My smiles?' Barabal spit out. 'You believe I'd allow him to have anything to do with me? Did you tell them you were special to me? No. That would imply they cared I had someone in my life. So I state again: what greed brought them here?'

They were talking in circles and getting slashed with her anger. He couldn't fix this if he didn't know what was wrong. Other than being naive, or a fool in love. Of being as impatient as her brothers to start their lives together. So he'd brought them here when he should have questioned at least some of it.

'Curse me, woman. I did wrong and we will sort it out,' Seoc said. His entire body was drawing cold, numb. His limbs turning to ice. 'But these are your brothers whom you talked about. I thought them lost to you. They made it sound as if you were lost to them.'

'She was!' Evander and Dugald said together.

'Quiet unless you can tell me the truth.'

'We've told you the truth,' Dugald growled.

His heart barely beating, and his breath nothing but a reedy hiss in his lungs, he rasped, 'All of it?'

Evander looked away and Dugald thinned his lips.

Seoc rubbed his chest. Something was terribly wrong. He wished his frustration could be solely laid at their feet, but he knew some of this…this despondency was because he didn't push for the truth himself.

Barabal released a brittle laugh. 'I've never been lost. They could have found me a thousand times over. They could have prevented me from leaving. They. Wanted. Me. Gone.'

Her words stunned him. Barabal never lied. Certainly she had never told the whole story—each word from her was like the last precious drop of honey from a hive, but they were true.

It wasn't she who'd walked out of their lives because of what they did. Her brothers had wanted her gone, had forced her to leave her clan, her home.

Dugald cursed. Evander released some pained sound like a wound he didn't expect.

'That's what she believes?' one said. 'That can't be,' the other added.

He didn't care who said what. He only cared for her. After he pleaded with her, he would turn his anger to them. Only when whatever happened became clear.

For he couldn't wrap his thoughts around it. Even when he almost died, he heard his father, his friends, whispering to him to heal, to come back to them. They'd been there for him while her family had pushed her away.

It wasn't missing her brothers he'd heard in her voice that night in the cellars. It was grief, hurt, pain. Something foreign to him in that happy moment so he hadn't recognised it. But now it was clear. They'd hurt her, wanted her gone and she grieved as if they'd died. No, as if she believed they'd wanted her to die.

'You wanted her gone,' he said, barely recognising his voice.

218   The Highlander's Mysterious Maiden

He thought he'd felt pain in his chest when that sword cut through him. It was nothing to the pain he'd brought to her.

He'd surprised her with family who'd hurt her. What a fool he was.

Her eyes, shining with agony and anger, locked with his. 'They wanted me gone. Just like I want you gone.'

He rocked back on his heels. Her eyes were shining now, shining with tears he'd brought her. Her brothers had wronged her and now he'd done the same. He couldn't... He didn't... His fingers curled like claws against his chest, bit into his scar. 'Barabal,' he said, clinging to the hope she'd hear the love in his voice.

'Gone,' she said with such force it cut through the entire clan. Through him.

Heavy snarled darkness lurking at the corners of his soul descended not like the gentle shift from day to night, but like the jaws of a tempest, blacking out any light or joy from his life. Gone. Until he knew nothing else. Not even words or meaning.

His eyes drifted to the empty barren fields beyond and there he walked.

Chapter Eighteen

Bitterness choking the breath from her, Barabal faced her brothers. Here, in the herb garden in the centre of the Graham Clan where outside the little stone fence people watched them. Could this be any worse?

Somewhere in her periphery, Barabal tracked Murdag and Beileag as well as Seoc walking far enough away they could not hear the words, if any, that would be exchanged between her and her brothers.

She found no comfort in that bit of privacy. Already she'd humiliated herself in front of everyone. She hadn't cried out in front of everyone since she'd begged her brothers to keep her. Now, she had lost any sense of her surroundings and thrown away her standing in a fit of despairing temper, which life had already taught her did no good.

Even if her brothers hadn't been coerced here by Seoc. Even if the women and Seoc hadn't betrayed her by teasing her with their arrival, she had to leave. No one in Clan Graham would want her now.

Evander laid his heart on his chest. 'Let us say, Sister, it is a joy to be—'

'What are you two doing standing here?'

'Seeing you all grown,' Dugald said. 'After so many years, it is nothing short of astonishing.'

220   *The Highlander's Mysterious Maiden*

The years had changed them as well. Both of them with their sturdy strong bones, brown hair and eyes that weren't murky like hers, but bright green. They were utterly changed from their youth, but she recognised their eyes.

Always their eyes. They were the last feature of her family she'd screamed and pleaded with. She'd beseeched that bright green for any acknowledgment they wanted her. But the light in them had been unforgivingly flat as they'd watched her be carted off to another clan, another family.

'So you're to satisfy some morbid curiosity about how I fared when you turned your back on me?'

'You believe we turned our backs on you? Never. Our separation has been a constant grief,' Evander said.

What game did they play to gain her sympathy? 'If you believe to soften me, I have no coin or gems, so be off with you.'

'We have no need for coin or gems.' Dugald shook his head. 'We want our sister.'

'Lies. You stared coldly at me on the day they took me. Our parents died and days later I'm on some horse-pulled cart dismounting in another clan's land. No family, no parents. No. One. So save your false care of me.'

Dugald crossed his arms, released them. Crossed them again. 'She doesn't remember, Brother. She was too young.'

Evander picked up a stick and something flashed in her memory. Like something he had done before.

She shook that off. He'd been a boy then, of course he'd played with sticks. 'I remember everything.'

Everything she was was because she had been pushed away that day. Every deed and word she'd made since was so she'd never be in such a vulnerable position again.

She didn't have to stay around for this. She turned to leave just as Evander slashed the dirt at his feet with a stick in an X pattern. Another memory...this one different. One of him

Nicole Locke 221

drawing. He used to draw in the dirt everywhere. Did he do that still?

She paused.

Dugald stomped forward. 'Can we go somewhere and talk? Our horses are in the forest and need rest and food.'

'Tell the man you travelled here with your complaints. I have no say in it.'

'We'll go.' Evander eyed his brother who gaped. 'We'll go as soon as you hear what we have to say.'

'So you can gloat?'

'No,' Dugald said, his voice gruff. 'But other matters happened after you left.'

She hadn't left, she was forced out. 'So you had a truth I was never afforded. Good for you.'

'She still doesn't understand,' Evander said.

'Nothing to understand, we're her brothers. She has to forgive us.'

'I don't,' she said.

Dugald crossed his arms again. He'd done that, hadn't he, when they were children. They were wider and thicker with muscle, but the movement was the same.

Again, she shook off the memory. She didn't want to remember these boys, these men. They'd been cruel to her.

'We came after you,' Evander rushed out. 'When we earned enough work to borrow a horse, we travelled to Mac-Farlane to see you.'

'We didn't earn enough work, we stole it,' Dugald said gruffly. 'Only a few years after you left.'

They were wanted, so why would they need to steal a horse? Why bother seeing her at all? 'So that was it, then. I wasn't there and you returned home?'

Evander clenched his thin stick. 'We were told you went on to Macnaghten, so we travelled there as well.'

'How easy for you.'

Glowering, Dugald released his arms to his sides. 'They didn't know where you went. If you wanted us to find you, you should have told them where you went.'

'You didn't say anything while they took me away. At what point in that exchange would I have thought you were wanting to find me? I didn't expect anything from you.'

'When did she stop listening?' Dugald turned to Evander.

'Why would I listen to you? Even this story you tell me is weak. So you tried to find me, couldn't, and now you have,' she said. 'Well done. You're exonerated from your guilt. Now leave.'

Expression mutinous, Dugald leant forward and stared right at her. 'No.'

'Back away, Brother,' Evander said. 'You're scaring her.'

No, he wasn't. He was making her remember him charging forward and barrelling through crowds. He'd acted more like a boulder than a boy back then and was doing it again. Curse him. She didn't want these other memories. She didn't want *them*.

'Please, Sister, you have to know we grieved as well as you, we thought as children did.' Evander tossed the stick. 'The tanner and his wife were childless, cold.'

So what? 'The tanners gave you a home. You were useful, so they took you.'

Dugald growled. 'We made certain they picked us and not you.'

They did what? Barabal's knees shook, and she placed a hand on the stone fence at her back. It was so much worse. So heartless. 'You schemed to rid yourself of me? Did you believe I'd take too much space in a shared bed, or that I'd eat more food than you?'

'No.' Dugald frowned.

'Then you had intentions I'd eventually catch the eye of some prosperous family and therefore increase the family wealth,' she said. 'Your plan failed; I haven't ever had two coins to spare.'

Growling, Dugald clenched the back of his head with his two hands and eyed his brother.

'How can you even believe such horrors?' Evander's eyes sheened.

She wasn't moved by his tears because she had lived exactly the life she'd described.

'We did it because you were our sister, because we cared,' Evander said. 'The tanners didn't want sons. They wanted workers to pick dog dung to immerse skins in and to urinate on leather. Gallons of ale we drank day in and out. We were provided little food, so that standing was difficult. More than once, I fell on top of it all. We didn't want that world for you.'

'We meant to protect you.' Dugald dropped his hands. 'We thought you went to our mother's family, to a better place, while we were under the tanners' thumbs.'

'We thought you'd stay in a happy home.' Evander said.

It hadn't been happy because they'd got rid of her. But apparently, her brothers weren't informed of this fact and she'd left for the Macnaghtens. She didn't know these men, not truly, but the details they spoke of were too exact. She didn't need to tell them her life, but that didn't mean she couldn't discover the lies they'd told about theirs. 'Even if true, you would have me believe no clan member did anything to help you?'

Dugald grunted. 'Do you believe they hit us where anyone could see?'

Her brothers were struck?

'Remember how we said we guessed at some things? Even

224   *The Highlander's Mysterious Maiden*

before you left, we knew that the tanners were no good, but also that the clan wouldn't help us.'

Clan members always helped each other.

Searching her gaze, Evander sighed. 'Our father wasn't kind to our mother, to anyone. People stayed away from them and even though they were gone, they stayed away from us. Or at least didn't pay close attention.'

She didn't remember any of this. 'No one came to your rescue?'

'We told you we stole their horse to search for you,' Dugald said. 'We maybe were also looking for a place to stay.'

It couldn't have been that bad. All these years where she'd travelled from one place to another trying to find a home, they'd had a home they didn't want.

'You live on Colquhoun land,' she said.

'They got weak though, didn't they?' Dugald said. 'While we got bigger.'

'We kept searching for you, asking about you if a stranger came by,' Evander said.

Dugald smirked. 'The tanners were old, and we knew they'd die eventually. Now we're tanning for the clan.'

'With different methods,' Evander said hastily.

'They're dead?' she asked, though it should have been no concern to her. She needed to bide her time and gather her thoughts. Their lives were not what she'd believed, and she didn't know what to make of all that. It was sudden for her; all of this was sudden.

Evander nodded. 'Only a few years ago, but by then we'd abandoned finding you on our own. So we stayed, in the hope you'd take away the darkness.'

'Brother?' Dugald said.

'For another time. Not now,' Evander said. 'Now we have her. We held out hope that you, our light, would return to us.'

Her heart ached. For them, for herself, but still… 'So your plan was to get rid of me and eventually find me again? Without telling me of this? Our parents were gone, you were the only family I had left. I cried out for you.'

Evander winced. 'You were five and were all smiles and light. You wouldn't be convincing if we'd told you our intentions. We needed you to throw a tantrum, to caterwaul like you did, so the tanners would be glad to rid themselves of you.'

The whole of Scotland had heard her that day. She'd given every bit of her soul to her words and sounds, begging them to keep her. It had done no good. None. And until today, she'd never come close to making those agonised sounds again.

'So, you're saying you wanted me to suffer,' she said. 'To believe myself as unworthy.'

'We were children and made the best plan we could,' Dugald said. 'It's as though she forgot!'

'Twice my age and together.' She glowered right back. 'You had each other and left me with nothing.'

Dugald hissed.

'But no one else,' Evander blurted.

She didn't remember her father or mother. She had flashes of her mother yelling, but they weren't clear memories like she had with Evander and Dugald. Had her father been mean and the tanners horrific? Evander sounded truthful, so maybe so.

Maybe they had travelled all over Scotland and returned to Colquhoun Clan in the hope she'd find them? But how was she to have even guessed at any of that? She'd grieved for her parents and her brothers had walked away.

'You were my brothers,' she repeated. 'I begged you. Begged.'

Evander closed his eyes as if her words gutted him deeply.

226   *The Highlander's Mysterious Maiden*

Dugald stepped away as though he'd been struck. 'It's true. We had each other. Even now we finish each other's sentences.'

'No family of our own or children though,' Evander whispered.

'That will happen, Brother, it will,' Dugald said like a vow.

'And it didn't have to be only us,' Evander said, desolation in his voice. 'We travelled to Macnaghten, but you were gone. Why didn't you tell them where you were going?'

Because she'd had to leave in the middle of the night, but she wouldn't tell them this.

Evander's eyes narrowed. 'Did you have enough to eat, Barabal? Was there a bed to lie on?'

She refused, absolutely refused, to give in to their story, to her own. To the utter heartbreak and lost years together. Heart constricting in her chest, throat clogged with tears and anger and hurt, she couldn't stay here.

They'd told her things she didn't know before, but how was she to forgive them now and return to Colquhoun land? It sounded as though not even the Colquhouns were fond of them and they hadn't wailed and begged, but been useful to the tanners, to the clan. She knew nothing of tanning, it wasn't even a craft she'd tried to learn. No, she couldn't return to the Colquhoun Clan, yet she couldn't stay here either. Yelling at Seoc, at Murdag, and now again at her brothers revealed she was broken and unworthy. More than once she'd spotted a Graham or two stopping to stare. She was surprised they didn't run her off since they had reason to. She couldn't take it any more, she again turned to leave.

'Time to go,' Evander said.

'So that's it? Dugald said harshly. 'There's no making this right?'

Nicole Locke 227

'We asked her to listen to our side and she did that,' Evander said.

'Did she?' Dugald said. 'How long will we be tortured for something I did when I was but eleven and you ten?'

Evander's eyes misted. 'It's our turn to go.'

'You told her that,' Dugald said. 'I didn't; I'm staying as much as I want. You go.'

'I'm not going without you.' Evander raised his voice. 'Where would I go without you? When have I ever gone without you?'

'At the Campbells,' Dugald grunted. 'When you—'

'Oh, you stubborn ass, I already explained a thousand times that—'

'Have neither of you grown up?' Barabal rounded on them both. This was ridiculous. She wanted to be left alone to her thoughts, and they went on and on with all the noise. 'Always with the bickering between you two. Dugald threw the rock and hit Matthew's ear.' Barabal pointed at Dugald. 'But you blamed your brother and that argument went on for weeks.

'And you!' She narrowed her eyes at Evander. 'Always leaving sticks around even though Mother warned you. You didn't even apologise after Dugald tripped on them and burned his hands on the cauldron as a result. There he was bandaged and all you could do was remind him of the time he pushed you in the trough.

'Always quick to blame the other, to talk over the other— you'd try the patience of a saint!'

Evander and Dugald gaped. When her words stopped echoing off the chapel, Barabal's jaw went slack as well. What had she done, what had she said?

'Barabal?' Dugald said.

'Sister?' Evander said at the same time.

Bright green eyes staring at her with so much hope her

228   *The Highlander's Mysterious Maiden*

heart seized and emotions clogged in her throat. Something strong, something unstoppable, bubbled in her chest, sizzled under her skin. Goose pimples raised and raced along her limbs.

She couldn't breathe.

They were twice her age when she was five, but they were only children and had tried their best to protect her, then tried again to find her...for years. They'd spent so much time in their own company, they were unwed and without family. They had been children trying to protect her as best they could. It wasn't their fault it hadn't been a good home. How would they know she'd be tossed about?

They'd suffered. She'd been hurt, grieving for her parents' death. But they, grieving, hurt, had felt powerless with the tanners. While she, whenever she was aggrieved, had simply left and kept moving forward.

'Will she not say anything?' Dugald said. 'She forgives us, right?'

'Bull-headed,' Evander cursed. 'Can't you see she's only now realising the truth? Give her time.'

'Too much time has already passed,' Dugald said. 'I want no more time, do you?'

'No,' Evander said.

Dugald gave a brusque nod. 'Then it's two to one.'

They never shut up. Never. Anger, hurt, happiness, relief bubbling, bubbling, ruptured in one harsh sound. Barabal slammed a hand over her mouth, but it didn't cover the snorting. One after the other, in between each breath as she tried and failed to hold the braying. Nothing. Horrified, she gasped and pressed two hands to her face.

Tears spurting from her eyes, snot dripping from her nose. Her face, she knew, was mottled purple from the effort. But it was all locked in her and burst from her very soul. It was

Nicole Locke 229

too much. Her brothers were here. After all these years, she had family.

Evander swallowed hard.

Dugald beamed. 'There it is.'

'Thought we'd never hear that sound again,' Evander praised as if he heard something priceless.

She'd always made these humiliating sounds? Face flaming, she wheezed, 'Do you two need to finish each other's sentences?'

'We're brothers, of course we do,' Dugald said.

Something pained her at that and her laughter stopped.

Evander's face fell. 'It makes us odd.'

It made them wonderful. Barabal drew in a clear breath and another. Felt the heat in her face recede. Thank goodness. They might be fond of her laugh, but she wasn't. It'd been mortifying to make that sound like that out here with them. She'd never had to worry about it before. She couldn't remember the last time she had laughed like that.

No. She did. With the women last night, then in the cellars with Seoc, but nothing before that. Nothing since she'd been with her brothers. She hadn't laughed since then. Her memories were flooding back. They'd all been close. She'd forced herself to forget their shared moments.

She'd shared moments with Anna, Beileag, Murdag and Seoc, too. She'd accused them of terrible things. She would always remember their tight expression and the way Seoc had disappeared within himself even before he'd walked away. As though his roots were ripping out of the soil and were digging up all the good in him.

She had pushed them away. She had caused that loss to him and she needed to repair it, not linger here revelling in memories.

She might not be able to stay here. No one wanted a

230   *The Highlander's Mysterious Maiden*

screeching harpy, but she could apologise before she left. She was used to leaving and moving on because of others' mistakes. This time, they hadn't done anything wrong, she had.

'Be gone now.' She turned to leave. Evander's brows drew in, but she had no more time to waste. 'I have more work to do than tarry and talk to you two.'

'Here you are,' Barabal huffed. For hours, she'd been looking for the women and here they were, loitering in the stables, talking low among themselves. Doing nothing else.

'There you are!' Anna said.

On a gasp, Beileag spun to face her.

'It's about time,' Murdag said.

'About time?' Barabal should have realised sooner to come to the stables. Instead, she had walked the breadth of the houses and buildings first searching for Anna, then Beileag near the carpentry, then finally here at the stables.

Where all three were. All the while she'd been very much aware of people staring at her, most likely wondering why she was still there—she swore she saw Joan smirk.

She cared nothing about the Graham Clan. She was soon to leave and find a clan who would appreciate her skills. Maybe she'd take up with the kitchens again. She'd proven she could work in the confines of the alcoves and the women said they liked her sauces.

Sauces were a weak reason to actually stay anywhere, but they were a start somewhere else. Surely.

She didn't want to stay and have the Grahams judging her for her awful behaviour today. Her brothers couldn't surprise her again, so there was a chance she wouldn't humiliate herself a second time. She'd prove her worth somewhere else. If she could apologise and keep her dignity with these three.

Beileag gave Murdag a dark look. 'We need to talk.'

Murdag never took her eyes off Barabal. 'I believe we still need that flagon.'

So they could share a celebratory drink when she left them? Congratulate themselves because they'd rid themselves of her?

For one bright moment, she thought she could stay with this clan, but she'd proven their earlier reservations true. Certainly, they'd encouraged her to stay when they thought Seoc liked her. But Seoc had walked away from her after all her accusations. She'd been wise to keep away from anyone until she'd proven herself.

For now, she needed to get this apology over with. Too many hours had passed and it was dark outside. Travelling now would be dangerous. She'd done it before and would again, but she needed to find Seoc first to apologise to him as well. She'd been cruel when he had been kind to her. A good apology and she'd be off.

Except staring at these women, she wasn't so certain she could face the man. She was barely facing them.

'I need to talk,' Barabal said. 'You need to listen.'

Murdag smirked, Anna raised her brow. Beileag looked hurt. Again. Obviously, Barabal could never be a friend to such a tender heart.

Barabal locked her shaking knees. She would cause another scene if she stayed much longer. How could she be harsh to such a good person?

'Well?' Murdag said. 'Let us have it.'

Anna poked her elbow into her sister. 'Tell us what you need to.'

What would her own life have been like if she'd had a sister? So different. Maybe she'd be as close as her brothers were to each other. Her eyes pricked. Now she'd cry.

232   *The Highlander's Mysterious Maiden*

No, she was tired, that's all. And she wouldn't be tired if these three hadn't kept her from her duty to apologise.

'You need to apologise,' Barabal said to Anna.

Anna raised her brow again; Beileag clasped her hands.

'This should be good,' Murdag said under her breath.

Barabal ignored her. She simply stared Anna down, willing her to at least start this conversation so she could get out of here before she humiliated herself.

'You want me to apologise,' Anna said slowly.

She wouldn't be the one to do it. If she had to be weak, she needed one of these three to soften a bit towards her first.

'Seoc brought my brothers here because you told them I was from Colquhoun land,' she said. 'Tell me that it wasn't you who disclosed what I entrusted of where I came from.'

Anna looked startled. 'I didn't know it was a secret. I'd never tell a secret.'

'You all like to talk too much.'

'Didn't I tell you we needed a flagon of mead?' Murdag said out the side of her mouth.

'Shh,' Beileag said.

Anna paled. 'You told me and I knew you and Seoc were close. You both seemed happy with each other. We hoped… he hasn't been the same since he was hurt and you arrived and we all saw the change in him. All those others after him even after Dunbar, but he only lit up when he met you. As though he'd found happiness as we had with our spouses.'

'I don't need meddling to find some husband.'

'We pushed too much; I see that now,' Anna said. 'I didn't believe telling him your clan would hurt you.'

It had, viciously, so she'd given back to them as good as she got. Even though she now knew her brothers weren't who she'd thought, that didn't change the fact that these people had surprised her.

She hated surprises. Why wouldn't she? Her parents died and, with no warning at all, she'd been forced away.

'I don't like surprises,' she said.

'I am sorry,' Anna said.

Barabal's eyes pricked again, and she turned her head away. Had anyone apologised to her before, or meant it? Anna looked as though she'd do anything not to have hurt her.

'I don't care what you say, I'm looking for some mead anyway.' Murdag walked behind her. 'Maybe I was wise in my past and knew we'd need it.'

They couldn't wait to celebrate. Another pang to her heart, another feeling of loss she couldn't shake. It was all too much. It was late; maybe she could pay someone to compose a message to Seoc. She didn't believe she could face him now.

'Well, good,' she said brusquely. 'This whole matter wouldn't be as terrible if you had all been where you were supposed to be.'

'Where were we supposed to be?' Beileag said.

'We've been waiting here since we found Anna,' Murdag said.

'When's that?' Barabal said. It was all their fault she was faltering. Right after she'd left her brothers, when she was still fresh from her ire at them, she could have faced these women more resolutely.

'Since you told us to leave the garden,' Beileag said.

That long they'd been hiding from her? Well, too bad for them she'd found them. 'Are you saying that parsley's been picked and is wasting in the garden? You said I needed to make the sauce. It was your idea, not mine.'

'I can't find anything in this room,' Murdag called out. 'I'll search the other room. Maybe I'll find four flagons' worth.'

What if Murdag didn't hear what she had to still say? She

234   *The Highlander's Mysterious Maiden*

was barely getting her words out in the first place! 'Don't go so far you can't hear me,' she called back.

'No worries for that,' Murdag yelled.

Barabal's heart seized. Now she was yelling again? She couldn't apologise about yelling with more yelling.

'I don't believe you need to worry about the parsley, Barabal,' Beileag said. 'I'm certain someone gathered it already to use it.'

Doubtful since she'd been arguing with her brothers with the wilting parsley at her feet. Now that was all wasted, too. It was time to end this. 'Let's get this over with.'

Beileag's hands fluttered. 'What exactly would be over?'

Her time here. 'My apology.'

'Oh, that's what you're doing.' Murdag said from somewhere behind her.

She was failing at this. 'I'm apologising. I said some harsh things in the garden because I overreacted.'

They couldn't know what Seoc bringing her brothers here meant. She hadn't needed to shout at everyone.

Murdag strode back to Anna's side. 'Couldn't find anything by the tackle either.'

Enough with the celebratory drinks. 'Regardless of all that, I don't like surprises.'

'Noted,' Anna said.

Good then, she could go. Throat clogged, heart tight, Barabal choked out, 'Well, then.'

Anna's eyes had gone soft. As though she was sorry for Barabal. Beileag's eyes were just as bad. At least Murdag's were lit as though she had a secret. As though maybe she had found the flagons, but didn't bring them out in case she had to share them with her.

Pivoting, Barabal swiftly strode towards the closed stable door and shoved it open. The cooling air brushed her wet cheeks, announcing to her she'd failed to hold back her tears.

Nicole Locke 235

'I don't believe she understood why we were waiting here,' Beileag said.

'Not without trying,' Anna responded. 'It has to be a good sign she didn't take a horse?'

'Told you we needed that mead.' Murdag chuckled. 'I'm beginning to see why your husband believes she's a little scary.'

Beileag said something in return, but fortunately, Barabal was out of earshot now.

She was scary, she knew that. Even more so now she'd made all that noise right next to the chapel and now again in the stables. She hurried her steps away from their words and her shame.

They'd thought she'd steal a horse? That hurt, terribly. Maybe these women could have been something more to her, but she'd failed and she'd have to make a home somewhere else. A little dangerous, true, with the war escalating and it was dark, but she had to leave, now.

The good bit was she'd already grabbed her satchel and had it strapped across her. She didn't have to face Eunice with her clumsy ways, Joan and her smirks and Mary with her cutting words.

What else was true was that she would most definitely be sending a message to Seoc. She could right her wrong and not face further humiliation. He'd probably think she was stealing his mead. Glad not to see her again, he wouldn't care that she didn't apologise in person.

Certainly she and Seoc had shared more than kisses and it meant something to her, but clearly not to him. After all, she wasn't his first and hadn't Murdag said he liked big breasts? Well, she'd seen plenty of those around here for him.

Having breasts and making decent sauces were no excuse for her accusations and yelling. Barabal bet they couldn't wait to be rid of her.

Chapter Nineteen

'Give her time.' Hamilton poked the fire with a long thin branch. 'Sometimes that's all that's needed.'

Seoc didn't look at his friend who sat on the makeshift bench off to his right with Evander beside him. Dugald, sitting on the ground, leant back on the same bench with his legs stretched before him. He was the picture of calm, but that man felt as comforting as walking around a bog. Camron, wisely, sat opposite and alone on the single bit of perched stone.

When Camron made some dismissal tone at Hamilton's advice, Seoc silently agreed with him. He had no intention of giving Barabal time. He'd been gone barely a week and look what had happened. If he'd stayed by her side, he would have begged for more moments in the cellar and they'd have shared dinners with his father. He'd have discovered why she had been preparing food in the kitchens at night. If he had stayed, he could be holding his lass instead of wandering fields and sitting by the fire with these men again.

'Time worked for me.' Hamilton waved the tiny flame off the stick.

'Beileag chasing you is what worked for you,' Camron said.

Frowning at his brother, Hamilton arched his arm to toss the stick.

Nicole Locke 237

'Give that to me.' Evander held out his hand. On a shrug, Hamilton slapped the stick in Evander's hand.

Evander grimaced, Dugald chuckled.

'What say you, Graham?' Dugald said. 'You giving my sister any time?'

He was cross with these men; he didn't want to give them his time.

'She told you to be gone,' Evander said.

'I won't.' He was incapable of it when his lass hurt so.

'See,' Dugald groused. 'I'm not leaving either.'

'She won't chase after you,' Evander said. 'She didn't with us.'

'Beileag didn't chase me either,' Hamilton said.

'There will be no chasing,' Seoc bit out. When Barabal first said for him to be gone, he thought his world would be black again. But it hadn't taken any time at all for him to realise he wasn't the same as he was last spring or even before Beltane. He was beginning to partake in his world again.

However, these men would drive him mad if he stayed in their company. But he'd already roamed the fields for hours and there was nothing out there for him. He was always able to find some solace among the grass and dirt, but this time he found no answers to repair his mistakes. When it turned dark, he headed back to see a fire and without thought his feet had veered here.

He'd expected the twins and a few scouts had set up to find quiet after long days of training and council meetings. What he hadn't expected was Hamilton, Camron and Barabal's damned brothers.

By then he'd been too close not to be spotted and when Camron faced him with one arched brow as if daring him to run away, he'd forced himself to complete the steps and sit with them.

238   *The Highlander's Mysterious Maiden*

Hamilton had seemed pleased to see him. Not so much Dugald and Evander. Seoc was fine with that, he wasn't pleased to see them either.

He'd led a life surrounded by a clan who respected him and friends who were loyal. He'd made mistakes, ones he still suffered from such as introducing Anna to the bastard Maclean and not saving the life of their Laird. He'd hurt and caused people pain.

But bringing Barabal's brothers here and witnessing Barabal's pain hurt worse than the unexpected agony of the sword across his gut. For he'd done it purposefully, gleefully, with utter joy and delight.

What an ill-footed fool he'd been. But then, with Barabal, he'd always been off balance.

When he'd first pursued her, he'd understood he would have to trust her for her to reciprocate. So when he'd told her of Dunbar, of every mistaken deed he'd made, he hadn't expected her to share any of her own life.

When they kissed and touched, he knew pleasure and a sense of forever. The way she felt in his arms burned through him even now. The desire and need for more of her was so strong he knew a thousand lifetimes wouldn't erase it.

Then, sweetest of all, her voice in the dark telling of her past. Those precious words from her lips, of her family, of the barest hint of the possible origins of her vulnerability.

He might have been unable to forgive himself for his own mistakes, but he'd known immediately how to repair what harm had happened in her life. So certain, he'd hadn't consulted his friends or family.

Now, he sat on a damp stump, listening to these men give their opinions and filling him in on facts he didn't know. Dugald and Evander had pushed her away as children because they were protecting her from spiteful tanners, only to discover she wasn't living with the clan they thought, nor the one after that.

She'd been too young to be roaming Scotland. Where else had she travelled? What more cruelty had she had to endure? His Barabal! How he wished he had not added to her pain.

Now here was Hamilton, happy with Beileag, offering advice as if he was an expert on how to repair relationships. As if he'd take any advice from a man as clueless as he. Hamilton had thought to pursue Murdag and belatedly noticed Beileag. At least Camron was wise and kept his mouth shut and Evander seemed to avoid his gaze as he drew circles in the dirt at his feet. Dugald, however, glowered like an old crone at him. As if this was entirely his fault.

Seoc glowered right back before sliding his gaze to Hamilton. 'I don't intend to stay gone. But I should have realised she wanted nothing to do with her brothers. The Colquhouns border us. If she'd wanted to see her brothers, she would have.

'No offence,' he said to Evander.

'All of it taken, Graham,' Evander said. 'So you won't respect her wishes to leave her alone, but you expect us to.'

'You made us believe we had a chance; you made us believe we'd have our sister back,' Dugald growled.

He'd told them only she was here. 'How was I to know there was a rift between you?'

'Rift, more like a chasm,' Camron said.

Ah, they'd gossiped about him while he'd been roaming the fields as well. 'Does everyone here know everything?'

'What they need to know,' Hamilton said.

'Is there more?' Dugald said.

Camron narrowed his eyes on the man. 'Only what concerns you and your sister. The rest is up to them.'

'If it affects any reparations between us, then we should know.' Evander's knuckles went white on the thin branch.

240   *The Highlander's Mysterious Maiden*

What was it with this man and sticks? And everything affected everything when it came to them, but curse these men. He'd been wrong to not ask Barabal's permission, but these men had lied to him. 'Just one question answered. One I repeatedly asked you of how long it'd been since you'd seen her would have told me what needed to be told.'

Dugald looked away, but Evander faced him. 'You were a stranger, and we thought it a private matter.'

'Then don't expect me to tell you more, either.'

Seoc barely kept his civility with them. If he truly had a chance with Barabal, and until she told him otherwise, it wouldn't do to ostracise her brothers. For better or worse, their fortunes were tied.

'So you all talked, and it seemed she forgave you,' Hamilton said. 'And afterwards, she walked away.'

'She didn't walk away, she stomped,' Dugald said.

So his lass had been on some mission then. Not to find him, else she would have. It wasn't a secret he frequented the fields.

'What of the women?' he asked. Perhaps his friends had had more interaction with Barabal.

'They had eyes like daggers,' Dugald said. 'We steered clear when they went into the stables and didn't emerge from there.'

'So what did you do after she left you in the garden?'

'Watched our sister walk the length of your clan and back again.'

'Did she talk to anyone?'

'If she did, we didn't see it,' Evander said. 'We tried to stay away so she couldn't see us. She may have talked to some people we missed.'

'They were fumbling about like lost lambs,' Hamilton said.

'Am no lost *lamb*,' Dugald said.

Nicole Locke 241

'We brought them to the fire to enquire why a couple of Colquhouns arrived on Graham land without announcing themselves,' Camron said.

'Good of you to let us know you brought some neighbours here, Seoc,' Hamilton said.

They were supposed to be family, not neighbours. Seoc rubbed his chest, but the pain didn't ease.

'So if she wasn't talking to anyone, what could she be doing now?' Hamilton said.

'Fleeing,' Seoc said at the same time as Dugald.

Dugald's frown deepened.

'Perhaps the women went to the stables to stop her from taking a horse to get very far?' Camron asked.

'Perhaps so,' Seoc agreed. Though his lass had walked her way from Buchanan land to here. Five clans he knew she'd been with: Colquhoun, MacFarlane, Macnaghten, Buchanan and here. But as much as he'd listened, he knew she'd lived elsewhere because the years didn't match up. What had she been fleeing from?

'You think she'd flee and you hid in the grass?' Dugald said.

'You two waddled behind these men to the fire and gossiped,' Seoc said pointedly.

'I do not waddle,' Dugald said.

'No horse, she can't be far.' Evander whacked the ground and Hamilton slid to the end of the log and away from Barabal's brother.

She shouldn't be gone at all. Why would she? She'd told them all to leave. If she'd listen and forgive him, he had no intention of being gone from her life, but that didn't mean he wanted to go charging forward and demanding she give him a chance.

She wouldn't be far, but that didn't mean she wouldn't

242   *The Highlander's Mysterious Maiden*

eventually try. If she was able to flee before, so much so that her brothers couldn't find her, he knew she could do so again.

'She's run before, she won't do it again,' he said, more for his benefit than theirs.

'Why not?' Evander said. 'We lost her once and searched for years.'

'We gave her all the apologies she needed, and she didn't listen,' Dugald said. 'It's your turn to make her listen.'

'I will not order her to hear me. She'll feel trapped.' He'd listen to his heart that demanded he mend the hurt between them, not her brothers.

'You could,' Camron said. 'That worked for me.'

'Aye, and that's how I met her the first night. When she disapproved of how you trapped Anna.'

Camron shrugged. 'She's good for you, my friend. I only wish for you to keep her in your life.'

He would do everything to ensure that.

'While I hope he'll find a woman who holds less of a grudge,' Hamilton said.

Seoc clasped his hands before him so as not to strangle the man.

'Her strength of character and grudges have been shattering his silence, Brother,' Camron said.

Head snapping up, Seoc caught Camron's steady gaze and then he knew. They'd spent time as they always had, but they'd seen him drifting. Overwhelmed, Seoc gave a curt nod to his friend, who nodded in return.

Dugald watched them both, but Seoc would be damned if he explained his own private matter with this Colquhoun. They could both keep their secrets for now.

'She's too wise to run now.' He hoped he was right. What did he know? She had responded to his kisses, not so much his words. And now she'd ordered him gone and he won-

Nicole Locke 243

dered if he'd get close enough to hold her again. 'She knows there's a battle at every border. It wouldn't take much for her to run headlong into the hands of the English, then what's to become of her?'

'One snap of that tongue of hers and—ow!' Hamilton said. 'You didn't need to kick me.'

'Yes, I did,' Evander muttered.

Camron chuckled. 'My thanks for that.'

'I said nothing wrong,' Hamilton said. 'She's strong and terrifying.'

She wasn't terrifying, she was covering vulnerability she'd told him nothing of and now he didn't know if she ever would. Curse his friend and himself for making her feel more distrustful of people. 'So you say, *Hamheart*.'

Hamilton's face flushed.

'My favourite was Hamhog,' Camron said. 'Or what was the other name she called you, Hamhead?'

'It was a jest,' Hamilton said. 'When will she let it go?'

'Never, Hamtoes,' Seoc added.

Evander and Dugald chuckled and for a moment the tension between all of them eased.

'We are sorry, Graham,' Evander said. 'I understand you care deeply for our sister. We took too much of a risk not telling you. But it was a decision when we were children to protect her from the tanners. Not the best decision, but one we thought best.'

That felt sincere. 'Do you know anything of her life between the time she left Colquhoun land and now? Anything you can tell me to help her?'

Dugald hung his head. 'Nothing and it tears us up not knowing.'

Him as well.

'Are you concerned for anything else?' Camron asked.

244   *The Highlander's Mysterious Maiden*

'That everything I said or could say to her is wrong. She may not listen to me either.' Seoc leant his elbows on his knees. 'She may leave the Graham Clan despite the dangers.'

'If that happens, do you intend to give her her freedom?' Camron asked. 'It is something I couldn't do.'

'You devoted your life to give Anna her freedom. You allowed her to be happy with another man and we watched your heart break when she didn't choose you. Whereas I have done everything in my power to be at Barabal's side from the moment she arrived.' So greedy to feel alive, so certain she was what he wanted, he'd never considered what she needed. He wouldn't make the same mistake again. 'She doesn't need to be kidnapped. Do you honestly believe that would work with her?'

'I hope she'd call you names and forgets all about me,' Hamilton said.

She'd curse him and he'd deserve it.

'When did she get so uncaring?' Evander said.

She wasn't uncaring. Her brothers truly didn't know her at all and he didn't either. But then they'd lost her when she was only five. Some of her hurt came from them. But if it was solely them, then after they told her the truth, she would have embraced them and not walked away. She held a grudge, but he couldn't believe she'd continue to with something as dear as lost family. There was something else, and he wanted to be there for her when she felt safe enough to tell.

What had she said to him at Beltane: *'Will you help or keep standing there?'* If there was a chance to help her, he would.

And he'd start now. 'She told you two to leave?'

'To be gone, she had work to do or some such,' Evander said.

'Poured our heart out to her and everything and she dismissed us.' Dugald crossed his arms.

His lass was hurt. 'Then by tomorrow, you best be gone.'

'But—'

'I need to win her hand, and I can't do it if her first wish, your departure, isn't met.'

'I believe her first wish was for you to be gone,' Dugald said.

'Enough, Colquhoun,' Camron said. 'You're on Graham land by our choice.'

Evander sighed. 'You know where to find us.'

Dugald crossed his ankles. 'I don't like it.'

Seoc didn't care. 'When you get to Colquhoun land, stay put.'

'If there's a chance at seeing our sister again, not even a war would move us,' Dugald growled.

'Dugald,' Evander said.

'I don't like it,' Dugald repeated.

Seoc had no time for this. He'd told them to leave, he'd push the issue later. For now, he would repair this.

'Er, Seoc?' Hamilton said.

No more talking. 'I know what to do now.'

Kidnapping wouldn't work for her, nor waiting until she chased him. If, and when she travelled, he'd follow her. His lass needed someone by her side, and he was the man for it. Standing, Seoc shook out his legs.

'Where are you going?' Hamilton said.

'Back to the village. If she's in bed, I'll sit outside her door until she wakes.'

Camron straightened. 'Remember when you said she was too wise to leave the clan now?'

'That might have been hastily said,' Hamilton added.

No, not hasty, it'd taken him hours to come to that conclusion and he'd been wasting those hours talking to these men. He was done wandering the fields and nattering with men

246   *The Highlander's Mysterious Maiden*

who didn't understand his lass. He knew what she needed, and it was him listening to what she wanted.

Ignoring them all, he stepped over the bench.

'Seoc,' Camron said, 'You should know—'

'They're telling you you're heading the wrong way.' Dugald pointed behind him.

Seoc pivoted. A presence, just a bit darker and curvier than the usual obstacles was gliding in the fields. No, not gliding, marching crisply. Away from their village, their clan. Away from him. Without thought, or even an acknowledgement, he raced towards her.

Away from the fire, the light dimmed. She'd travelled far already. The moon almost full, but still too dark for her to traverse out here.

'Where are you going?' he said before he reached her.

She didn't still or pause. She didn't even turn to see if it was him. Although his rushing through the tall grass meant she knew he, or at least someone, was coming her way. But as usual, his Barabal didn't let anyone slow her down.

She increased her pace, and he loped up beside her. He loved that she was tall and big boned. Loved they matched in many ways. Something he couldn't take advantage of in the cellar on a worn bench. How he wished for a home and bed of their own. Soon. If she'd have him.

'I'm going away,' she answered.

Then so was he.

He'd already traversed much today, but not this section. He tended to avoid it because— Clamping her waist, he shuffled them both five steps before he set her down again.

'What are you doing?' she hissed.

'Moving you, lass. Another two steps would have you tumbling in that crevasse which you can't see given the grass

Nicole Locke 247

there. In the past, I fell into it twice before I realised where it is.'

When he saw her glowering at the hidden dip, he pointed to the horizon. 'It aligns with that tree there. In case you come this way again.'

'I won't be coming this way again,' she gritted out.

'Knowledge is always good though, isn't it?'

When she kept stomping away from his home, his friends, her brothers, he simply kept pace. He thought he'd feel some sense of loss or worry. It wasn't as if she'd given him much notice to say his goodbyes. But he was at peace with it.

What he wasn't at peace with was her seething silence. It would have been easier if she cursed him a bit, or said whatever words she needed to. He meant it; he wouldn't demand anything from her, that he'd be there for her when she was ready. For all he knew she could have terrible secrets, other men, other families, and he ached to help her.

'Fine!' She spun to face him. 'I apologise.'

He was ready to listen. 'For what?'

'What do you mean for what?' she said. 'You're obviously waiting for me to say something, what else could it be?'

For you to acknowledge you love me.

But it was too early for that, it might be too early for him to say it as well, though it was true.

'This apology would be for?'

'For yelling and accusing you.'

She'd been betrayed by him, and she thought a raised voice and reciting his deeds warranted her apology? How should he reply? Refusal because he should apologise, or acceptance because he didn't want to refuse her feelings.

There was no winning with a reply. 'Did you give the same apology to your brothers?'

She adjusted the strap across her breasts. It was dark and

248 *The Highlander's Mysterious Maiden*

he couldn't see as much as he'd like, but still he tracked the minute movement. The leather width separating and lifting curves he hadn't had enough time to explore. Would he have that chance again?

'I did to Murdag, Anna and Beileag.' She looked at him, down at her chest, then back to him. When she frowned, fiercely, he knew he was staring, but as much as his soul ached for hers, his body yearned just as fiercely. He loved this woman, every bit of her.

Clearing his throat, he added, 'And your brothers?'

Releasing her thumb trapped between the strap and her sternum, she answered, 'They told me of their past and I believed them. They obviously told you as well.'

He didn't deny it. 'Then what are you doing?'

'I'm leaving,' she said.

'Because you yelled and made accusations.'

'Exactly,' she said. 'I was wrong, and you all were not.'

It would take a lifetime for him to understand all she meant. Yelling wasn't the reason she was leaving, there was something behind that. When she eyed him a bit longer and he returned her gaze, she released a frustrated breath and started walking.

'Where are we going?'

'We are not going anywhere. I am.'

'I'm asking because if we continue this way, we'll have to backtrack to avoid the water that meanders past those trees.'

Only a few more steps before she said, 'Are you telling me you're taking me in circles?'

Having too many tallies against him, he pointed out, 'You started this path, not I.'

They walked more, the ground became muddier. Over their squelchy steps, Barabal said, 'Are you here to ensure I

Nicole Locke 249

leave Graham land? You could inform me where the border is and I'll keep walking.'

That's where her thoughts went, to some place darker yet? 'I'm leaving because of you.'

'There's no need when I am leaving. You can have your clan and family and friends with no more of my annoyances.'

He wouldn't listen to her hurting herself. 'Wherever you go, and whatever you want to do, I intend to be by your side.'

He'd lay himself bare to this woman if need be.

'At my side?' She stumbled. Stopped. Gripped her satchel strap, hard. 'Why?'

Because she was his and he was hers. Because he knew he'd have to fall first, and tell her everything before she did, and he wanted to. 'Because I want to be.'

Her eyes narrowed. 'No, you don't.'

'And yet I am here.'

She gazed around them, most likely seeking answers, but they wouldn't come from the fields, he'd tried. When her eyes dragged back to his, they were filled with stark vulnerability and frustration.

'I don't even know where I'm going.'

'Then we'll plan together.' He'd have to be pried from her side.

More conflicting emotions from those greenish-brown eyes he loved, more gripping of the satchel's strap. More of his Barabal looking at him as if he was both an obstacle in her way and something she desperately wanted to believe. He needed her to believe in them. He knew he could tell her until the day he died how much he loved her, how much he wanted her to stay, but she wouldn't trust it. She had to believe they were meant to be together.

'Why are you doing this?'

'What am I doing?'

250   *The Highlander's Mysterious Maiden*

She bit her lip, drew it in. 'I've only travelled alone to clans.'

'You've travelled alone to a few clans; we'll travel to some more.' He poked, knowing it was more than a few she'd travelled to, and that his lass wouldn't falter in correcting him.

'A few!' she hissed. 'I was dragged away from Colquhoun Clan to MacFarlane. When they were done with me, I went to Macnaghten's, then MacDougall's, then Campbell's.'

She stopped, drew in a harsh shaking breath, then shook her head at him. Oh, no, he wanted her to share them all. 'Then where else? To Buchanan's to here?'

Barabal pivoted, turned her back on him, took a step in a different direction, then another.

He wouldn't let her get far. 'Then to Buchanan to here, is that it?'

She rounded on him again. 'Why do you care where I've been, Graham? Are you attempting to discover where not to travel to miss me entirely? Or is it curiosity because you can't imagine a life without family, friends, or a clan who was loyal to you.'

Her body was shaking, her voice broke. Seoc wanted to end his questions and wrap her in his arms and take her to safety, but he wanted her to say more. He had vowed not to push, but whatever truth she was withholding was breaking her and killing him.

'Tell me,' he repeated. 'Buchanan to here?'

'No! Campbell to McNab to Stewart to MacGregor to Buchanan to here.' Her laugh was bitter. 'When I say I don't know where we're going, I mean it. For all I know, we're on to England.'

So many places, so many reasons she'd left them. Maybe some of them along the way she was forced to leave, but not all. There was something more here and maybe she didn't see it, maybe talking to her brothers again brought only pain. But he was beginning to understand. Barabal left too many clans, too many people. She intended to leave him behind as well.

'So now you know,' she said. 'All of it.'

No, but he was closer to the truth. 'That's not all of it.'

Her hand went to the strap again, but her fingers only tapped at it. 'There are other women within Clan Graham. And all of Scotland for that matter. Ones with breasts and some such.'

That stalled him. 'You think I'm following you because you're a woman.'

'Murdag said you liked my breasts,' she said. 'And Joan doesn't have any.'

He wanted to laugh, he wanted to lament. He loved everything about this woman and wanted to show her that love, if they ever got past the point she was leaving him.

Or trying to, at least. 'You think I'm following you because of the cellars?'

She spun, walked faster, her hips rocking with each rapid step. 'Go and find Joan or someone else.'

As if there could be anyone else, as if his desire was so interchangeable. He sped his own steps until he was beside her again. 'And how about yours, then? How about Tasgall or Calan?'

'Who?'

He didn't take any pleasure from her not recognising the men who'd offered themselves that night on Beltane and had eyed her more than once since. It was almost proving his realisation: Barabal didn't see what he did. She didn't know what was shown so brightly to him, but why?

'Is everyone interchangeable for you?'

She stopped, her skirts and satchel flaring out. 'Interchangeable? You think I'm flinging people aside?'

252   *The Highlander's Mysterious Maiden*

He suspected that was exactly what she was doing. Oh, some of it was because of her brothers and she rejected first before she was hurt again, and he feared some might have harmed her, but he was beginning to believe something else motivated her to keep going, to keep looking. Something he'd lost in Dunbar, but she never had. Something good.

Because besides her pain, she'd shown him what she held so brightly: hope. It was what drew him to her. Always, that hope, that heart of hers when he had none, she simply demanded it of everyone around her. How could she not see it?

She thumped her chest with her palm. 'Clans reject me. I've been telling you all along I am not worth yours or anyone's regard,' she said. 'You talked to my brothers, and know my mistakes. My failings are so plain for all of Clan Graham to see. No matter what apology I make, or however much help I offer, it won't be enough. *I'm* not enough.'

Chapter Twenty

It wasn't Barabal's words letting her know she'd gone too far. It was the look on Seoc's face that whipped reason across her consciousness. Reason she hadn't been able to collect since Seoc brought her brothers to the garden.

Seoc, who looked at her thunderstruck because she shouted her darkest thoughts. The ones she hadn't acknowledged since she was five years old. She swore she'd never make herself feel helpless again, that she'd make herself worthy. She thought she had.

But even her brothers' explanation didn't erase the unworthiness still inside her. Because she went on to accuse and shout. Proving they'd been right all along to leave her behind. She needed to leave the Graham Clan.

Except like that night she'd arrived, everything felt a little off. As though she wasn't on time, or she couldn't complete a task she'd meant to. Leaving had never been like this before. As though she was forgetting something, or had faltered on an instruction.

Still, she knew what had to be done: loop her satchel across her body and move on. She'd never found her footing with Clan Graham, then she'd yelled and accused them. She'd tried to make it right with an apology and to leave with dignity.

But Seoc wouldn't leave her alone and she'd made it worse.

254   The Highlander's Mysterious Maiden

What had she said? What had she done? Horrified, she darted away from this confusing man. It didn't matter, Seoc had legs as high as tree trunks and easily caught up with her.

What wasn't easy was his firm grip on her wrist, the digging in of his heels which propelled her back. A twist of his hand, and she spun into his waiting arms.

'Not enough? That's what you say to me.' His words were harsh, his grip insistent. His eyes searching hers for the answer she didn't mean to give. She hadn't meant to confess to her shame.

Seoc's brows drew in. 'No.' A minute tightening in his hold was all the warning she got before he kissed her hard, his arms crushing her against his chest, the satchel biting into her side.

But she didn't care. It was Seoc, holding her again when she didn't think he would. She'd told him to go and now she was leaving. He said he wanted to go with her, but that was too puzzling to believe. But this kiss, it felt good, better than perfect. She clung to him with every part of her urging her with *yes* and *this*. He groaned and dragged his lips off hers, while her fingers bit into broad shoulders to keep him close.

'You're wrong, my Barabal, my lass,' he said, pressing kisses wherever he could reach. 'Wrong about not being enough, wrong about leaving, wrong about why.'

She was— She wanted— 'Wait, stop.' She wasn't wrong. Letting go of her grip on his shoulders, she answered, 'You're kissing me.'

Another soft drag of his lips against the cord of her neck sent a shiver through her, his warm breath as he pulled away a shudder up her spine. But it was the bite of his grip at her hip that enticed.

When he straightened and his eyes held with hers, she almost whimpered. His eyes were full dark, his body locked against her more pliant one.

'I'm kissing you and intend to kiss you more,' he said.

'Seoc,' she said, not knowing what she wanted. To prove him wrong, or give in to his kisses and beckoning words.

Another calloused grip to her waist, a low timber from his chest. Maybe a word, more of a growl as he gazed from her eyes to her lips. 'Kiss me back, Barabal.'

This wasn't right. She was leaving. *Leaving.* Because no one wanted her, because she yelled and accused and wasn't useful. His kisses weren't making sense. 'You walked away. I told you to go and you walked away. Twice because you walked on the first night we met as well.'

'And how long did I stay away, hmm?' he answered. 'How long did I make it before I had to see you again?'

A confusingly short time. This was confusing.

'You could ask me a thousand times to go, Barabal, but until you mean it, I'll think of a thousand and one ways to be back at your side.'

'I meant it,' she said, her voice no longer affected by the kiss, but by no means resolute, not when he held her so intimately. 'You hurt me.'

'And I'm sorry for it. But until you set me straight with directions and instructions and ways to do things better, it'll happen again.'

Did he tease her or mean it? She shoved against his shoulder, but he didn't let her go.

Brows drawn in, he said, 'Ask me.'

'What?'

'You seem intent on leaving this land, leaving this clan, and I told you I'll leave with you. Now ask me if I care where we are going.'

Her heart was breaking. She'd never thought to be this

256 *The Highlander's Mysterious Maiden*

close to him again. To feel his hands on her skin, take in his warmed ale and leather scent. She was meant to send him a message of apology, not say it out loud. Or like this with his arms around her. She felt like saying more than she should when she'd told him too much already.

'All you have to do is talk,' he said. 'I don't care if you take us to England or to anywhere, Barabal, now ask me the reason.'

'Why?' Were his arms bringing her closer to him because her hands were now clasped behind his neck as though she was curling up into him? But she had to leave.

'Because you are my destination.'

Her heart reeled.

'No more drifting. You are who I want beside me in this life,' he continued. 'Can you imagine what it was like to be as dead as I? I hadn't a heart anymore and you came poking and demanding, forcing me to live again until I don't want any other existence. Why would you deprive me, *us*, by leaving?'

His words were like an echo in her head making no sense. They wouldn't, not while he held her like this. Not when she clung to him. 'Let me go.'

He did.

Instantly the cold broke through her thoughts. She needed to turn and walk away, but this man would follow her until she set him straight. 'I apologised. I said my goodbyes. I owe you nothing.'

He eyed her wrist as if to pull her towards him again and she tucked it behind her back. Confusion marred his face. 'How would I know until now? Before I interrupted your nightly walk, I received no apologies or goodbyes.'

Did he think she had others like him, or anyone at the Graham Clan? Women who brought drinks and shared stories with her. She'd never had that before. When she'd left other clans, no one said they'd leave with her. 'I intended to send you a message.'

He exhaled slowly. 'What would it have said?'

Why was he acting hurt on this? 'My apology.'

'That's all?'

'What else would there be?' She released her arm, held her hands steady at her side, but she didn't feel steady, she felt unbalanced. Why wasn't he acting like everyone else? They shared kisses, and the cellars, but she'd seen others in such embraces and they walked away.

Why wouldn't he take her at her word as everyone had before and leave her alone? After their kiss her knees were still so unsteady, she feared she'd need to crawl across the Graham border. And they stood in this field of nothingness. A fire with some men in the distance and her home where she'd lived for these weeks further than that. It wasn't raining, maybe she could stay still, but he had to go.

Instead, a glint entered his eyes, as though he knew she was about to crumble.

'This is what you've done with other clans, isn't it? Just left them behind.'

'I left them behind?' she said, not hiding the bite in her voice. She needed it to cover the hurt. Why would no one listen to her? 'You were there in the garden and travelled with my brothers, you know what happened. My parents died of a fever. My lasting memory of them is of their soaked sheets. My brothers—'

'Tried to protect you,' he cut in.

She reeled from her brothers' tale, but that shouldn't change things. It wasn't only them, it was the other times, other clans as well. She'd been one way for too long for her brothers' reasoning to change everything. She still accused and demanded; the Graham Clan still didn't accept her.

258   *The Highlander's Mysterious Maiden*

Sauces weren't enough, especially since the rest of the clan hadn't tasted them.

'I know what happened to your brothers, tell me what happened to you,' he said. 'Why do you leave people?'

She pulled the satchel before her, wrapped her hand around the strap for something to hold on to. She didn't leave. Everyone left her first. 'I was sent to my mother's cousin, Ciorstaidh and Gillespie, her husband. I stayed until they didn't want me any more. It was a harsh season, and they had no food. They sent me to the Macnaghtens and now I am here.'

Seoc's expression didn't ease, but he looked at her expectantly. 'You were at other clans before us, tell me of them first.'

'Why do you want to know? It was nothing and should be forgotten.'

Scowling, he took a step closer. 'Let me know you, as I want to, as you need me to.'

For one blinding moment, it didn't matter that it was night and she could only see the outline of him because she felt the truth in his words. She did want someone—no, she wanted Seoc to know her. And she almost believed him, but life had taught her no one wanted to know her and she'd tell him why.

'The Macnaghten family I stayed with had a son. Over and over, he cornered me, threatened me. The parents turned a blind eye to his cruelty. So one day, I left in the middle of the night.'

Now that she revealed this ugly bit of her past, she expected Seoc to grow distant, to walk away again. Instead, his stance changed, grew larger. 'Some day, you will give me his name. Some day, swear to me, you will. For I will not forget him. But right now, tell me, did you leave the other clans in the middle of the night. Were you cornered again? Because there were other clans you left, Barabal.'

Nicole Locke 259

She had told the women of Archie and never had to say more. Of course there were other clans, and they were difficult, too. She'd tell him. He'd know her then.

'I fled to the MacDougalls after that. Stayed for a few years—they were little better than the Macnaghtens. After two years I left for the Campbells.'

'You went to Campbells from the MacDougalls?' he said. Finally, he understood how she was rejected or forced away.

'Clan Campbell were decent people, but they never trusted me. How could they? They didn't trust the MacDougalls or the Macnaghtens and I lived with both,' she said. 'I never left; I was always forced to go.'

But…was that the truth? She glanced at Seoc again, waited for his protest, or word for her to continue, but he stood silent, strong. Faced her and waited. Goose pimples raced up and down her arms and sweat beaded in the small of her back.

They weren't all Macnaghtens, and she hadn't exactly been forced to leave the Campbells either. Which meant, she hadn't always been brave like Murdag said. She'd been altogether something else.

She showed him every flaw, every bit of uselessness in her. Maybe, maybe when he knew there were more clans, more instances of her unworthiness he'd see what she was beginning to see. Because she wasn't always forced. No, it was much worse. But she did leave them because she felt their rejection, so she…rejected them first. She'd been afraid.

'I stayed with the Campbells for a few years. No one talked to me there. They didn't dare, but they weren't cruel and I thought it was the best it could be.'

'But you didn't stay there,' he said as if he knew the truth.

No, she'd run from the others. 'Then it was the McNabs, Stewarts, MacGregors, Buchanans.'

260 *The Highlander's Mysterious Maiden*

He slowly shook his head as though he didn't believe her.

'What do you want from me? I tell you unbearable times of my life and you want me to tell you more, or is it details you're missing? Like where Archie's hands went that last time he cornered me in the kitchens, or that entire Campbell rooms would fall silent when I entered. Or how I broke down and accused your clan because my brothers arrived.'

'You didn't break; you're not broken.' He glowered. 'We took you by surprise. You are the strongest woman I have ever met.'

He wasn't listening. 'I was weak and you're right. I wasn't always forced to go like my brothers did to me. I left, too. That's what you wanted me to confess, isn't it? About what a coward I am? I left all those clans before they hurt me. I left because I didn't want to be the one hurt. I was leaving you as well.'

His brow drew in, his eyes misted as if what she said pained him. 'Because I hurt you. Because I brought your brothers without asking if you wanted to see them. And here I am—'

Cursing, Seoc rubbed his hand through his hair and stepped away. 'Why do I not have patience for this time? Maybe I'm not right because I seem to be making it worse and hurting you. I want—no, need to stay by your side, Barabal. But if you tell me not to, I will leave you be. I will do this for you.'

When she said she pushed people away because she was weak and afraid, she hadn't meant him, had she? Except, he wasn't seeing it as she was. He thought he deserved to be pushed away for his deeds when it was her own shortcomings that were truly the cause.

'Seoc—' she started. 'It's not you who is wrong, I am.'

'For what? For being hurt?'

'For accusing others so I don't get hurt.' It was devastatingly clear to her now what she'd been doing all these years, what a coward she was to keep running.

He tilted his head. 'So you believe you leave these clans, all these clans, including mine because you're either forced or you're too weak to stay.'

Maybe he did listen. 'Now you know why you don't need to leave with me. You can go back to your fire, to your home.'

He let out a huff of air. 'If this is how it is to be, I've changed my mind, I will grant you no say in my not travelling with you. I'll stay by your side until you mean to make me go. Until then, you need to see. I need you to see.'

'See what?' This man was confusing. The Graham Clan was confusing. 'More of my unworthiness because I know you don't want to leave with me forever.'

He stilled. 'I swore I would not push you, Barabal, but your words beg me to. I thought by now you would see yourself as I do. As I have always done.'

'I've told you all the truth; I've told you all the clans,' she said.

'Not the truth to yourself,' he said. 'Tell me details, then. Why'd you leave Buchanan and come here?'

'Because I didn't want to go to Colquhoun and see my—'

'No.' He grabbed her hand. His calloused fingers scraped across her skin, and she shivered.

'What happened at Buchanan to make you come here?' he said.

There was no reason. She'd wanted to be useful that's all, and that clan had made it impossible. 'The Buchanan baker didn't believe me when I told him how to burn the bread for Beltane.'

'You told a baker how to burn bread?' His lips curled.

It reminded her of when she'd told him of the bees, it made

262   *The Highlander's Mysterious Maiden*

her want to smile back as if they shared something. Her hand warmed in the palm of his.

'There's a method to burn the ends consistently without ruining the entire loaf.'

'Always clever, my lass,' he said his voice lower, more rumbling. 'Now tell me the rest.'

Not his lass. She was leaving. His hand which was wrapped around hers gentled. She could tear away from him now, but she didn't think herself capable. Standing out here in a field of rocks and grass, and she wanted him to keep touching her, telling her she was his and commenting on her cleverness.

But he wanted more from her than this field and her hand. However, her life didn't change because a few facts were different. It didn't change her or her past actions, deeds she did because she hadn't been brave, and as such, she shouldn't stay here. Shouldn't lean into his hand or step closer to him.

'From Buchanans I came here,' she said.

His eyes grew soft, his fingers brushed wrist. 'Then marched up to me and told me what to do.'

She had.

'And we've been trying to keep you here ever since.'

'Keep me here?'

'Murdag and Anna and Beileag.'

That wasn't true. 'When I left, they were hiding from me in the stables.'

Seoc stared at their hands. 'Did it not occur to you they were in the stables to stop you leaving with a horse?'

'Stealing a horse, you mean.'

'Borrowing.' He tilted his head and looked at her through his lashes. With his height, he shouldn't have been able to do that, and it shouldn't have made her heart skip a beat. 'They want you here as badly as I do. But you probably didn't give them a chance to tell you that, did you?'

Nicole Locke 263

They'd been over this. 'Because I didn't want to get hurt so I pushed them away.'

'You think they would hurt you?' Seoc said.

She lifted her chin. 'They turned my back, so I didn't see you and my brothers approach.'

His face fell. 'That's on me again, not them. You've talked with them and know their stories. Do you believe Anna couldn't see the signs of your mistrust and understand your pain of betrayal? Or that Beileag with her soft heart and that mother of hers wouldn't recognise you were given harsh words and abuse somewhere in your past? And you know it was Murdag's idea to be in the stables to stop you. You can't believe they would hurt you.'

Betrayed for her brothers' arrival, it was possible she'd misinterpreted their reason for being in the stables. 'They do want me to make sauces for the clan.'

'You think it's for sauces?' he huffed. 'Do you know why you tried with the Buchanan baker, or why you demanded me to help Anna?'

What else could it be? 'What do you want from me?'

He took her other hand and wrapped them both in his now. It felt like comfort. Like that tree with its roots holding her.

'You think you have to be useful to be loved or needed. After my injury at Dunbar when I could do nothing but breathe, don't you think I didn't recognise that need in you? That very first night, I saw your wariness, your hurt you carried. It called to me, but do you know what else I saw?'

His expression turned so fierce she could barely look in his eyes. 'I wasn't myself that night. Everything was off because I'd arrived later than I intended. I wanted to help with Beltane and there was nothing to do. I was ill footed, and then you asked to kiss me. Nothing I did from that point on was

264   *The Highlander's Mysterious Maiden*

the same. I told Anna where I was from, I walked in circles with— You're laughing at me.'

His grin dropped a bit. 'No, I'm understanding. The moment I met you, I felt the same. Ill footed. But mostly because I felt anything at all. You made me feel.'

'Annoyance?' she said. 'Frustration?'

He chuckled. 'Certainly frustration, but…' He looked wildly around them, narrowed his eyes. Then he bent down, cradled his arms around her and swung her up.

'What are you doing?'

'Moving to that partially built fence.'

'But I'm leaving,' she said.

'If you are, so am I; it'll be good to rest our legs a bit.' He sat on the thickest part of the stone. When he was done adjusting, his feet were on discarded rocks, and she was resting on his lap, and he still held her hands.

His holding her securely was too intimate, felt too good. She should protest, but the angle forced her to lean into him and rest her head on his shoulders. So she did.

'At Dunbar my chest was carved open,' he said. 'And I swear my heart dropped from my chest that day. Whatever soul I had left was ravaged by the fevers. I was nothing when I woke.'

This time she shifted her hands to wrap her fingers around some of his.

'I understand why you feel as though you need to leave. I know what fleeing feels like. After Dunbar, my body was here, but I was gone in my thoughts. When I woke, I didn't see the point because we'd lost so much from my failure. When you stormed up to me in that field, you didn't see or know any of that. You acted as though I could do something.'

It was the timbre of his voice her heart felt, the light touch of his hand, the tremble of his fingertips that her body clung to. But his words, she couldn't grasp them. 'I think everyone can do something.'

'I wager you made suggestions to your home the moment you saw it.'

'I told them to make hooks for clothes,' she said. 'But that's because if I didn't, they'd see I wasn't worthy. And I'd just arrived, it was too soon for me to run away.'

'So clever and yet you still do not see what I do.' He released one of his hands, caressed her cheek, and raised her eyes to him. 'It's that you try, Barabal. You have hope. I knew you were protective, demanding, wary because of some hurt in your past, but you tried that very night you arrived. And every day since with everyone around you whether we listened or not. Hope spills from you like some shining light, it blinded me that very night of Beltane.'

He leaned his forehead to hers, kissed her lips reverently, once, twice. 'Then my love for you blindsided me.'

She pulled away. 'You love me.'

His eyes glinted. 'How could I not, with all that hope of yours you gave to me? You took me to the cellars telling me you could help my sword arm. You tried to even help me. Someone who hadn't felt for so long.'

'I never did help you,' she said. 'You distracted me.'

'With this?' He gave a quick kiss. 'Stay, Barabal. Don't quit on us or me. Stay. After all, I'm not possibly healed, am I? You still have much more work to do here.'

'I haven't even tried yet and you know it,' she said. 'And you said you'd travel with me.'

'So I did.' He rubbed his thumb across her jaw. 'But my father hasn't had a chance to know you and that you have to stay here for.'

He loved her. Seoc loved her and now he wanted her to stay. 'We can send him a message.'

266   *The Highlander's Mysterious Maiden*

His eyes glinted. 'Or how about more kisses, more of my touch and what we shared in the cellar?'

'I'm certain you can find ways to kiss and touch me elsewhere if I still go.'

A rumbling sound came from his chest. 'That I could, I will. Because your curves are—'

'No.'

'I do like your breasts,' he said.

Ducking her head, she hit her forehead on his shoulder. 'Don't.

'I like the rest of you, too,' he chuckled.

'Please!'

His tender teasing, the weight of all their words eased into her soul like little shoots in the soil next to his. He saw her hope and thought it something good. This *was* different. He made her comfortable. Not the strained hope of her past, or her fears or her hurt moving her forward and away, but something steady and sure. Sitting on Seoc's lap, her feet dangling against his, she felt as though she was home.

'Then how about all that parsley?' he continued. 'Certainly you'll need to stay a day or two to make some sauces.'

Didn't he know, couldn't he feel, he'd already convinced her? 'That parsley is already used for something else by now.'

'You could teach me how to make some sauces. That you'll need vast kitchens for, not campfires on the side of the road.'

She liked envisaging them in the Graham kitchens together. 'There's a few good ones with mint I think you'll like, but I could show how to do that anywhere.'

Why she was teasing him about leaving when she knew she'd stay, she didn't know. But she loved the way he couldn't stop touching her. One hand along her face, another caressing her hip, along her side, and up her back. Soothing her, giving her the courage to ask the truly difficult questions.

'So you love me?' she said.

If possible, his eyes softened even more. 'From the second you made your first demand at Beltane.'

There were people that night she could have demanded from, but she'd walked the entire length of the field to reach him, but that's not when she loved him. 'It wasn't Beltane for me. That night, I found you irritating, standing there and doing nothing.'

His eyes lit up. 'I imagine so.'

She turned fully in his lap, his hands dropped to her waist. 'I'm telling you I didn't love you from the first.'

He chuckled, gave her kiss. One that made her gloriously dizzy until she clung to him. His kisses were intoxicating and she never wanted him to stop. Peering at her dazed expression, he laughed low again, 'And now you get cross with me because you didn't love me quick enough.'

She was. 'I blame that terrible mead you made me drink.'

His eyes widened. 'Are you telling me you know how to improve my mead?'

'Use more fruit—the sweeter it is, the stronger.'

He let out an incredulous sound. 'Do you know how long I couldn't solve that issue? Stay, Barabal, and teach me.'

She liked when he complimented her and when kissed her. She liked sitting in his lap and talking of their future.

'Is it your brothers?' he added. 'I told them to leave for Colquhoun land.'

He'd done that for her. 'You did?'

'Hamilton and Camron were there when I made the order and agreed. You have Graham support.'

She did and she felt it. Maybe she always had and that's why being here with these people and this man made her off balance, and different from before. She belonged here.

'Do you want them gone?'

268   *The Highlander's Mysterious Maiden*

Her brothers had been children when they tried to protect her. She feared they held much back on the tanners' cruelty and their search of her. And she, too, hadn't told them all about her life, both the good and the bad.

And they cared. Both of them so emotional at seeing her again, it returned more of her memories. They never could hold anything back.

'No,' she said. 'I want to talk to them still.'

'That's good,' he said. 'I don't think they were going to listen. Dugald certainly wasn't.'

She snorted.

Seoc grinned. 'Do it again.'

When she shook her head, his expression grew soft again. 'I like it, lass. Very much.'

She searched his features. 'How is that possible?'

'It's joy bursting from you. Pure happiness and hope and I'll do anything to keep hearing it.'

He meant it and she never wanted to leave this man or his home. 'I don't want to stay.'

His smile fell.

'Not for only my brothers,' she blurted. How could she not get this right? 'But maybe I could stay. Perhaps for yo—'

He kissed her. This time longer, deeper, sweeter. As if tasting her words for their truth. When he pulled away from the kiss it wasn't very far. Only enough for his eyes to hold with hers.

'You didn't let me finish,' she said. 'I wanted to say I could stay…for the cellar.'

His eyes lit. 'It is true, you won't get that quality of a cellar anywhere else.'

Because his mother had helped build it, because it was special to the man she loved. Her heart stopped and stuttered; she could hardly get the words out of her throat. No more running or hurt or abandonment. No more feeling as though she wasn't worthy. If this was hope again blooming in her chest, it wasn't hope like she knew it before. This one was worthier, too.

'Put me out of my misery, Barabal.'

'I always thought my hope was foolish.'

'It is the most precious thing in the world,' he said tenderly. 'I will defend it with my life no matter what comes our way. Now tell me the rest.'

He wanted her to say she loved him. Wasn't it obvious? 'What a waste of words when you already know my feelings.'

'Are we dallying too long for my lass?' His lips curled. 'Do we have things we should be doing?'

It was the dead of night, and they sat in an empty field. She couldn't imagine a better place to reveal her soul to herself and her heart to him. They'd met in a field and this man, with his roots and strength, was holding her. She loved him. Truly loved him from her toes to the tip of her head, from all the painful parts of her past to her future.

Beaming at him, letting him know all of it, she answered, 'You're making me sit in a soggy field, when we have better things to do with—'

When Seoc kissed her…kissed her like he wanted to forever…there wasn't anything else she wanted to do. Except this. Pulling away just enough to whisper against his lips, 'I love you, too.'

* * * * *

If you enjoyed this story,
be sure to pick up the previous instalments in
Nicole Locke's Lovers and Highlanders miniseries

The Highlander's Bridal Bid
The Highlander's Unexpected Bride

Get up to 4 Free Books!

We'll send you 2 free books from each series you try PLUS a free Mystery Gift.

Both the **Harlequin® Historical** and **Harlequin® Romance** series feature compelling novels filled with emotion and simmering romance.

YES! Please send me 2 FREE novels from the Harlequin Historical or Harlequin Romance series and my FREE Mystery Gift (gift is worth about $10 retail). After receiving them, if I don't wish to receive any more books, I can return the shipping statement marked "cancel." If I don't cancel, I will receive 5 brand-new Harlequin Historical books every month and be billed just $6.39 each in the U.S. or $7.19 each in Canada, or 4 brand-new Harlequin Romance Larger-Print books every month and be billed just $7.19 each in the U.S. or $7.99 each in Canada, a savings of 20% off the cover price. It's quite a bargain! Shipping and handling is just 50¢ per book in the U.S. and $1.25 per book in Canada.* I understand that accepting the 2 free books and gift places me under no obligation to buy anything. I can always return a shipment and cancel at any time by calling the number below. The free books and gift are mine to keep no matter what I decide.

Choose one:
- ☐ **Harlequin Historical** (246/349 BPA G36Y)
- ☐ **Harlequin Romance Larger-Print** (119/319 BPA G36Y)
- ☐ **Or Try Both!** (246/349 & 119/319 BPA G36Z)

Name (please print)

Address   Apt. #

City   State/Province   Zip/Postal Code

Email: Please check this box ☐ if you would like to receive newsletters and promotional emails from Harlequin Enterprises ULC and its affiliates. You can unsubscribe anytime.

Mail to the Harlequin Reader Service:
IN U.S.A.: P.O. Box 1341, Buffalo, NY 14240-8531
IN CANADA: P.O. Box 603, Fort Erie, Ontario L2A 5X3

Want to explore our other series or interested in ebooks? Visit www.ReaderService.com or call 1-800-873-8635.

---

*Terms and prices subject to change without notice. Prices do not include sales taxes, which will be charged (if applicable) based on your state or country of residence. Canadian residents will be charged applicable taxes. Offer not valid in Quebec. This offer is limited to one order per household. Books received may not be as shown. Not valid for current subscribers to the Harlequin Historical or Harlequin Romance series. All orders subject to approval. Credit or debit balances in a customer's account(s) may be offset by any other outstanding balance owed by or to the customer. Please allow 4 to 6 weeks for delivery. Offer available while quantities last.

Your Privacy—Your information is being collected by Harlequin Enterprises ULC, operating as Harlequin Reader Service. For a complete summary of the information we collect, how we use this information and to whom it is disclosed, please visit our privacy notice located at https://corporate.harlequin.com/privacy-notice. Notice to California Residents – Under California law, you have specific rights to control and access your data. For more information on these rights and how to exercise them, visit https://corporate.harlequin.com/california-privacy. For additional information for residents of other U.S. states that provide their residents with certain rights with respect to personal data, visit https://corporate.harlequin.com/other-state-residents-privacy-rights/.

HHHRLP25